BRAVER

A WOMBAT'S TALE

Also by Suzanne Selfors

FORTUNE'S MAGIC FARM

WISH UPON A SLEEPOVER

BRAVER

A WOMBAT'S TALE

SUZANNE SELFORS & WALKER RANSON

【Imprint】
MAKE YOUR MARK
New York

[Imprint]
MAKE YOUR MARK

A part of Macmillan Publishing Group, LLC

120 Broadway, New York, NY 10271

Library of Congress Cataloging-in-Publication Data is available.

ISBN 978-1-250-21991-6 (hardcover) / ISBN 978-1-250-22033-2 (ebook)

Our books may be purchased in bulk for promotional, educational, or business use.
Please contact your local bookseller or the Macmillan Corporate and
Premium Sales Department at (800) 221-7945 ext. 5442 or by email at
MacmillanSpecialMarkets@macmillan.com.

Book design by Carolyn Bull

Imprint logo designed by Amanda Spielman

First edition, 2020

1 3 5 7 9 10 8 6 4 2

mackids.com

"All creatures take heed,
A warning indeed,
Whether feather or fur,
Web-footed or spur,
If you steal a book
The predators will look,
FOR YOU."

Proclamation from the Royal Librarian of Dore

*Dedicated to Brian Jacques, whose stories
we will always treasure and without whom
we never would have started writing.*

TABLE of CONTENTS

PEACE AND QUIET

"Lola, please stop asking so many questions." Arthur Budge, a dark-brown wombat, pulled a parsley sprig from the ground, then frowned at his daughter. "You're giving me indigestion."

"But—"

"Questions can wait," he said. "We have all the time in the world."

Alice Budge, a light-brown wombat, handed Lola a clump of freshly dug snow grass and whispered, "Do try to have patience. You know how much your father enjoys the peace and quiet."

Lola sighed. She sat next to her father, close enough that she could smell the parsley's sharp notes as he bit through its stem. Despite his reprimand, Lola didn't want to stop asking questions. On this night she'd already asked thirteen, from "Why do our teeth keep growing?" to "Why are our rumps so hard?" But the answers were often some variation of "Because that's just the way it is." Or "Because that's how it's always been done." Lola flicked a worm from the snow grass clump, then sank her teeth into the succulent green blades.

It was a lovely night in Tassie Island's Northern Forest. Lola and her parents were foraging in their favorite clearing, where wild grasses and herbs grew in abundance. Every wombat family kept a tidy garden patch next to its burrow, growing radishes, tomatoes, and lettuce for meals, but foraging was good exercise and provided "important nutrients," as Alice often said. Lola chewed and looked up. A new moon shone through giant gum trees that seemed to reach as high as the distant mountains. No songs drifted down, for the birds were all in bed. Except for the wombat family's quiet chewing sounds, the forest was swaddled in silence.

Silence.

There were few things more valued among the bare-nosed wombats of the Northern Forest. Singing and whistling were frowned upon, except on the queen's birthday. Reading, with its soft sounds of page turning, was the favored hobby. Wood carving, with its delicate sounds of chipping, was the vocation of choice. If quiet had been something tradable, like bowls or spoons, wombats would have hoarded it with dragon-like avarice.

Except for Lola, who knew she was a bit of an oddball because she *loved* talking. And she loved telling stories to the forest mice. But storytelling had to be done while her parents slept, for they would be ashamed if they discovered their daughter's unwombat-like activities.

With the grass eaten, Lola wandered over to a log and started munching on some moss. It was one of her favorite flavors of green and quite the thirst quencher. But though she was enjoying the meal, she sighed loudly. It was proving to be another *quiet* night, following another *quiet* day in her, as ever, *quiet* life. This sameness never seemed to bother her mother or father. Arthur and Alice relished the predictability of their wombat existence, but Lola was always on the lookout for someone to talk to and if she found someone, be it a bird or a mouse, she talked. At length.

Maybe that was why Lola's parents looked more haggard than other wombat parents, and why her father's stomach was prone to episodes of upset. Parsley, known for its stomach-settling qualities, was his herb of choice.

"What's that?" Lola dropped her pawful of moss, scrambled atop the log, and peered down at the stream. First came the squelch of steps along the muddy bank. Then she caught sight of a dark shape that was clearly wombatish in nature. "Hellooo!" Lola called.

Arthur gasped. "Lola, no, not again."

"It's our neighbor, Mister Squat. I'm being friendly. Don't you want me to be friendly? Hello! Hello!" Lola stretched her short arm as far as she could in a wave, hoping to get the old wombat's attention.

It worked. He stopped in his tracks, then glanced up at the log through his thick spectacles.

"Mister Squat! It's me, Lola! Lola Budge! Are you having a nice night of foraging? Did you find some watercress?"

Mister Squat grumbled something under his breath and turned around so his prodigious rump blocked Lola's view. Then he began digging in the streambed for roots.

"Maybe he didn't hear me." Lola took a deep breath, cupped her paws around her mouth, and bellowed, "MISTER SQUAAAAAT!" His fur bristled and his ears scrunched up in sudden displeasure.

"Oh, hooly dooly." Alice hurried to Lola's side and clamped a paw over Lola's mouth, her own ears partially clamped shut as well. "Please stop hollering. You'll wake the daytimers."

Lola squirmed free. "But Mum," she pleaded. "I'm just trying to be neighborly."

Alice shook her head in a worried way, which she tended

to do around her only joey. "Sweetie, how many times must I remind you that talking to our neighbor without invitation is bad manners?"

"Yes, I know," Lola grumbled. "I'm disturbing his 'peace and quiet.'"

"Why isn't she shy like the rest of us?" Arthur asked his wife.

"Because she isn't," was Alice's answer—the same answer she gave each time he asked that question.

Lola chewed another mouthful of moss, her gaze fixed on Mister Squat, who shone silver in the moonlight. As he sat, feasting upon a root he'd pulled from the mud, Lola's mind filled with questions. How old was he? Could he see without his spectacles? Did he like carving spoons and bowls? She certainly didn't.

As Lola flicked a piece of moss from her white whiskers, Mister Squat stopped eating, turned around quickly, and faced the stream. He adjusted his spectacles. He shook his head. He shrugged. He shook his head again. Lola took a quick breath. Wait. What was happening? Was something happening?

She scrambled along the log, trying to get a better view. Mister Squat was clearly looking at something in the distance. He shrugged again. Lola could barely contain her excitement. She reached the end of the log and stood on the tips of her toes, her long claws prickling the bark. Why was he shrugging? Was he talking to someone? Yes, he was talking to someone. But Mister Squat never talked to anyone. She'd never heard his voice.

But then he turned abruptly, abandoned the root, and hurried up the trail that led back to the burrows.

She wanted to call after him but wrinkled her nose, remembering her mother's words. Bad manners? Lola narrowed her eyes. No one else thought it was bad manners to say goodbye. Why did wombats have to be so antisocial? The only time the community got together was on Queen Myra's birthday, to feast and sing songs in her honor. Though Lola had never met the queen, she'd been raised to love and admire her, as had all the wombats of the Northern Forest. Queen Myra's birthday was considered the most important day of the year. But during the rest of the year, there was no need for group gatherings. The wombats let each other know that all was well by displaying their cubic droppings on rocks. While out foraging, Lola's mom might say, "Oh look, there's Mister Pudge's dropping. He appears to be doing just fine." Or, "Oh look, there's Missus Portly's dropping. She seems healthier than ever."

Lola was aching to find out who Mister Squat had been talking to. She slid off the log. "May I—"

A sharp look and gnashing of teeth from her father answered the question.

With Mister Squat gone and nothing interesting to watch, Lola finished her moss. Then she patted her belly rhythmically with her hind paw—a wombat sign that the meal had been satisfying and that the belly was contentedly full. Arthur and Alice also patted their bellies. Then the Budge family began to waddle along the forest path, climbing over fallen branches and ducking beneath tangled vines. But Lola had one more question on her mind, and it was one of the best questions she'd ever thought of, so it was worth risking another reprimand.

"Mum, Dad, if you were both shy, how did you meet?" Lola made sure that her voice was very hushed when she asked the question. But if her father didn't answer, she was prepared to ask it again. And again.

To her surprise, he chuckled. "We grew up a few burrows

apart. I was impressed because your mum's droppings were always perfect cubes."

"Thank you, my dear."

"You're welcome. Of course, I was too shy to talk to her, so I left her a letter. And she wrote back. After thirteen letters, I finally worked up the courage to forage with her."

This was the most talking her father had done in weeks and it was thrilling. Lola was about to ask another question, but a serious look from her mother reminded her not to push things.

Upon reaching the burrow, Arthur opened the door. Then Lola and her parents waddled downward, following a tunnel beneath the roots of a celery-top pine until it branched into a series of rooms. Each room had been dug by paw, then fortified with wooden beams. Skylights were set into the tops of the rooms, allowing moonlight to trickle in. Though Lola and her parents could see well in the dark, this extra light was helpful for activities such as reading and carving. And during the day, when they slept, curtains were drawn across the skylights to block the sun.

The largest room was their main living area. It had a river-stone table to carve upon, circled by three chairs. Specialty carving tools, such as chisels and gouges, hung from a tool rack. Wall shelves held some of the lovely bowls that Arthur and Alice had made. A broom stood in the corner, for sweeping up wood chips. But the central focus of the room was the looming grandfather clock. Carved by Arthur's father, it was a prized family heirloom and ticktocked with quiet perfection.

Two passageways split off from the main chamber. One led to a storeroom where the Budge family kept their winter food. The other led to the bedrooms, with their straw mattresses and moss-filled pillows. When she was much younger, Lola's parents often had to replace the moss in Lola's pillow because of Lola's midday snacking. Wardrobes contained extra blankets, needed during the deep freeze of winter, and traveling cloaks, though Lola's was unused, as she'd yet to travel anywhere. All in all it was a tidy and simple dwelling.

"Lola, are you going to work on your bowl?" Arthur asked. He picked up a piece of soft pine and began to hollow it. As he worked he would alternate using claws, chisels, and even his teeth.

"No, thank you," she replied. "You know I don't like carving."

"How will you buy the essentials of life if you don't have anything to trade in return? Woven fabrics and glass panes are expensive and have to be shipped from Dore." Arthur shook his head sadly. "Plus, you need to wear out your teeth somehow. You don't want to end up with them sticking in the ground like that Biggun Longtooth from the old stories, do you?"

Lola picked up her bowl and began gnawing at it, oozing boredom.

"Maybe she will be good at something else," Alice said hopefully.

"But what could that be? She's a wombat, and wombats carve."

"I'm good at talking," Lola almost said, but she knew a statement like that would bring a frown to her father's furry face.

While Arthur and Alice sat at the table and worked on their bowls, Lola tossed hers aside and tucked herself into the corner to read her favorite book, *The Tales of Tassie Island*, though perhaps she would skip over Longtooth's story today. Each story began in the same way: "Gather ye round and prick your ears, for a tale is about to be told." She knew all the stories by heart, but that didn't matter. How she loved the thrilling high-sea adventure of "The Penguin Pirates" and the heartbreaking romance of "The Quoll Princess and the Beast." Each story was usually a quick read, but on this night Lola was having trouble concentrating, her whiskers twitching uncontrollably. She couldn't stop thinking about Mister Squat. He'd ignored her hellos, but he'd obviously talked to someone else. Who had been able to get Mister Squat's attention? And why? She'd only finished two paragraphs when her mother patted her on the head. "The sun is rising."

Lola kissed her parents on their furry cheeks, then shuffled to her room and climbed into her bed for the day's sleep. Alice and Arthur retired to their own room and soon, the sounds of their deep breathing filled the burrow. Lola closed her eyes. She curled on her left side. Then curled on her right side. She rolled onto her back, opened her eyes, and stared at the dirt ceiling. The night's events tapped at her mind like raindrops onto the ground.

Mister Squat never spoke to his wombat neighbors, so did that mean he'd encountered someone who wasn't a neighbor? Someone who didn't usually live in the burrows? Were there clues left behind? There was only one way to find out.

Lola slipped out of her bed and tiptoed from her room. She stopped outside her parents' door, listening to make sure they were still in a deep sleep. Then, ever so quietly, Lola Budge made her way outside.

2

MESSAGE IN A BOTTLE

When Lola emerged from the burrow, she took great care to look around, her eyes blinking against the brightness. As she waddled on, her vision slowly adjusted. Even though she'd done this before, daylight always mesmerized her. The morning forest was covered in a small layer of water droplets that sparkled in the sunlight, much like the stars at night. The ruffled leaves of the tanglefoot trees blazed a brilliant dark green.

"G'day, Lola." Lola paused and looked up. A forest mouse peered down from her little cottage, built into a hollow stump. "Sneaking out again, are ya?"

"Yes," Lola whispered. If she woke the wombat neighbors, they'd surely complain to her parents and she'd get in trouble for wandering outside the burrow, no matter what her reason.

"Gonna tell us a story?" a young mouse asked, sticking his head out of the nest. "How about the one where the pelican turns into a glossy ibis. What's that one called?"

"'The Ugly Hatchling,'" Lola replied.

"We love that story, we do. Tell us that story." The mice sat on the edge of their porch, kicking their feet as they eagerly awaited their morning entertainment.

It was a lovely request, and normally Lola would be thrilled to indulge. "I'd like to, but I've got something to do," she told them.

"Well, don't you go mucking about for too long," the mama mouse advised with a wink. "Your mum and dad will throw a wobbly, they will, if they find ya gone again. Just like I would if mine was to sneak out." Her eyes shifted to look down at her youngster with a heavily raised eyebrow.

"I'll be quick," Lola assured them. Then she made her way down to the stream, following the path that had been worn into the forest floor over the years by dozens of wombat paws. Things looked so different in sunlight. The water glistened and shone, allowing Lola to see the smooth rocks below and the thin silver fish that darted about. She'd always loved this stream. She and her parents had waded through it many times, crossing to the other side where the watercress grew thick. Lola had asked her mother where the stream went and she'd said it emptied into the Fairwater River. But a rushing river was too dangerous for wombats, so Lola always swam in the quiet pools of the stream.

Lola found the exact spot where Mister Squat had been sitting, his paw imprints still visible on the muddy bank. She looked up and down, but there were no other paw prints that might reveal what sort of critter he'd been talking to. Maybe he'd been talking to himself? Lola did that sometimes.

She sighed. Even though the mystery had not been solved, perhaps the morning wasn't a total loss. She could return to the hollow stump and tell the mice a story. Then she could hurry back to her burrow with plenty of time to sleep the rest of the day away, her parents none the wiser. That seemed a good plan. But when she turned to head up the path, a splash drew her attention. On the other side of the stream, a dark shape was swimming in one of the deep pools. It couldn't be a wombat because all the other wombats were still tucked into their burrows. She guessed it was a forest rat but noticed that the tail was wide and paddle-shaped. The critter swam in a circle, then disappeared underwater. Lola's whiskers bristled with curiosity. She had to find out what it was.

She splashed across the stream, her claws gripping the slippery rocks, then plopped herself onto a boulder at the edge of the pool. How could the critter stay underwater for so long? "Hellooo!" She reached one paw into the pool and waved underwater.

"Oi! Stop doin' that!"

The critter had popped out of the water. A pair of swimming goggles covered his eyes and he had a funny flat bill instead of a nose. He pushed the goggles up his forehead and glared at her with his tiny black eyes. Lola found herself looking at a small, irate platypus.

"Stop doing what?" she asked.

"Stop churnin' up the water! How'm I gonna catch me brek-kie if yer splashin' about, interruptin' me electroreception?"

Lola lifted her arm from the water. "Sorry." She frowned. "What's electro—?"

"Electroreception," he said snippily. "Ya don't know about electroreception?" She shook her head. "Well I don't have time to explain it to ya 'cause I'm far too busy." Lola wondered why he was so cranky. Maybe he was hungry. Lola watched as he dove again, somehow not disturbing the water. A few moments later, he emerged with a blue yabby in his mouth, which he quickly ate. Then he climbed out onto the rocks. With his webbed paws, he reached for a green bag that was slung around his body. That's when Lola noticed the spur.

How could she have forgotten? Her mother had warned her to never anger a platypus. Their hind legs hid a toe-like spur, filled with deadly venom.

"Oh, hooly dooly." Lola scooted backwards. "I'd better go." But the platypus spun around and pointed at her.

"Wha'd ya say?" Even though he'd eaten, he sounded grumpier than before.

She couldn't take her eyes off that spur. She knew the tales. Once injected, the poison would travel through her veins and cause extreme pain, then paralysis. "I—I said I'd better go. I'm not supposed to be outside the burrow during the day."

"No, the other thing." He waddled across the rocks until he stood in front of her. His fur was sleek with water and his bill was shiny in the sunlight. "What's the *other* thing ya said?"

Lola kept scooting until she slipped off her rock and was standing in the stream. She had no idea how fast a platypus could run, so she needed to keep her distance. She took a step backward, then another. "I don't think I said anything else. But I do talk a lot. It's bad manners to talk so much. I'm supposed to be quieter. I'm not supposed to ask so many questions. That's what my mum and dad tell me." He wasn't coming any closer, so she stopped. Something else had caught her attention. "How come your bag has the word *messenger* on it?"

"'Cause that's what I am." He straightened to full height and his paw flew to the side of his head in a salute. "Bale Blackwater, Platypus Delivery Service, Northern Streams and Rivers Division," he said in an official manner. "Best in the business. I've won the Golden Platy Award three years in a row."

That sounded very impressive. "Congratulations," Lola said.

He stopped saluting. "It's very rude of ya to keep me waitin'.

Don't ya know I've got other deliveries to make? How'm I gonna win another Golden Platy if I get deductions for tardiness? Huh? How?"

Lola had never heard of the Golden Platy Award, so she had no idea how to answer his question. But something else didn't make sense. "Did you say I kept you waiting?" She scratched her cheek. "But how could I keep you waiting if I didn't know you were here?"

He narrowed his eyes again. "Oh, so yer gonna play that game, are ya? Look, ya can pretend all ya want that ya didn't know I was here, but I know ya knew, and you know ya knew, so it all comes down to the fact that ya kept me waitin', plain and simple! I asked that old bloke where ya were and ya know what he said?"

"Old bloke?"

"Yeah, last night."

"Oh, you mean Mister Squat." She had been right. Mister Squat had been talking to someone. "Did he tell you to stop interrupting his peace and quiet?"

"Yep. Can ya believe that?" He began to rifle through the contents of his bag. "No respect for me profession. Now, where is it?"

"Do you need help finding something?" Lola asked, forgetting all about the spur.

The platypus whipped the bag behind his back and pointed at her. "Keep yer furry paws outta me bag. I got lots of stuff in here. Messages for all sorts of critters that are none of yer business."

"Sorry," she said. He was the crankiest critter she'd ever met. "I won't look in your bag, Mister Blackwater, I promise."

"Indeed, ya won't." He rifled some more. "Where's that

blasted thing? Aha! Found it!" He pulled out a small bottle that had a long string attached. Lola cautiously crept forward so she could get a better look. The bottle contained a rolled piece of paper and was sealed with a cork. Bale Blackwater stared at Lola, looking her up and down as if waiting for something. He tapped his webbed foot. "Well?"

"Well what?"

"Ya gotta say the secret password. I can't give this secret message to ya unless ya say the secret password."

"Secret password?"

"I think ya said it before, but I didn't quite hear ya so ya gotta say it again, to be certain." He held up the bottle. "The bloke who paid me to deliver this is a real beast, if ya know what I mean. A real bloodthirsty brute." He shivered.

Lola felt more confused than ever. "I don't know any bloodthirsty brutes. I'm Lola. Lola Budge. Are you sure you're talking to the right wombat? Don't get me wrong, I'm really enjoying our conversation. It's so rare that I get to talk to a total stranger. But there must be some mistake."

"Mistake?" He opened his flat bill and gasped, his long tongue curling in surprise.

"Maybe you're in the wrong place?"

"The . . . the . . . the *wrong place*?" he sputtered. "Bale Blackwater doesn't swim to the wrong place. This is the Northern Forest, right?" She nodded. "This is the part of the Northern Forest where the bare-nosed wombat burrows are located, right?" She nodded again. "And you," he pointed, "are a female bare-nosed wombat." It was true. She nodded. He folded his arms. "Then do us both a favor and give me the secret password so I can be on me way."

"I'd give you the password if I knew it," Lola insisted. "I would. But I didn't come down here for a delivery. I was just trying to figure out who Mister Squat had been talking to and . . ." The platypus scowled at her. "What I'm trying to say is that I'm not—oh, hooly dooly!"

"Bingo!" He thrust the bottle into her paw.

Lola's eyes widened as she stared at the bottle and the rolled piece of paper inside. She didn't know whether she should be excited or nervous. "What does it say?"

"What does it say?" A pained expression passed across the platypus's face, as if Lola had just told him that someone dear to him had died. He blinked very quickly. "What does it *say*? Are ya suggestin' that I read yer message? Yer *secret* message?" he shrieked, his webbed paws waving wildly in the air. His flat tail slapped against a rock.

Lola shook her head. She hadn't meant to insult him, but this entire encounter was very confusing. "I . . . I . . ." she started to explain. Suddenly, all she could think about was the venomous spur on his foot. *Never anger a platypus.* "I'm sorry, I—"

"A messenger *never* reads the messages," Bale interrupted. "That would be a clear violation of our code of ethics." He slung his bag over his shoulder. "I swam all the way up here, practically to the middle of Woop Woop, and I waited all night, and do I get a 'thanks'? No, I don't. Everyone always *blames* the messenger but they never *thank* him."

"Thank you," Lola said, clutching the bottle to her chest. Trying her best to smile so as not to displease him more.

The platypus glared at her and grumbled, "Yer welcome." Then, with a huff, he headed toward the deep section of the stream, his webbed feet gripping the slick rocks as he waddled.

Despite having been on the receiving end of a platypus temper tantrum, Lola burst into a grin. What a morning this was turning out to be! She'd had a long conversation with a stranger *and* she'd gotten a secret message. But the only way to find out if the message was meant for her was to read it.

She pinched the cork with her claws and was about to pull it free when a sound shot through the air, the likes of which Lola had never heard before. It was a screeching sound and it sent a shiver up her spine. Bale Blackwater whipped around and both he and Lola stared in the sound's direction.

"Only one sort of critter sounds like that," Bale said, pulling his goggles over his eyes. "And it's the wrong sort. Ya'd best get outta here, and fast." With his messenger bag in place, he slipped into the stream and began swimming away.

"Wait!" Lola called. "What kind of critter?"

But the platypus was making quick time, and just before the stream rounded a bend, he raised his head and hollered, "Platypus Delivery Service guarantees messages get delivered, but we don't guarantee what happens next!" Then he disappeared below the water.

Leaving Lola alone as another screech rent the air.

3

A MONSTER IN THE FOREST

More screeches echoed from beyond the embankment, followed by growls and snarls. The forest canopy rustled as songbirds took to the sky, seemingly eager to escape the horrid uproar. Instinct kicked in, filling Lola's entire body with the urge to dig as deep as she could. She would dig a burrow, safe and dark, then seal it tight with her rump. But a new squealing sound broke through. A wombat squeal. And it was coming from the burrows.

Bale Blackwater had told Lola to get out of there, but how could she leave if a wombat was in trouble?

She looped the string over her head so the bottle hung like a necklace. Then she hurried back across the stream and started up the embankment. When she reached the path, she broke into a run. The growling and snarling arose again in the distance. Bale had said that only one sort of critter made that noise—the wrong sort. So why was Lola running directly toward it? *What am I doing?* she asked herself as she pumped her legs. *I should be running away from danger, not into it.*

Another squeal sounded. Then she heard a voice she recognized. "Lola! Lo—" Her mother's cry was abruptly cut off, as if she'd had the air knocked from her.

"Mum!" What was happening? Lola forgot her fear and ran as fast as she could, but even at a gallop, she was still a few minutes away from home. She ducked under a branch, tripped on a root, and took a tumble. The fall smarted and would probably leave a bruise, but that was the least of her worries.

There was another squeal. Lola scrambled to her feet. "Mum!" she called again.

Someone scurried in front of her. "Lola, don't go that way! Hide! Hide!" a forest mouse cried before darting into a hole.

Lola couldn't hide. Not if her mother was in trouble. Despite the pain in her side, she started running again. Deciding to take a shortcut, she turned sharply off the path and forced her way through the dense brush. Branches poked her from all sides, but she pushed through. Upon reaching the edge of the dirt road, she froze. The daylit forest had gone eerily silent. No insects buzzed through the air. No songbirds sang from the trees. Lola's heart drummed in her ears.

What was that?

A steady beating sound arose. Lola stared at the end of the road, where dirt clouds swelled up from the ground. The marching came closer and closer. She gasped as strange figures emerged from the clouds, singing to the rhythm of their pounding feet.

Our stomachs rumble evermore

To slurp some stinky slime,

To fill our plates with mold galore

With scraps long past their prime.

The overripe and putrid bits,

Decaying seeds and oozing pits.

If black with rot then it's a treat,

That's what we want to eat.

That's what we want eat!

Swamp water rats—the most mysterious of all the island rats, for they rarely left the swamp. The only time Lola saw these critters was on the day after Queen Myra's birthday. The rats would bring their shovels and buckets and collect all the leftover food—soggy root pies, wilted salad greens, and crumbled seed cakes. They relished the bits others wasted, and their cleanup service was always appreciated. But the queen's birthday was in winter and this was summer, so what were they doing here?

The rats were roped together in three lines, nine rats to a line, each line attached to an enormous wooden cart. Having finished their song, they grunted and groaned as they pulled the cart down the road. Each rat had a bucket and a shovel strapped to its back and strands of swamp grass clinging to its fur. The rats were scavengers, not predators, so what did Lola have to fear? Nevertheless, something was terribly wrong, so before anyone noticed her, Lola darted behind a shrub and pushed the leaves aside so she could see what was happening.

As the rats neared, so too did the unique stench of the swamp water they lived in. Lola was about to put her paw over her nose when she smelled something familiar. The cart held a large wooden cage, but it wasn't filled with garbage. It was filled with wombats.

There was Mister Squat and Mister Pudge. And Missus

Portly and Pickle Portly, her son. And Stout Junior and the entire Rockbottom family, all crammed together. Some were crying, some were trying to console others, but most were huddled and trembling.

Mayor Ponderous peered out from between the bars. Because the bare-nosed wombats of the Northern Forest didn't like to engage in public debates or campaigning, there'd been no election for the mayor's position. Leadership was simply granted to the largest member of the burrows. "Hellooo!" he called. "Could you take it easy up there? A bumpy ride is not good for one's digestion."

"Let us go!" another wombat pleaded.

That had definitely been her mother's voice, but Lola couldn't see her. "Mum?" She stepped out from the shrub just as the cart passed by. "Mum?"

All the wombats turned to look at Lola. They scooted out of the way for Lola's parents.

Alice and Arthur pushed through until they were up against the bars. Their eyes met Lola's.

"Stop the cart!" a voice ordered. The rats stopped pulling.

Arthur's eyes widened with fear. Alice put a finger to her mouth. Lola understood and stepped back into the shrub until she was hidden again.

Someone leaped off the top of the cage. She was a black furry critter with bloodred ears and a white fur collar. Lola had never seen one in the flesh, but she'd seen enough drawings in her storybook to know exactly what she was looking at.

A Tassie devil!

"Correct me if I am wrong, but did I just overhear someone whining about the quality of the ride?" The devil growled as she began circling the cart, twirling a whip menacingly in her right paw. "We have provided you dirt-dwellers with this luxurious means of transportation and you have the audacity to complain? If you are not satisfied with the treatment you are receiving, perhaps you would like to fill out a complaint form?" She snarled and flicked the whip at the cart. Many of the wombats squealed and huddled closer together. Alice and Arthur turned away, making sure not to look in Lola's direction.

Lola shuddered as she remembered the stories she'd read. Long ago, before her grandwombats and her great-grandwombats were born, a group of carnivores rowed across the ocean and set upon the shores of Tassie Island. Everything was upended as the invaders hunted and terrorized the peace-loving critters who had long made the island their home. But thanks to the first king TheoDore, the invaders were eventually conquered and they agreed to live on Mount Ossa forevermore. Their descendants, born on the island, became known as Tassie devils. Some called them night monsters.

So what was this one doing here?

When the devil had circled to the other side of the cart and was out of sight, Alice whipped around and mouthed, "Run!" But Lola was too scared to run. Unlike swamp water rats, Tassie devils didn't dine on garbage. They dined on flesh. Is that why Lola's family and neighbors had been captured? Because this monster was going to *eat* them? Lola's little heart started pounding so quickly it felt like it might burst from her chest.

Mayor Ponderous removed a handkerchief from his vest pocket and wiped a speck of blood from the edge of his wide nose where the whip had struck. "I say, why are you treating us good and peaceable folk in this manner?"

The creature stopped walking and tapped her whip against one of the wheels. "I was informed that wombats are quiet and shy. That they do not like conversation."

"Indeed, that is true," the mayor said. "But under the circum—"

"Enough!" She jumped onto a wheel. Now level with the cage and its occupants, she flexed her claws and stretched her mouth wide, revealing a golden tooth that gleamed in the sunlight. Then she exhaled carnivorous breath straight in the mayor's face. The mayor broke into a coughing fit and quickly turned away.

While the devil laughed villainously, Alice, once again, mouthed, "Run!"

Lola's body wanted to run, but her heart wanted to stay. She shuffled fretfully, and as she did, a twig snapped.

The devil stopped laughing and spun around, her gaze burrowing into the foliage. She jumped off the wheel and stealthily crept toward Lola's hiding place. Her black eyes narrowed. "Who's there?" Lola held her breath, trying to make herself as small as possible, not an easy task for a barrel-shaped critter.

Arthur and Alice's expressions turned desperate. "No one's there," Alice said. "You've captured all of us."

Arthur pressed against the bars. "And you've broken the queen's law. You're not supposed to leave Mount Ossa!"

The devil stopped in her tracks. She flicked her whip, then spun back around. "Who dared to speak to me in that manner?" She darted back to the cart and snapped her whip against it.

Arthur stood his ground, though his shaking legs belied his fear. "I spoke the truth." Lola knew exactly what her father was doing. He was trying to keep attention away from his daughter. And it had worked.

"The queen's law?" Spit flew from the monster's mouth. "The

queen's law?" Enraged, she jumped back onto the wheel and shrieked. "Your isolation has made you ill-informed." She snapped the whip again. Missus Portly and Pickle Portly squealed. Mister Squat jumped about a foot in the air. "Our lovely little queen has rescinded that accursed treaty."

Arthur's mouth fell open. "That can't be true."

"Are you calling me a liar?" The whip landed on Arthur's paw. He winced.

"Queen Myra would never rescind the Treaty of Mount Ossa," Alice said. "It exiles your kind so you won't eat us."

"Is that what you think? That I am going to *eat* you?" She turned toward the rats who were now stretched out on the ground in various resting positions. "Did you hear that, you slime-covered scoundrels? The wombats think I cannot control myself."

The rats shook their heads and murmured to one another. "Against the rules." "No hunting allowed."

"Come to think of it . . ." The devil tapped the whip's handle against her foot. "It has been a long time since my kind has eaten wombat. I have heard fireside stories that you are delicious roasted with red potatoes."

Stout Junior squealed and his mother put her paws over his ears. Lola's legs suddenly felt weak, as if they could no longer hold her.

The Tassie devil laughed again. "Do not be alarmed, young one. No one is going to eat you, not on my watch. You see, I will get paid a great deal of gold coin if I deliver you *alive*."

"Gold coin?" the mayor asked. "Why—"

The whip cracked again and another spot of blood appeared on the mayor's nose. "No more talking!" Then the Tassie devil climbed back onto the driver's bench. She'd apparently forgotten that someone might be hiding in the bushes. "Get a move on!" she ordered. "Or you won't feast on garbage tonight." With a unified groan, the rats got to their feet and began pulling the cart down the road.

Our stomachs rumble evermore

To slurp some stinky slime . . .

"Mum, Dad," Lola whispered as she poked her head out of the shrub.

As the cart's wheels rolled, and as the swamp water rats sang, Alice clung to the back rails of the cage, her desperate gaze meeting Lola's. For a long moment the two were locked in a stare, each wondering if they'd ever see the other again. Then the cart took a bend in the road and disappeared from view.

Lola crept out of her hiding place. She took a few hesitant steps, then a few more. The swampy stench lingered in the air, a putrid reminder of what she'd just witnessed. Lola didn't know how to help her parents and neighbors, but she knew one thing—she couldn't let them go without her. So she started to follow, her paws slipping into the ruts left by the wagon's wheels. She cautiously picked up speed, only slowing as she approached each turn and twist in the road, catching glimpses of the cart as it rolled down a hill or around another bend. She didn't have to follow far because, after a short while, the cart turned off the road.

Lola crept forward, ducking behind a tuft of tall grasses. She drew a deep breath. The cart had stopped at the edge of Fairwater River. The river flowed north, its current strong and steady. Along the riverbank, a flat-top barge waited, secured in place by a rope. A big wheel stuck out of the water along the boat's side. The only boats Lola had seen before were the little skiffs the wombats carved for the forest mice.

The Tassie devil scrambled off the cart and began shouting orders to the rats. One by one, the rats untied themselves. Then they pushed the cart across a set of planks until it was sitting on the boat. "Where are you taking us?" Alice demanded.

"I said no talking!" She pounded her fist against the cage. The rats tossed the lengths of rope onto the boat, then gave it a shove. As the boat floated away, each rat gracefully dove into the water and effortlessly slipped onto the boat's deck. A pair of rats took position on either side of the paddle wheel and began to pump their legs, pressing their narrow hind feet against the pedals. As the wheel rotated, the boat began moving upriver. The devil slid off the cart and entered the wheelhouse, closing the door behind her. Lola had always been told that swamp water rats were an important part of life on Tassie Island in that they helped keep things clean. But here they were, helping a night monster take her family away! They were horrid, Lola decided. As horrid as the monster herself!

Lola pressed her paws to her mouth, holding back her sobs. Everyone she knew and loved was floating away. Desperation taking hold, she ran to the river's edge. She didn't care if the devil saw her. She wanted her parents.

"Take me with you!" she cried. "Please take me with you!" With every heartbeat, the barge moved farther and farther away. Lola threw herself into the water, paddling her arms and legs as fast as she could. Despite her valiant attempt, the river's current pushed her downstream and back onto shore. She tried again but found herself right back in the mud.

Once again, Arthur and Alice clung to the cage, staring at their daughter as they floated farther and farther upriver. Then Alice opened her mouth. Lola flicked her ears forward, straining to pick up the sound of her mother's voice. "Find your uncle!" Alice hollered. "He'll know what to do!"

Lola's eyes overflowed with tears until the image of her parents became a blur. Until the paddle-wheel boat, with its cage of wombats and its slimy crew, disappeared into the horizon.

Mud oozed between Lola's claws as she sat at the river's edge and sobbed.

4

A "T" and a "B"

Find your uncle. He'll know what to do.

Those words repeated in Lola's mind. And then, through her sniffles, she asked out loud, "I have an uncle?"

In the quietness of their lives, Lola's parents had rarely mentioned their childhoods. There'd been rare stories about learning how to swim and how to carve, but no mention of siblings. Who was this uncle and how was Lola supposed to find him? Was he her mother's brother or her father's brother? Was he older or younger? Why didn't he live in the Northern Forest with them?

And why would he know what to do? One shy wombat against a Tassie devil and a bunch of stinky swamp water rats seemed an unlikely victory. He'd probably get tossed into the cart like the rest of them.

Despite her broad shoulders and stout legs, Lola had never felt so small. Her parents were gone, her neighbors were gone, even the mayor was gone. What would become of her? How would she survive? How could she save the others when she was just a joey?

Find your uncle.

There was no time to waste. If she could find any clues about this uncle, they would be in the family burrow. She wiped her eyes, then scrambled up the riverbank. Once on the road, she broke into a gallop. *Go faster*, she told herself. But her heart ached as she ran, for she knew that each step took her in the opposite direction of her parents. She didn't slow until she reached her burrow.

The rats had made a mess. The table and chairs had been overturned, the tool rack broken, tools scattered. Bowls, platters, and spoons were discarded here and there. The beloved grandfather clock lay on its side, its pendulum hanging lifelessly. Lola's ears flattened as her fear turned to anger. Those rats and that monster with the gold tooth had torn her family and her home apart! She clenched her paws in outrage. That's when she remembered the little bottle.

What if the message *was* important? What if it was some kind of warning? Maybe it would explain what had happened.

She uncorked the bottle, turned it upside down, and shook until the rolled paper fell out. She set the bottle aside, and then, careful not to tear the delicate paper with her long claws, unrolled the message. A single sentence had been written on the tiny piece of paper:

T.B. is ready.

What did that mean? Who was T.B.? Lola groaned. The message was no help at all. What a waste of time. She crumpled the paper and let it fall to the floor. Then she marched into her parents' room to begin her search for information.

Find your uncle.

Lola found nothing out of the ordinary under the bed or

under the braided carpet. She continued her search in the storage room, behind baskets, inside crates, and back in the main chamber. She looked inside every bowl and drawer. Where would her parents keep something about their families? Her gaze settled on the grandfather clock.

She'd looked inside the clock many times, curious about how it worked. Alice had shown Lola the gears, the springs, and the winding mechanism. She'd also shown her how to keep the workings oiled. It was a brilliant piece of machinery. Lola sat next to the overturned clock, and when she opened the door, the clock's contents spilled out onto the floor.

There was a jar of wax for polishing the wood. There was also a small box whose lid had fallen free. Some papers were tucked inside. Lola held her breath for a long moment. Then she pulled out the folded papers, which turned out to be two letters.

She unfolded one. According to the date at the top, it had been written a few years before Lola's birth.

Dear Sister,

We are just over halfway to the royal city, but we ran into a messenger pelican along the way and decided to send word early, to let you know that we are both all right. As usual, our brother Teddy has been very quiet during the trip and keeps to himself, but what an adventure I'm having. I've met many critters. I have engaged in the most interesting conversations and have learned a great deal about making one's fortune. Once we reach

Dore, I intend to apply for a job at the palace, for that seems to be the perfect place for someone like me who wants to move up in the world.

Wish you were with us but someone must stay home and take care of Mum.

Good health to you.

Your brother,

Tobias Bottom

Lola couldn't believe her eyes, so she read it three more times. Then she sat against the burrow wall, her mouth open in disbelief. She had *two* uncles, named Tobias Bottom and Teddy Bottom, who left the Northern Forest to seek their fortune, leaving Alice to take care of their mother. Why had Lola never heard any of this?

She grabbed the other letter, which had been written after Lola's birth.

Dear Sister,

I have been incredibly busy, so this might be my last letter for some time. Queen Myra, in her wisdom, has promoted me to ambassador. She appreciates my gift of gab and believes I am an asset in the negotiations of trade. Aren't you proud of me? I have become the most popular wombat in all of Tassie Island. And there are so many beautiful things that my salary can buy. I am becoming quite the collector.

I am sad to report, however, that our brother continues to have lesser aspirations and works in the bowels of the castle as a lowly mop-pusher. He seems content, for there is peace and quiet down there. But what a shame that he does not apply himself more.

Good health to you, your husband, and my new niece.

Your brother,

> Sir Tobias Bottom, Ambassador to the
> Northern Forest and the Realms Beyond

Now Lola understood. One of her uncles had chosen a quiet job, as most wombats would. But her other uncle loved conversation. He was just like her! And to make matters better, he was a famous ambassador who knew Queen Myra. Clearly, he was the uncle she was meant to find. He would be able to explain the situation to the queen and then she'd send help. Everything was going to work out. Queen Myra would never let anything terrible happen to critters as peaceful and loyal as the wombats.

Hope renewed, Lola scrambled to her feet, and as she did, she noticed the crumpled message lying on the floor.

T.B. is ready.

"Crikey!" she exclaimed as she grabbed the crumpled paper. T.B. stood for Tobias Bottom, she was certain of it. So maybe Bale Blackwater was right and the message had been meant for Lola after all. But if her uncle was ready . . . *what*, exactly, was he ready for? And why would he send a message to the niece he'd never met?

There was no time to figure out the entire puzzle. Lola knew the important piece—that she had an uncle and that she had to get word to him. If only the platypus had stuck around, she could have used his delivery service. But swimming would be too slow. She needed something faster. She needed a bird.

Lola hurried from the burrow and stood outside, her eyes adjusting to the bright sunlight once again. The forest was eerily quiet. "Hellooo?" she called. "Hello? Is anyone here?" No birds or mice replied, having been scared away by the monster's shrieking. Even knocking on the door of the mice who had greeted her earlier received no response. Lola stomped her foot in frustration, but then she realized that the forest songbirds were too small to fly all the way to the royal city. She'd need a professional messenger, a bird who was designed for long distances. She needed a pelican. And the nearest place to find one was the trading post in Fairwater.

Lola began packing a small backpack for her trek. She'd need coin to pay the messenger pelican, so she searched for the coin jar. Empty! She'd have to sell something at the Fairwater Trading Post. She grabbed a bowl and two spoons her father had carved and set them into the pack. They should fetch a nice price. Then she tucked her uncle's letters inside, along with the secret message and her copy of *The Tales of Tassie Island*, her favorite possession. Her parents had told her it took a day and a half to walk to the trading post. She took her traveling cloak out of the wardrobe. She'd need it for warmth, in case she didn't have time to dig a sleeping burrow.

Lola took a long look at her ransacked home. Then, with the backpack secure, she marched up and out of the tunnel and set off southward.

She knew one thing for certain—she was the only hope for the bare-nosed wombats of the Northern Forest.

5

THE TRADING POST

Lola ran as long as she could. When her muscles began to ache, she slowed to catch her breath, resuming a wobbling gait. There was no way her short, stocky legs could maintain the pace. But she'd made some progress, already passing the section of the river where she'd last seen her parents and neighbors. The narrow dirt road followed the river, matching its curves and bends. As time passed, the backpack grew heavier and pain spread from Lola's legs to her sides. Soon, every part of her furry body urged her to stop and rest. But the image of the wombats crowded into that cage kept Lola moving forward. One step after the other. As fast as she could manage.

It was a lonely trek. The wombat burrows lay downriver from the Fairwater Trading Post, with no villages between. While Lola had never visited, her mother went twice a year to sell their wood carvings. Alice had promised that this year Lola could accompany her for the first time. It was going to be a glorious outing, one that Lola had dreamed about. What kind of critters would she meet? What kind of exciting stories would she hear?

But she had never imagined she'd make the journey alone, under such dire circumstances.

With each new bend in the river, Lola hoped to catch sight of the paddle-wheel boat and the wombats, but no such luck.

After a few hours, the road turned away from the river. The forest canopy began to disappear, trees growing thinner of trunk. At the same time, the underbrush grew thicker. Lola began to hear songbirds again, dusky robins and honeyeaters, but like many birds, they preferred to speak their own intricate languages rather than the common tongue of Tassie Island. So, to pass the time, she began to recite a story called "The Tale of the Long Waddle."

"Gather ye round and prick your ears, for a tale is about to be told, of bravery and endurance, not for the faint of heart."

Even though she had no audience, the sound of her own voice helped her to feel less lonely. It was a tale of a time, generations ago, when the invaders terrorized the southern region of the island. As a matter of survival, the wombats, with joeys in pouches, left everything behind and made the journey north to find a new home. They traveled through mud bogs, across quicksand deserts, and over mountain passes. They endured hailstorms, floods, and illness. And when they came to the Northern Forest, a place more peaceful than any they'd ever seen, they made it their home.

Lola furrowed her wide brow and ground her teeth. The wombats had been taken from the paradise they'd worked so hard to find. Taken by the same menacing critter they'd long ago sought to escape.

What had the gold-toothed monster said? That someone was going to pay gold coin for the wombats? Who would do such a thing? And why?

Her stomach groaned. She took a moment to eat clumps of

grass, enough to calm her hunger pangs. But as day began to turn to twilight, Lola realized that she couldn't take another step. Exhaustion took hold. She set down the backpack and sank onto the ground. Instinct told her to dig a burrow. It would be cozier underground, and drier if the spring rains came. But it would also be safer. For Lola knew, as every wombat knew, that the reason her wombat ancestors dug burrows was to have a place to hide from predators. And the reason her wombat ancestors had such hard, wide rumps was to block the entrance to their burrows. And even though the wombats of the Northern Forest had lived most of their lives without the threat of predators, the instinct remained. As did the hard rumps.

Though now it seemed their predators had grown smarter.

But Lola was too tired to dig. She wrapped her cloak around herself and leaned against a stump. Then she gazed up. A sprinkling of stars had appeared overhead. With no tall trees blocking her view, the sky seemed to stretch on forever.

Being a nocturnal critter, sleeping at night wasn't normal for Lola. Moonlight and starlight usually gave her energy. But after such a long waddle, her eyelids closed like heavy curtains and sleep washed over her with the rushing urgency of a river.

As the sun poked over the horizon, its rays gently warmed Lola's cheeks. She rubbed her eyes and stretched. She brushed a leaf off her bare nose. After a long yawn, she sat up and looked around. Confusion took hold. This wasn't her bed. This wasn't her bedroom. A tree stump stood behind her; a dirt road lay in front of her. Lola's heart skipped a beat.

She remembered.

She scrambled to her feet. "Mum, Dad," she mumbled. Where had her parents and the other wombats spent the night? Had they all slept in that cramped cage? Were they still on the barge or had they landed somewhere? Tears tugged at the edges of her vision as the enormity of the task before her finally settled in her heart. Her mother's parting words echoed through her mind.

Find your uncle. He'll know what to do.

Her tears did not dry quickly, but her resolve soon reasserted itself, prompting her to waddle back toward the road. It would be another half day's walk, she guessed, maybe less since she'd kept such a fast pace. She dug some water-ribbon roots and tucked them into the backpack for later snacking. Breakfast at the forefront of her mind, she continued her foraging, chewing on grasses and tender leaves. She ate only enough to quell the hunger pangs, not enough for a full-belly pat. She found a flat rock upon which to display her cubic droppings, but with no wombats around to admire them, the ritual seemed unnecessary.

She shook dirt from her cloak and folded it into her backpack. Then she set out, continuing to follow the road along the river. About an hour into her walk, Lola's whiskers quivered and her nose scrunched. She stopped dead in her tracks as a new terror made itself known.

Smoke!

It was the scent all critters of the Northern Forest dreaded. Fire had been forbidden in these parts since the Great Burn many generations ago. Luckily, the wombats and forest mice had no need of cooking fires. And because none of their arts or crafts required fire, they were perfectly happy without it. Lola had never seen the flicker of flame, but she instinctually recognized its scent. The memory of the Great Burn had been passed down from generation to generation, seared into every critter's memory, never to be forgotten. A line in the story "The Great Burn" came to mind—"a time of flame and fury."

Lola's heart thudded like the marching footfalls of the swamp water rats. She stood on tiptoe, pointing her nose as high as she could. She sniffed. The scent was light, as if carried on the breeze from far away. The sky was clear and blue. Where was the fire?

Her parents had taught her that if she ever encountered a forest fire, she was to seek shelter in the deepest burrow she could dig. And if for some reason there was no time to dig, she was to go straight to the river.

Though terrified that fire would find her, Lola had to move on. But at the first sign of flame, she would dig for her life.

A short time later, just as her legs started to complain again, the road ended at the river's edge. A wooden dock jutted into the water, matched by an identical dock on the other side. A sign hung on one of the dock's posts:

**FERRY BOAT TO FAIRWATER TRADING POST
SHOUT FOR SERVICE**

Lola shaded her eyes to get a better view. Sure enough, a little boat was tied to the opposite dock, but there was no sign of its captain. She wrapped her paws around her mouth and shouted, "Hellooo!" No one answered. She stepped to the end of the dock and tried again. "HELLOOO! IS ANYONE THERE?"

A door opened in the opposite riverbank and a brown head popped out. It was a platypus. "OI! PUT A SOCK IN IT! I'M

TRYIN' TO NAP!" He popped back inside and the door slammed shut.

Lola frowned. She didn't want to disturb anyone's sleep but she needed to get across the river. "HELLO! HELLO! MISTER PLATYPUS, SIR?"

The door opened again. "WHADDAYA WANT?" he shouted back.

"I WANT TO GO TO FAIRWATER!"

"I'M ON ME BREAK! COME BACK LATER!"

Lola frowned again. How long did a break last? Though the current at this section of river appeared to be gentle, if would be difficult to swim with her backpack and its contents weighing her down. "EXCUSE ME, BUT I REALLY NEED TO GET TO FAIRWATER!"

"AND I REALLY NEED TO NAP!" The door slammed shut again. Why were platypuses so cranky?

Lola had never hollered this much in her entire life. Hollering was considered rude by most critters, but by wombat standards it was downright vulgar. "BUT IT'S AN EMERGENCY! MY FAMILY AND ALL MY NEIGHBORS WERE TAKEN BY A TASSIE DEVIL!"

The door flew open. "A TASSIE DEVIL?"

"YES! WITH A GOLD TOOTH!"

"WHY DIDN'T YA SAY SO IN THE FIRST PLACE?" The platypus reached into his home, grabbed a captain's hat, and plopped it on his head. Then he waddled down the dock and climbed into the boat. A rope was strung across the river between the docks. The platypus leaned over the boat's bow, grabbed the rope, and began pulling. Paw over paw, he guided the boat on a linear path. With such small webbed paws, he made progress slowly. When the ferry finally reached Lola's dock, she was wiggling with impatience.

The platypus was old, evidenced by the gray streaks around his bill and the wrinkles around his black eyes. He squinted at her. "It's the middle of the day. Shouldn't ya be sleepin' in a hole in the ground?" Before Lola could answer, the platypus pointed at her. "Yer a bare-nosed wombat. I thought all of ya got put into that cage."

She took a quick breath. "You . . . you saw them? You saw my parents and my neighbors?"

"Passed through here last night on the paddle-wheel barge. Stopped in town where a devil and a bunch of rats made a real ruckus. They ate all the food. Then the devil set the storage shed on fire."

"On fire?" Lola desperately looked around. It had taken generations for the forest to recover from the Great Burn. How could someone purposely set something on fire? "Is it coming this way?" She glanced down at the river, wondering how deep she'd have to wade to be safe from the flames.

"No worries. Didn't spread. Took most of the night to put it out. That's why I'm tryin' to catch up on me sleep." He opened his bill wide and yawned.

"It's out?" She released a deep breath. "But what about the wombats? Where are they?"

"Went upriver." He stood on the bow, giving her a closer look. "Say, what're ya doin' here? Yer too young to be out on yer own, 'specially with a predator on the loose."

"I came to get help. I need to get a message to my uncle, who lives in Dore. That devil is going to sell the wombats for gold coin."

"Blimey. Never heard such a thing." The platypus scratched his bill tiredly. "Who'd pay gold coin for a cage full of wombats? A bowl collector?"

"I don't know." Lola shuffled in place, ignoring his annoying little jab. "But I'm going to find out. So can I please have a ride on your ferry? So I can get to the trading post?"

He held out his webbed paw, palm up, and waited. Lola's shoulders sank. "I don't have any coin."

"I'm not in the habit of givin' free rides." He pointed to her backpack. "Whatcha got in there?"

Lola shuffled through the contents until she found the bowl. "My dad made it." The platypus smirked at her before snatching it from her paws to examine it.

"That's a nice carving job," he said, seeming a little more jovial. "I could keep me snackin' worms in here. Okay, it'll do. Climb aboard."

"Oh, thank you!" Lola climbed into the boat. It tilted from side to side as she tried to find her balance. Once she was seated, the platypus moved to the stern, grabbed the rope, and began pulling them across. Lola's gaze flicked to his ankle spur.

"Name's Captain Jeb, by the way. Platypus Delivery Service, Northern Forest Ferries Division. What's yer name?"

"I'm Lola. Lola Budge."

"I don't usually chat with the wombats who ride me ferry. They're not much for conversation." He stood upright, keeping himself balanced with his flat tail. "But ya seem different."

"Yes, I guess I am." She wrapped her arms around her backpack as he pulled the rope, paw over paw, the ferry moving as slowly as a tortoise. "Can I help you?" she asked. "Maybe I can pull it faster?"

He stopped pulling and whipped around so quickly his hat fell off. "Help me? Help me?" He glared at Lola. "Ya think I need yer help? I've been pilotin' these waters most of me life." He grabbed the hat and plopped it back on his head. "I won the Golden Platy a few years back. Best ferry boat captain in the union. Never lost a passenger. Never lost a vessel."

"Congratulations," Lola said. Platypuses were definitely a testy lot, and just how common was this "Golden Platy" anyway? "It's just that I'm in a hurry. I need to get to Fairwater so I can hire a messenger pelican. How much do you think that will cost?"

"I haven't seen any pelicans in these parts in weeks."

"Oh no." Lola clutched the backpack tighter. "What am I going to do?" She had one plan, only one. "What about you? Could you swim there and take a message to Dore?"

"Swim there?" A watery snorting sound shot out of his bill. "This river doesn't lead to Dore."

"Then how can I—? How, how . . ." Her lower lip began to tremble.

Captain Jeb's grumpy voice turned soft. "Ya poor thing." He waddled over to her and patted her shoulder. "I'll get ya to Fairwater and then we'll figure somethin' out."

Maybe the cranky old critter wasn't so bad after all. Lola wiped a tear from her eye and nodded.

Once the ferry was docked, Captain Jeb helped Lola disembark. "C'mon," he said. He put the carved bowl in his house, then led Lola up the road, waddling in his odd platypus way. Lola's steps felt heavier, weighed down by a brand-new worry—what chance did the wombats have if she couldn't get a messenger pelican?

"C'mon, c'mon," Captain Jeb urged. The road climbed a grass-lined hill. When they reached its crest, Jeb halted. "We're standing smack-dab in the middle of where the river forks. That's the eastern fork and that's the southern fork. The trading post lies between." He pointed.

Lola looked down the hill. There were two structures—a small, split-log cabin, made from saplings and young branches, and a much larger log building, two stories high. A third structure was now a pile of ash—the remains of the storage shed. She shuddered. Then she looked past the buildings, toward the surrounding woods and along the river, but found no signs of a gold-toothed devil, the rats, or the wombats. She took another deep breath, yearning to smell her mum's peppermint perfume and her dad's whisker cream. But the breeze only carried the scent of smoke.

Captain Jeb led her down the hill to the little log house. Jeb stepped onto the welcome mat and opened the little round door. He stuck his head inside. "Josie? Rupert?" His voice echoed. There was no answer. "Those two pincushions are around here somewhere." Lola followed him along the path that led to the larger building. Lola was so busy looking around that she didn't notice the strange ball of spikes lying directly in her path.

"Ouch," she said as she accidentally brushed against it. What was that thing? Some kind of plant? She reached her paw cautiously toward the spiky surface, but just before she touched it again, it shuddered. Startled, Lola jumped back.

Then the ball slowly uncurled, revealing the odd critter it was.

6

CUPPA BAD NEWS

The small echidna rolled upright and looked at Lola. She blinked her beady black eyes, then made a snuffling sound with her long gray snout. Her spikes were brown and tipped with specks of white and yellow, contrasting with the gray skin beneath. Even though Lola was not yet fully grown, she still towered over the critter.

"Ah, there ya are, Josie," Captain Jeb said. "Whatcha doing all curled up?"

"I heard footsteps and got scared," Josie replied in a quiet, squeaky voice. She started to tremble.

"Nothing to be scared about. That night monster is gone." Jeb looked around. "Say, where's Rupert?"

Some shuffling sounds drew everyone's attention as the ground nearby heaved upward, the tips of spines sticking up from below. Within moments a small elongated head poked out of the dirt. "You sure it's gone?" a new squeaky voice asked as Rupert revealed himself. His spikes were a darker brown than Josie's. He wiped flecks of dirt from his snout but ignored the large patches between his spines.

"Long gone. Way up the southern fork by now." Captain Jeb

held out a paw to help Josie to her feet and then, more carefully, pulled Rupert out of his hole. "This here's Lola. She's come from the burrows. It's her family that was taken by the Tassie devil."

"And all my neighbors," Lola added.

"I've never heard anything so sad." Josie's eyes pooled with tears and she continued to tremble. "I'm so sorry. What a terrible upset for you, to be orphaned at such a young age." Rupert handed Josie a handkerchief. She shook dirt from it, then used it to dab her tears. "So very terrible. So very terrible indeed."

"I'm not an orphan. My parents are alive and I'm going to find them." The echidnas and the platypus looked at Lola in disbelief, as if she'd just told them she was going to grow a pair of wings. "I'm going to do everything I can to save them. I walked all the way here and I'll keep walking if I have to. I'll do whatever it takes. I *will* see them. I will."

"Yes, yes you will, my dear," Josie said tenderly, using the handkerchief to blow her snout. "My, my, you do talk a lot for a wombat. Please forgive me for blubbering. I've never been so frightened in all me life. Never ever."

Lola didn't blame Josie for crying, having shed many tears herself over the last two days. "Did . . . did your family get taken, too?" she asked.

Rupert shook his head. "Our puggles are long grown and moved away. Captain Jeb and us, why, we're the only critters who live here."

"Lived here most of me life," Captain Jeb said, scratching beneath his hat. "And I've never seen swamp water rats act that way before. They're usually harmless critters. They come here and collect garbage and molding food, then go back to their swamp. But they were followin' the orders of that Tassie devil. She told them to help themselves to food and drink, then she set the shed on fire."

Lola looked over at the charred remains. "Why did she do that? Fire is forbidden here."

Captain Jeb shrugged. "Tryin' to scare us, I guess."

"It worked," Josie said, her spines trembling anew. "All I could do was curl into a ball." As she began to sob, Rupert put his arm around her. His paw flowed through her spines without hesitation or worry, gently stroking her back.

"There, there, love, we're unharmed. We can rebuild. Come on, let's get you inside for a nice cuppa." He smiled gently at Lola. "Would you like a nice cuppa? When the other wombats come here to trade, they always like a nice cuppa."

Lola did love tea, but there was a much more important matter to attend to. "I need to get a message to my uncle in Dore," she said with urgency. "Do you know where I can find a pelican?"

"We haven't had any pelicans in weeks," Rupert told her.

Captain Jeb made a little smacking sound with his bill. "That's exactly what I said."

"Is there any other way I can get a message out?"

"You could have sent one on the paddle-wheel boat," Rupert said. "If it hadn't been stolen. It's the only boat that travels this river."

No messenger pelicans and no boat? Lola's legs suddenly felt wobbly. Her hopes had been swept away like chips of wood. Had she come this far only to find a dead end?

Rupert motioned for her to follow. "Let's go inside, get a cuppa, and maybe we can come up with a plan."

Rupert and Josie ambled toward the larger building. From behind, it looked as if they were wearing thorn-covered capes, one much dirtier than the other. "C'mon," Captain Jeb told Lola. "With some grub in us, we're bound to think of somethin'."

A sign hung above the building's door: FAIRWATER TRADING POST. Passing through, Lola realized that the doors had been made large enough for the wombat customers. There were three tables with matching chairs, some small enough for forest mice, some large enough for wombats, but most had been knocked over. Pretty red-checkered curtains framed the windows, but many of the glass panes had been broken. A painting of the queen lay on the floor. Rupert picked it up and rehung it on its nail.

The kitchen was also a disaster. Most of the cupboard doors had been torn off their hinges, the cupboards noticeably vacant. As Lola looked around, a gust of wind blew in, suddenly knocking a dish onto the floor. At the sound, Josie squealed and curled into a ball. It took a few minutes for Rupert to calm her down and unfurl her.

While Rupert shuffled into the kitchen, Lola helped set four chairs upright. Then Josie set four bowls onto the table along with four spoons and four teacups, each carved by wombat claws. Lola, Captain Jeb, and Josie sat. Rupert returned with a tin in his hand. "The rats ate most of the food," he told them, "but they missed the worms." He set the tin on the table, then opened the lid. The contents squirmed. "Mealworms and earthworms," he said, scooping a heaping, wiggling spoonful into each bowl. Captain Jeb clacked his bill expectantly.

Lola looked at the slimy, tangled mass in her bowl and cringed. Worms were not wombat food. But the truth was even if it had been a lovely salad of mint and parsley, she couldn't have eaten a bite. Her stomach was all in a knot. "Don't worry, my dear," Josie said as she reached into her apron pocket. "I always keep a few of these on hand for snacking." She slid a biscuit across the table. "Acorn and oatmeal."

"Thank you," Lola said, and truly meant it.

Rupert picked up a teapot that had been sitting in a beam of sunlight. "Lucky for us, rats don't seem to care for sun tea." He carried the teapot to the table and began filling the cups. The sweet scent of peppermint filled Lola's nostrils.

Table manners did not seem to be a consideration for Captain Jeb, who slurped loudly as he dipped his bill into the bowl. Josie and Rupert had a different method of eating. With snouts poised, their long, pink tongues snaked around their bowls, picking up worms one by one. Lola desperately wanted to use this perfect occasion to ask them questions about their lives, but her head spun with images of the gold-toothed devil, the caged wombats, and the singing rats. Her task was paramount. "Where are the pelicans?" she asked.

Rupert shrugged. "We dunno. They just stopped coming. Captain Sam, the platy who owns the paddle-wheel boat, usually shows up a couple times a month to pick up the wombat carvings so he can deliver them to fancy shops. He brings all the things we need at the trading post. But Sam hasn't been here in weeks. We're all out of wombat whisker cream and we don't have any tail conditioner for the forest mice."

"How did that monster get Captain Sam's boat?" Lola asked.

Rupert slurped a long worm. The thing wriggled desperately before disappearing. "She stole it, I reckon."

Captain Jeb looked up from his bowl and narrowed his tiny eyes. "Or Sam rented it to her."

"Why would he rent his boat to a night monster?" Rupert asked.

"Greed, pure and simple," Captain Jeb said. "If it's true, if Sam's taken gold from a Tassie devil, he'll get kicked out of the Platy Union, mark my words."

Rupert smacked his paw on the table. "If history tells us one thing, it's that no good ever came from associating with those red-eared carnivores. They only care about themselves, and they'll betray you in an instant if they believe they'll get away with it. There's no honor to be found amid those mammal-eaters."

Everyone suddenly looked at Lola. She knew what they were thinking. "She isn't going to eat the wombats," she insisted. "She said she was going to sell them."

Captain Jeb snorted. "How can ya be sure? Everyone knows that wombat is a Tassie devil's favorite food and always has been."

"Jeb!" Josie scolded.

"What? She might as well face the truth. The chances of her seeing her family again are—"

Josie whacked Captain Jeb on his head with her unused spoon. The gesture got his attention. He stopped talking and rubbed his head. Josie reached across the table to pat Lola's paw. "There, there, my dear. Don't listen to that cranky old platypus. Queen Myra is the dearest queen we've ever had. She'd never let anything happen to the wombats. Never. She knows that we critters of the Northern Forest are her most loyal and always have been. She'll make this right. I know she will." Her husband said nothing, prompting her to elbow him. "Everything will be fine, won't it, Rupert?"

"I'm loyal to our dear queen, don't get me wrong." He shrugged. "But if those monsters start leaving the mountain, what can she do?" Josie huffed, but seemed to agree, and didn't reach for the spoon again.

The knot in Lola's stomach tightened. "I can't just sit here." She pushed her chair back.

"Hold on," Captain Jeb said, lifting his bill from the bowl at last. "Where ya goin'?"

"I'll walk to Dore if I have to. My uncle is the ambassador to the Northern Forest. He'll help the wombats. I know he will."

"Ambassador? You mean old Tobias Bottom?" Rupert asked.

"Yes," Lola said. "Do you know him?"

Rupert leaned back in his chair and smiled fondly at some distant memory. "It's been ages since I saw him. He visited here when he was setting out to seek his fortune. He was a chatty one. You remind me of him—quite a bit, actually."

Josie poured another round of sun tea, her snout scrunched in a fretful way. "I don't like the idea of you going off on your own. You're younger than my grandpuggles."

"I don't know what else to do," Lola said. "I've got to find my uncle."

"It might not be such a bad idea," Captain Jeb said as he dropped three sugar cubes into his teacup. "Maybe someone high up in the government can fix this mess. If Tassie devils have come to hunt wombats, then who might they hunt next? Besides, Lola seems mighty determined to continue on."

"Yes, I am mighty determined," Lola confirmed.

"That being the case . . ." Rupert slipped out of his chair and walked over to the stairway, climbed up, and disappeared. The sounds of shifting furniture could be heard scraping across the floor above. And Rupert's muffled voice: "Where is it? Where is it? Aha, found it." Then the footfalls began to patter around once more, until Rupert reappeared from the stairway with a roll of paper in his paw. "I hope this will serve you for the journey ahead." Pushing aside the bowls and cups, he unfurled the paper, revealing a large, timeworn map. Spying a nasty little mite eating away at the paper, Rupert quickly snaked his tongue out and got rid of the problem.

Lola jumped out of her chair, hurried around the table, and carefully leaned over Rupert's spiky shoulder so she could get a better look.

"Here's the southern fork of Fairwater River," Rupert explained. "That's where the night monster was taking your wombats. But she can only take them this far, right here where the river meets up with the Royal Road."

"What's the Royal Road?" Lola asked.

"It's the road that leads to Dore. But before it reaches Dore, the road passes through the Mouse Farmlands and the town of Bounty. Someone there might have seen the wombats and might know where they are. But if not, this is the road that will lead you to your uncle." His finger traced over the map. "Now, to get to the Royal Road you follow the old path along the river."

"How long will that take?" Lola asked.

Rupert's tongue darted out to catch a wayward worm just as it was about to make its escape over the edge of the table. But Josie was faster, smirking shyly at him as she chewed. "It depends," Rupert said. "How fast do you walk?"

"Wombats can run," Lola said. "Faster than most critters."

"Then it shouldn't take you more than a week."

"A week?" Lola asked with alarm. Her gaze traveled over the map. "Can't I take a shortcut?" She pointed. "Across this section?"

Captain Jeb and Rupert exchanged a concerned look. "That's swamp," Jeb said. "It's full of bities."

"But it's shorter, right?" Lola asked.

"Yes," Rupert said. "Should take you two days at the most. But those bities are nasty."

"Oh dear, oh dear," Josie mumbled. "I hate bities."

Lola hated them, too. But wombat fur was a natural defense against the annoying little bugs, and she knew to coat her nose and ears with mud. "I'm going," she announced.

Rupert rolled the map and handed it to her. Lola winced as she accidentally brushed against his spikes. She carefully tucked the map into her pack. Then she glanced out one of the broken windows. There was still half a day of sunlight left. "Thank you for the map and the ferry ride. I think I should be going now." The three grouped around her to say their goodbyes. "When I get to Dore, I'll tell my uncle about your burnt shed and broken windows. I'm sure he'll help."

Josie's eyes filled with tears again. "You listen to me, my dear. If you get scared, don't hesitate to come back." She hugged Lola, acting as if one of her own was leaving the nest. The hug prickled something fierce, but Lola held her breath until Josie let go. Then Josie tucked some bags of peppermint tea into the backpack, along with two oatmeal acorn biscuits and a small tin of worms, which Lola politely accepted.

They walked her to the start of the shortcut. "Safe journey to you, and give Tobias our best," Rupert said. He and Josie stood side by side, smiling sadly, as if they'd never see her again.

"May the wind be at yer back," Captain Jeb said, waving his captain's hat. "And beware the bities!"

The three continued to wave goodbye as Lola started down the path, her backpack a bit heavier, and her heart as well.

7

SWAMP SOUP

A few hours into her trek, the ground grew increasingly wet. Lola's paws left little furrows that slowly filled in behind her. At first the small pools of fetid water were easily avoided, but soon the majority of the ground was covered in thick muck, with large ponds disguised by floating green plant growth. Long tendrils of moss hung from the trees. It was a peaceful and quiet landscape, which would appeal to most wombats. But dampness was seeping through Lola's fur and she shivered. She wondered if her parents had ever been to this place. If she found them, she'd tell them all about it.

When she found them, she corrected herself.

There was no time for doubts. No time to get scared and sad. So with a determined jut of her furry chin, she paused and unrolled the map. Careful to keep the paper dry, she checked the route. Unfortunately, no lines had been drawn to indicate a way through the swamp. She climbed onto a log, stood on tiptoe, and searched for a trail. The slimy landscape lay before her, green and watery, with no signs or arrows to point the way. According to the map's compass, she needed to head southeast, which meant that she needed to keep the setting sun on her right and slightly behind.

She'd learned about using the sun during her daytime sneaks out of the burrow.

At first Lola tried to avoid swimming through the stinky water, and ended up having to backtrack several times to find ways around. But as dry land disappeared, she found herself waist-deep in the swamp. Balancing her pack on her head, she walked, her claws feeling along the bottom for sharp rocks. She hoped she wouldn't step on anything that might sting or pinch. Was that a fish that brushed past her leg? She shuddered.

That's when the bities appeared. Little black insects, humming eagerly as they caught the scent of a warm-blooded critter. Lola scooped some mud with her claws and rubbed it onto her nose and ears, but not before a squadron of the little demons had bitten her. Her nose felt itchy and bumpy, but the mud soon soothed it and her coarse fur protected the rest of her. The bities were still annoying little things. "Go away," she grumbled. "Go bother someone else." But who else was there to bother? She hadn't seen a single rat since leaving Fairwater, and this was their home. Were all of them helping the gold-toothed devil? Swamp water rats and wombats had never been enemies, but after what they'd done to her family, she wanted to stay as far away from them as possible. She thought about reciting a story to break up the silence, but she didn't want to attract attention. If there was one Tassie devil on the loose, there might be others. With that thought, the swamp began to seem eerie—like the moss tendrils were waiting to grab her. She squeaked in sudden fear.

The sun was Lola's best indicator of direction, but it was almost setting. While she was well suited for moving about at night, she needed the sun to guide her from the swamp, so she decided to find somewhere to rest. But there'd be no burrowing in this landscape. She didn't want to sleep in the muck and she certainly couldn't sleep in the water. She needed to find a dry spot, perhaps in a hollowed tree trunk. And she needed to eat. The bug-eaten and egg-laden swamp grasses didn't look appetizing. Fortunately, she had water-ribbon roots and Josie's biscuits to feast upon for supper.

As she began her search for dry land, a faint orange glow caught her attention. She sniffed. Notes of fire rose above the tangy scent of swamp. There were voices, too.

A dry patch of ground appeared up ahead. Lola took care not to make any squelches or other noises as she stepped out of the water. Rather than shake her fur dry, she resigned herself to shivering. The smoke was near. She peeked out from around the trunk of an ancient, gnarled tree. And there, in the middle of a clearing, she saw it.

Real, living fire.

It was her first sight of what she'd long heard about. The flames danced inside a ring of stones and sang a strange, crackling song. As fear tightened her stomach, Lola told herself that fire shouldn't be a danger in a place as wet as this. Any flame that tried to travel would quickly be extinguished. She stared at the reddish-orange light, her gaze sinking into its depths. The effect was mesmerizing. She might have stood like that forever had a voice not woken her from the trance.

"Hurry up. I'm starving!"

Three swamp water rats sat around the campfire. The first rat was large with a broad chest and thick arms. He was also missing an ear. The second rat was shorter but equally muscular. And the third rat was small and lanky, seemingly younger than his companions. While the larger rats had a green tinge to their gray fur and were covered in dried bits of swamp slime, the leaner rat had perfectly combed gray fur and was slime-free.

They sat on fallen branches. Three buckets were stowed behind them and three shovels leaned against a tree. One of the buckets was wrapped in bright-red cloth that included patchwork pockets on the outside. Each rat held a wombat-carved bowl on his lap. Unlike the others, the smaller rat had a white napkin tied around his neck.

"I hate soup," the shorter rat said. "Nothing proper about cooking something in water, even if it's swamp water." He sniffed at steam that rose from a cauldron hanging over the fire. He turned his snout up in disgust. "It doesn't even smell that bad. What kind of decent food doesn't smell bad, Bob?"

"Stop complaining and eat your supper," Bob, the larger rat, said. Then he pointed to the skinny rat. "You don't hear Melvin complaining, do you?"

"Of course Melvin's not complaining. He's the one who cooked it."

"I think it's delightful," Melvin said. He ladled some soup into his bowl. Then, after blowing on the soup to cool it, he tipped his bowl to his mouth and took a delicate sip. Then he coughed. "The roots and greens give it a crisp flavor, with notes of, um, licorice."

"Crisp flavor? Notes of licorice?" The shorter rat frowned. "What's the matter with you?"

Melvin dabbed his mouth with his napkin. "There's nothing the matter with me, Stanley, just because I like trying new things. Even if they don't turn out as well as I hoped." He mumbled the last sentence to himself, but continued to eat the soup.

Stanley glared at him. "Well, *Melvin*, if you hadn't taken so long making the soup, we'd be halfway to Dore by now. I don't want to eat this. Where's the rotten bits? Where's the greasy film? The unrecognizable floaties?"

"I've got an idea." Bob reached into his bucket and pulled out a small, green lump. "Been saving this piece of moldy cheese for a special occasion." He tossed it into the cauldron. He stirred, then ladled soup into Stanley's bowl. "That better?"

Stanley took a sip. "Not bad. But it would be better with a petrified spud or two."

"That goes without saying," Bob said.

Melvin rolled his eyes.

Swamp water rats sure liked to eat horrid things. Lola wondered what she should do. Should she talk to them? Or were they up to no good, just like the rats who'd helped take her family and neighbors? Bob ladled soup into his bowl. "Things are going to change for us, Stanley. No more scrounging. No more scavenging. The queen promised us our fill. Mountains and mountains of slimy garbage, the kind that feels like it's trying to crawl back up your throat. All we have to do is to join the Royal Guard."

"Glory to Queen Myra, may her reign be long." Stanley smiled, revealing his yellow teeth. "And may our feasts be ever rotten."

"May our feasts be ever rotten," Bob repeated. The two rats raised their bowls, knocking the wood together with a loud crack. Soup flew through the air, spilling all around. Bob and Stanley didn't seem to mind, but Melvin scooted down the branch, narrowly avoiding the downpour.

Lola leaned against the trunk, still unsure what to do. She had questions. But she still didn't know if these critters were friend or foe. She leaned a bit farther, trying to take in more of the scene. There were no signs of any Tassie devils. Perhaps these were nice rats after all. Maybe she could join them for supper. Maybe they could show her the best way to the Royal Road.

Bob spoke next. "Think of it, mates. Dore! A place rats like us could only dream of."

"It's a dream that's coming true," Stanley said. "With all the critters who live in Dore, there will be garbage heaps as high as the sky."

"Personally, I'm looking forward to the bakeries," Melvin said. "Dore is renowned for its winter wheat loaves. Fresh out of the oven, warm and buttery." He looked sheepishly at his companions, who stared at him, mouths agape. "I'm sure they taste great when they get *moldy*."

Bob snorted. "I'm beginning to think your brain is moldy, Melvin." He and Stanley laughed. Then he raised his bowl. "We'd best eat and get to bed so we can get an early start come morning. Bog in, blokes."

As they ate, Lola's legs began to cramp and she wasn't sure how much longer she could stand still. Her stomach ached, reminding her that she hadn't eaten much that day. Darkness had fallen over the swamp and a chorus of frogs began an evening lullaby. The temperature had also fallen. Lola shivered again. At least the little bities had gone to bed.

She couldn't stand there forever. She needed to make a decision.

But as Bob stopped slurping, Lola's decision was made for her. "Do you smell that?" he asked. He stuck his snout up in the air and took a few deep sniffs. Stanley and Melvin sniffed as well.

Then they turned toward Lola's tree.

8

ALL ABOUT MUD

Stanley dropped his soup bowl and grabbed his shovel. "Who's there?" he demanded, holding the shovel in both hands, ready to swing. "Show yourself!"

"Oh, hooly dooly." Taking a deep breath to compose herself, Lola stepped into view. Stanley's arms relaxed.

"You're a joey," he said with surprise. "Why were you spying on us?"

"I'm sorry, I wasn't spying, exactly . . ." She held tight to her backpack. "My name's Lola. Lola Budge. I'm looking for a place to sleep." She could feel the fire's warmth on her cheeks, so she took a step back. What if those flames leapt free, pranced across the ground, and nibbled on her feet?

"What are you doing in the swamp?" Bob asked.

"I'm trying to find my family."

"Here?" Bob scratched the spot on his head where his ear had once been. "Wombats never pop around these parts."

"No one ever pops around these parts," Stanley added. "Why would your family be here?"

It was the story she hated to tell, for each time she told it, she relived those terrifying moments—especially the last view of her mother and father. Her shoulders sank, her ears drooped, and she scratched at the itchy bites. "A—a Tassie devil and some rats took everyone from the burrows. Everyone but me, because I was down at the stream talking to a platypus. He had a message for me and after he gave it to me, I heard a snarling sound and—"

"I thought wombats were quiet," Stanley grumbled, wriggling his claw inside his ear.

"This one's a real yabberer," Bob said.

"You asked me a question and I'm answering it," Lola retorted, slightly annoyed.

"Guess I did," Bob said with a snort, sitting back down. "Go on."

Melvin hadn't said a word, but he was sitting at the edge of his branch, paying close attention.

"Well, as I was saying, this monster took all the wombats away, on a paddle-wheel boat. Have you seen them? Do you know where they are?"

Bob wiped his mouth with the tip of his bald tail. Then he whispered something in Stanley's ear. Stanley whispered something back. They nodded in agreement.

"Information is valuable," Bob told Lola. "Do you have anything you could trade for information? Anything *to eat*?"

"Oh, yes, I do have some food," Lola said hopefully. She set her pack onto the ground, then searched through it. "I have some roots, some bags of tea, and a tin of worms." She held out the tin.

"Worms?" Bob grimaced. "We don't need worms. The swamp is filled with them."

"Oh." Lola put the tin back and kept searching. "I have two bikkies."

Stanley scurried forward and stuck his snout up to the biscuits, sniffing eagerly. Then he frowned. "They smell fresh."

"No mold?" Bob asked.

"No mold," Stanley confirmed. "No rot. No maggots." He turned his back to Lola and shuffled to his branch. "*No* decent food, *no* information."

"There must be at least something you can tell me. Why are rats helping a night monster? And where are they taking my family?"

Stanley and Bob ignored her. Stanley refilled his bowl and took a slurp. "Ouch," he said. "This soup's been on the fire too long. Just about burned my tongue."

Lola looked down at her backpack. "Wait," she said. "I think I have something you'll like." She pulled out the two wooden spoons. "You can have these. My dad carved them. If you use them with the soup, you won't burn your tongue." Despite the flickering flames, she edged closer, holding out the perfectly-hollowed spoons. "Could I trade *these* for information?"

Bob and Stanley eagerly snatched the spoons from her paws. After testing the spoons with loud slurps, the two of them agreed. So Lola asked her first question. "Have you seen my parents and the other wombats of the Northern Forest?"

"Nope," Bob and Stanley said.

Lola gritted her teeth. "Okay, well, do you know where they might be?"

"Nope," they said again.

Lola clenched her paws in frustration. "Well, what *do* you know?"

Bob scratched his back with his new spoon. "I know that a Tassie devil came here a few days ago. She promised us rats that we could eat all the food we wanted if we worked for her. Many of our friends left. We haven't seen them since."

"Did she have a gold tooth?" Lola asked.

Stanley pointed to one of his own teeth. "Gleamed like the sun."

Lola's paw clenched tighter as she pictured the critter who took her family away. "But *why* would rats work for her?" she asked. "Night monsters are dangerous."

"It's simple," Bob said. "She offered them food. We rats think with our stomachs first, and our brains third."

"What's second?"

"Our tongues, of course!"

"Not *all* rats." Melvin cleared his throat, then waved a paw to get Lola's attention. "Not all rats think with their stomachs or tongues. I have made many decisions that are not food based."

"That's because you're a weird one, you with your fancy bucket," Bob said. "The rest of us care only about food."

"If you care only about food, then why didn't *you* go with the monster?" Lola asked.

Bob snorted. "Do we look stupid enough to work for a Tassie devil? Can't keep eating good food if you get eaten, after all." He tapped his foot, waiting for Lola to respond.

The popping of the embers, the crackling flame reaching for the starry sky, and the croak of a lone, insomniac bullfrog were the only sounds as Lola tried to figure out the answer to the question. "Um . . ." she paused, hoping she wouldn't insult the only critters who'd had some real information for her. They didn't *look* stupid. In fact, other than the green slime that clung to their fur, they had very nice faces, with little, round eyes and long, thick whiskers. But they had rejected a perfectly lovely oatmeal and acorn biscuit because it hadn't been full of maggots or mold. "No?"

"You got that right," Bob said. "Now, if you don't have anything but those fresh bikkies, leave us in peace." With their new spoons, he and Stanley began slurping the last dregs of soup.

Melvin slipped off his branch and walked over to Lola, his movements graceful and sleek, his tail held upright. He smelled surprisingly fresh and clean. He picked up one of the biscuits, turning it in his paws to examine it from all angles and sniffing curiously. "May I?" he asked Lola. She nodded. He nibbled delicately. His eyes grew wide as the sweet taste of acorns and oats filled his mouth. "It's delicious. The hint of cinnamon contrasts beautifully with the honey. And the nutty texture of the acorns pairs well with the creamy oats." He waved the biscuit at his companions. "You should give it a try."

Bob and Stanley groaned. "You're a disgrace to all swamp water rats," Stanley said over his shoulder, his wormlike tail curling in on itself in apparent disgust.

Melvin smiled. "I do believe that's the nicest thing you've ever said to me."

This third rat was so different from the other two, Lola immediately sensed a kindred spirit. "You can have the bikkie," she told him.

"Thank you." He carefully clasped the biscuit in his paws as if it were a treasure. Then he ushered Lola to the edge of the dry land and they sat side by side on another fallen branch. The crackling of the fire and the voices of Bob and Stanley faded into the background. Melvin ate one biscuit while Lola ate the other. After each bite, he paused, as if thinking about what he was eating. Lola watched with fascination. She'd never seen anyone savor a biscuit in that manner.

"It's rare that we get fresh food here in the swamp," Melvin told her. "You see, it's impossible to grow anything in these mucky conditions. And because the terrain is so difficult to cross, merchants don't venture here. So for generations, swamp water rats learned to eat whatever they could find. As the years passed, taste buds changed and the rats who lived here got used to eating what others throw away. They began to prefer it." He shrugged. "It's nothing to be ashamed about. Scavenging is a noble profession."

Lola nodded. "And useful, too."

"Indeed. But it is not my calling. I am not like the others. My taste buds long for flavors that go beyond the palate of sour, putrid, and rancid. And these bikkies are divine. Do you make other delights?"

"I didn't make them," Lola said. "The only things I've ever made are bowls, but they always come out lopsided and wobbly. Wombats are supposed to be good at carving but . . . I'm terrible at it."

"Seems we're both a bit different," he said. He smiled at her and she smiled back. Then he began grooming himself. His paws worked quickly, the sharp claws picking at crumbs and fluffing his fur. He removed the napkin from his neck and cleaned his face. Then he took a jar from his red bucket. It contained thick, green paste, a dab of which he rubbed into his paws.

"You won't find a better paw cream on all of Tassie Island," he explained. "It's also good for itchy tails. It's my own concoction, made from swamp mud and a few other secret ingredients. Want to give it a try?" He glanced at her slime-covered legs and raised an eyebrow. "You could use a bit of grooming."

Lola knew her mother would be mortified by her messy appearance, but Lola didn't care how messy she looked or how stinky she smelled. She needed to know things. Many things. And she needed to know them now. She politely dabbed some cream onto her palm, then asked, "Do you have any idea where the wombats might be?"

"I'm sorry, I don't. But I do know something else." He pulled a piece of paper from his bucket. "About an hour before you arrived, a pelican dropped this into the swamp."

Lola jumped to her feet. "A messenger pelican?" She couldn't believe her luck. "Is the bird still here? I really need to talk to it. Where is it?"

"Gone, I'm afraid. You know how pelicans are. They do their jobs, hack down any fish in the area, then leave." He held out the poster. Lola took it. The paper was so damp that the ink had run and splotched all the words.

"I can't read this," she said.

Melvin leaned forward and took a peek. "I'm afraid that's what happens to paper in the swamp. It's why I don't own any books. They dissolve before you can finish reading them. You know, I don't think I've ever gotten to the end of a story." Lola thought about her beloved storybook and Rupert's map. She didn't want either to dissolve, and fidgeted uncomfortably.

"What did this say?" she asked, squinting her eyes at the blurry words.

"It was a job description. It said: 'Attention all rats. Queen Myra needs you to join the new Royal Guard. Eat all the food you want in exchange for work. Come to Dore immediately.'"

"What's the Royal Guard?" Lola wondered as a few drops of ink rolled down her arm.

"There used to be one, long ago," Bob said loudly. He'd clearly been eavesdropping. "The Guard was formed to protect the royal family and the royal city, way back when the invaders came. But there's been no need for a royal guard for generations."

"Looks like they need one now. So that's where we're heading in the morning," Stanley said. "To Dore, to offer our services to the queen. And we'll get all the food we want without having to scavenge for it." He and Bob slapped paws high in the air.

Melvin leaned close to Lola and lowered his voice. "I'm tagging along but I'm not going to join the Guard."

"Then why are you going?" Lola asked.

"To seek my fortune." He reached out and picked a strand of moss off Lola's shoulder. "Living in a swamp is not for everyone, but it does have its merits. The climate keeps the skin moist and the claws supple. I intend to create an entire line of beauty products made from swamp mud. I'm going to open my own grooming salon."

"Really?" Her eyes widened. "My uncle went to Dore to seek his fortune, too. And now he's an ambassador."

Perhaps it was the starlight, but it seemed to Lola that Melvin's eyes lit up at that moment. "That's quite a step up the social ladder. If a wombat can go that high, perhaps a mere rat can climb higher still. You've given me hope."

"An ambassador?" Stanley jabbed his elbow into Bob's side. "Can you believe that, Bob? A wombat working in government, a swamp water rat starting his own business, and a Tassie devil who's left the mountain."

Bob scratched his back, again, with his new spoon. "Everything's changing."

Lola frowned. One thing was never supposed to change. "It's against the law for a devil to leave Mount Ossa. But I heard her say that Queen Myra had changed the law. That's a lie. Queen Myra is good. My mum says she's the best queen we've ever had. She would never let night monsters roam free."

"Maybe she would, maybe she wouldn't," Bob said. He stuck another piece of wood on the fire. Then Bob pulled a blanket from his bucket. "Most critters in these parts are loyal to the queen. Me included. But the truth is, she's never set foot up here, and none of us have taken the journey to meet her. She lives behind her golden walls, eating whatever she wants and doing as she pleases. It was her greatest grandfather who sent the devils away, long before any of us were born. Maybe that gold-toothed devil wasn't lying. Maybe our little queenie did change the law, and maybe more of those monsters are coming this way." He stretched out on the ground. "If more are coming, I'd rather be working behind those royal walls than sitting in the swamp, waiting for one to come cook me up for tea."

"Me too," Stanley said, grabbing his own blanket and stretching next to Bob. "I'm going to dream about royal garbage." Then, after some good-nights, they pulled the blankets over their heads.

Lola had never heard anyone doubt the queen or her intentions. She thought about the portrait hanging in her burrow, and the same portrait hanging in the trading post. Queen Myra had the kindest, largest eyes Lola had ever seen. "Queen Myra would never do anything to hurt the Northern Forest critters," she quietly said to Melvin.

"I hope you're right," Melvin whispered back. "But it is a mystery why she would suddenly want to form a royal guard."

"My uncle will know the answer," Lola said with the utmost confidence, "and find my family. I know he will."

Melvin smiled at Lola, but it was a sad sort of smile, as if he didn't quite believe her. Then he put his paw over his mouth and yawned. "It's getting late." Unlike the others, he didn't lie on the bare ground. His blanket was sewn together, like a tube, and he slipped inside. "Good night."

Lola looked around. "Are we safe from the bities?"

"The fire will keep them away."

As much as the fire made her nervous, she was grateful for its presence. "May I walk with you? In the morning?" Lola asked. The rats would know the best way out of the swamp and it would be nice to have company.

"I don't see why not. You shouldn't be on your own." He yawned again.

"Thank you," Lola said, yawning as well.

Lola lay on the ground, her cloak spread over her. Except for Bob's and Stanley's muffled snoring, a heavy silence descended upon the swamp. No frogs, no buzzing insects, no trickling water. Silent but not peaceful, for Lola's mind hummed with terrible thoughts. She pulled the cloak tighter, tucking it beneath her feet and sides, as if it were a shield. After closing her eyes she tried to channel her thoughts toward happy places—a mossy bed, a warm burrow, a family home. Stanley's snoring became her father's snoring. The lapping sound became the burrow's stream.

Lapping sound?

Lola's ear pricked and her eyes flew open. She took a shallow breath and held as still as a boulder. There it was again, the soft sound of water lapping against the shore. A wave? How could there be a wave in the swamp? Was something moving through the water?

The sound came again. Yes, something was out there, but none of the rats seemed to notice. Their hearing was clearly not as sensitive as hers. She held back a squeal as she imagined a night monster swimming slowly toward their camp. Minutes passed. Hours, it seemed. But the sound didn't repeat. Holding herself in that frozen state was exhausting, and fatigue finally overcame her. Whatever was out there, it had passed by.

She closed her eyes, curled up, and fell asleep.

9

BABY BLUE

Lola spent the next morning following the rats through the swamp. Sometimes they waded, sometimes they walked on dry patches of land, but mostly they swam through the mucky, stagnant water. The rats were adept at swimming with buckets balanced on their heads and shovels secured to their backs, but Lola's pack was not watertight, so she balanced it on her head. It wasn't the most comfortable way to travel, but she didn't care. Getting to the Royal Road as quickly as possible was her only concern.

Even though Lola was far larger than her companions, she had trouble keeping pace with them. The rats were smooth, sleek swimmers, able to dart beneath low-hanging branches while Lola had to swim around. They could slip over fallen trees faster than Lola's short legs could manage. She spent most of her energy trying to keep up. But she did manage to squeeze in questions. "Why do you have shovels?"

"Best way to dig for rotting food," Bob said. "Our claws aren't like yours."

Lola flexed her paw. Her five sharp claws and her padded palm were perfectly designed for digging and scooping. "I am particularly fond of my shovel," Melvin said, reaching back and giving it a pat. This didn't make much sense to Lola, for Melvin had expressed a dislike for garbage.

"Melvin doesn't like to get his claws dirty," Stanley explained, as if reading her mind.

Though the terrain was tricky, Lola was happy for the companionship. The rats didn't mind conversation. And she quickly learned that they were fond of singing. Bob and Stanley sang a particular song so many times, Lola soon had it memorized and joined in.

When you dig in a garbage heap

Who knows what you shall find

Half a pie, a crust of bread, a slimy melon rind.

So raise your shovels to the sky

Then plunge them in the ground,

There's garbage to be found, mates,

There's garbage to be found.

If you feast in a garbage heap

You'll be a lucky bloke

Wriggling maggots, putrid roots, a rotting artichoke.

So raise your shovels to the sky

Then plunge them in the ground,

There's garbage to be found, mates,

There's garbage to be found.

Finally, they emerged from the swamp. What a relief to be free of its sour scent. Lola took a deep breath of cool, crisp air, while Bob and Stanley coughed, apparently unhappy about the new, fresh scents. They'd met the southern fork of the Fairwater River. Just as Rupert had said, the swamp had proven to be a shortcut. Lola's nose itched, she felt waterlogged, and she smelled bad, but she'd survived the bities and hadn't seen any signs of more Tassie devils. All in all, she was in good shape.

This was no longer the Northern Forest. The landscape had opened up. Smaller trees were spaced wider apart. Tall grasses and shrubs were separated by stretches of dirt and exposed rock. The swamp's thick foliage had filtered sunlight, but here the sun shone bright. Too bright. Lola found herself blinking more often and her eyes felt drier. Traveling in daylight was going to take some getting used to.

The river's current flowed at a gentle pace. Melvin wasted no time and jumped into the water to scrub himself down. Hesitant at first, for this was not like the calm pools of the stream, Lola joined him, not so much because she wanted to remove the swamp slime, but because the cool waters were soothing in the heat of the day. The water lapped gently over her paws as she slowly settled down in the shallows, letting it run around her as if she were some great boulder in its path. After a while she rolled onto her back and stretched her legs out, the water caressing her back. She narrowed her eyes and scanned the sky. Still no sign of any pelicans. Bob and Stanley did not bathe, but did pause for a brief snack of rancid applesauce and larvae.

Though it felt nice to rest, Lola was eager to be on her way. Bob and Stanley seemed equally eager, for they picked up their pace, their long tails dragging on the ground, collecting dirt, and leaving a furrow behind them. Melvin, however, held his tail aloft. "Melvin," Lola said, walking alongside him.

"Yes?"

"Did you hear that sound last night? In the swamp?"

"What sound?"

"Like someone was moving through the water."

He thought for a moment. "It could have been a fish, or a bullfrog. Or . . ." He reached out and patted Lola's shoulder. "There's nothing following us, if that's what you're thinking. If it had been another one of those devils, we wouldn't be here, walking together." Lola nodded, for that seemed true enough. But she couldn't shake off the weird feeling she'd had last night. She glanced over her shoulder.

Now that they were back on a path, it was easy for Lola to keep up with her rat companions. Being larger, she could outpace them with little effort. They'd been so nice to guide her through the swamp. Would it be rude if she ran ahead? She desperately wanted to get to the Royal Road. Her legs twitched, urging her to run. Urging her to gallop. "Melvin, now that we're out of the swamp, I think I might—" She stopped in her tracks. "Did you hear that?"

Melvin stopped walking and tilted his head to listen. The sound was faint and coming from behind an outcropping of rocks.

"Someone's crying," Lola said.

"I think you're right," Melvin said. "Hey, Bob! Stanley!" The two were well up the path.

"Wait!" Lola hollered at them.

Bob turned his head slightly, but kept his pace. "We wait for food and nothing else."

Then he and Stanley began singing another garbage-themed song. They marched around a bend in the path and disappeared from view.

Melvin shook his head. "They only care about their stomachs."

The crying continued, soft little sobs, reminding Lola of how she'd felt when she'd been alone in her burrow. The sound practically broke her heart. No one should feel that sad. She pushed aside branches, heading into a thicket that stood between the path and the rockery. The small shrubbery proved no trouble for Melvin. Lola, however, found herself having to turn aside several times as the branches grew too thick or too pokey. The first thing they found was a basket lying on the ground, its lid off and its contents spilled about. "Are those . . . apples?" Melvin asked. He picked one up. "They are. I haven't seen a ripe apple in ages. We usually just get the cores, or rotting skins." He sank his teeth into the red skin. "Oh, it's delicious. Try one."

Lola loved apples, and it did look tempting, but the mysterious someone was still crying. "I'll try it later," she told him. He grabbed three and put them into his bucket. They kept walking. Soon they came upon another basket; this one had also spilled its contents. "How strange," Melvin said. "First a basket of apples in a place where apples don't grow, and now a basket of pears, which don't grow here either." He dropped four into his bucket.

Lola bristled with curiosity, cocking her head as she tried to get a read on the sound. The crying was still muffled, but closer. They hurried around a large rock and found another basket, but this one's lid was secure. The crying leaked out between the woven reeds. Melvin grabbed his shovel and held it in both hands, a serious look on his face. "Just in case it's a trick and I need to whack it on the head," he whispered. Lola was surprised by this, for Melvin didn't seem like a critter who would whack anything on the head.

"Trick?"

He mouthed the word *snake*.

Lola had never heard of a poisonous tiger snake living that far north, but anything seemed possible after these last few days. She nodded at Melvin; he tightened his grip and nodded back. Then she grabbed the edges of the lid and pulled it free.

The first thing they saw was a beak, which was open so wide they could see down the bird's gullet. With the lid removed, the crying increased in volume, prompting Lola to pull her ears down. Melvin relaxed his arms and let the shovel drop. Then he and Lola took a step closer and peered inside.

The bird sat with his head flung back. His belly was white but his face was blue, as were his feet and flippers. His back, however, was covered in downy gray feathers. A few had been shed and were caught on the breeze, rising into the air along with a strong, fishy scent.

"It's a penguin," Lola said in surprise. "A fairy penguin."

"And he's a baby," Melvin said as he plucked one of the downy feathers from the air.

The penguin's beak snapped shut. He scrambled to his feet and glowered at them. "*Not* a baby!" His voice was astonishingly loud.

Melvin held back a smile. "Oh dear, I'm very sorry I called you a baby. What would you rather be called?"

The penguin sniffled and looked at Melvin with tear-filled eyes. "B-B-Blue."

"Well, hello, Blue. It's very nice to meet you." Melvin bowed formally. "I'm Melvin and this is Lola. You're a long way from Penguin Bay. What are you doing up here?"

The penguin chick wiped his tears with one of his flippers. "L-L-Lost!" he bellowed. He threw his head back and started crying again.

"There, there," Lola said, crouching beside the basket. "We're here and we'll help you. Please stop crying."

"I-I-I want my Mum!"

Lola wanted the exact same thing, but she didn't want to scare the little fella with her terrible story. "Would you like to get out of that basket?" She carefully tipped the basket so Blue could waddle out. Once he was on the ground, Lola and Melvin got a better look. He was a plump little bird, his rounded belly barely hidden beneath his still-downy feathers and general fluffiness. He hopped around a lot as they stood there, some of his feathers falling out as he did.

"How did you get here?" Melvin asked.

"Up." He pointed at the sky.

"Up?" Lola frowned at Melvin. "I thought penguins couldn't fly."

"They can't," Melvin confirmed.

"I fly! I fly!"

Melvin raised an eyebrow. "Are you telling us that you flew all the way here from Penguin Bay?"

"I fly, I fly, I fly!" Blue began to stomp around in a circle. As he stomped, a few more downy feathers were set free. "I fly, I fly!"

Melvin whispered to Lola from the corner of his mouth, "I'm no psychologist, but I'd say that he's got a bit of an anger-management problem."

Or maybe he's scared to be all alone in the wilderness, Lola thought. Either way, he was definitely a funny critter. "Why were you in that basket?" Lola asked.

Blue stopped stomping and looked up at Lola with an expression of bewilderment, as if she should know exactly what he'd been doing. "I sleep."

"You climbed inside to sleep, then someone closed the lid?" she guessed.

He shrugged. Then he threw his head back and cried, "Hungry!" Lola wondered if his mother and father wore earmuffs around him.

"Do you want to eat some worms?" she asked, grabbing the tin from her backpack. How fortunate that Josie had given this to her.

"No!" Blue started stomping in a circle again. Lola was a bit surprised by his reaction. Most of the birds she knew in the Northern Forest loved worms. She'd seen the chicks in their nests with their beaks open, begging for food. One worm always seemed to do the trick. Blue chanted, "Hungry, hungry, hungry!"

"Well, this is most unpleasant," Melvin said dryly, looking over his shoulder as if he almost missed Bob and Stanley.

"Hungry, hungry, hungry, hungry, hungry!"

"You sure you don't want a worm?" Lola asked.

"Hungry, hungry, hungry, hungry, hungry, hungry, HUNGRY!"

Melvin scowled. "Maybe his parents left him here *on purpose*."

"We've got to feed him," Lola said. "You grab him and I'll put a worm into his mouth."

Melvin did just that, wrapping his arms around Blue to hold him still. The penguin opened his beak to complain and that's when Lola dropped a worm in. Melvin let go.

"Yuck!" Blue cried, spitting it out. He started hopping up and down. "HUNGRY!"

"What do you want to eat?" Lola asked.

"Fish!"

Melvin went cross-eyed for a moment as he plucked a downy feather off his nose. Then he sighed and said, "Guess we're going fishing."

Lola and Melvin helped Blue waddle through the thicket to the river's edge. Bob and Stanley were long gone. Had they reached the Royal Road by now? Lola was itching to get going. She stared down the path.

Melvin followed her gaze. "Lola, you don't have to stay here. I can help Blue. You go ahead and find your family. I can seek my fortune later."

It was a very kind offer, and for a moment, Lola considered accepting it. But Melvin had stayed behind because Lola had insisted on finding out who was crying. It didn't seem fair to abandon him with a temperamental baby penguin. And the penguin was too large for Melvin to carry. It would take forever for the two of them to get anywhere. Lola, being much stockier, would have no trouble carrying him. "I'm hungry, too," she said. "Let's eat and then we can make up for our lost time."

Blue stood at the river's edge, staring at the water, a pout spread across his face. "Why doesn't he dive in?" Melvin asked.

"He's too young," Lola explained. "Those downy feathers have to be replaced with waterproof feathers. Until that time, he won't be able to swim."

"How do you know so much about penguins?" Melvin asked.

"There's a story about them in my book."

"I see." Melvin rubbed his chin. "I guess we'll have to go

fishing for him." He pulled a hook and line from his bucket and strung them through the handle of his shovel. "You're probably wondering what I'm doing with fishing gear," he said. Lola nodded. "Unlike my compatriots, I prefer fresh seafood to rotting seafood." He held out his paw. "Worm?"

Lola opened the tin and handed over a plump red worm. She winced as Melvin skewered it with the hook. The worm continued wriggling. With the makeshift rod complete, Melvin climbed atop a rock and cast the string daintily into an eddy. Lola grabbed one of the apples and sat down to watch the process. As she chewed, she thought about Bale Blackwater, who'd dove to catch his fish. Too bad he wasn't here to help.

"Hungry!" Blue yelled.

"I'm doing my best," Melvin said.

"Fish!"

Melvin sighed with exasperation. "My dear little friend, I suggest you stop yelling. If you scare the fish, you won't have anything to eat."

Blue seemed to understand because his beak snapped shut. But his impatience showed as he smacked his webbed feet together.

Lola offered a piece of apple to the penguin but he refused. So she chewed and watched while Melvin jiggled the shovel. A few minutes later, the line went taut. Blue scrambled to his feet and waddled to the water's edge. Melvin pulled the line. A silver fish appeared. Blue bounced up and down. "Fishy!"

Melvin carefully removed it from the hook. "Shall I clean it and fillet it for you? I have a knife in my—"

Blue grabbed the fish with his flipper and swallowed it whole.

"Well, that's an option, too," Melvin said.

"More!" Blue demanded.

Lola couldn't help but laugh at the penguin's enthusiasm. Even though he didn't seem to know the words *please* or *thank you* and didn't seem capable of speaking quietly, he was a funny, fluffy little fella. But she was beginning to understand why some wombats preferred the quiet.

Melvin proceeded to catch a dozen more fish, casting his hook until the worm tin was empty. Blue sat contentedly, calmer now, his legs splayed, his belly round and full. "It's good manners to pat your belly after you eat a meal," Lola told him. She demonstrated, for the apple and the remaining water-ribbon root had satisfied her. Blue patted and burped a fishy burp. Then he gazed curiously at his rescuers as if noticing them for the first time.

"Not penguins," he said.

"I'm a wombat and Melvin is a swamp water rat."

Blue seemed to absorb the information, scratching his head with his flipper. Then, in the way youngsters tend to do, he changed the topic.

"Home." Tears flooded his eyes.

Lola looked at Melvin. They stepped away from Blue so they could talk in private. "I don't know where Penguin Bay is," she admitted.

"It's quite a detour." They examined her map. The Royal Road forked, with the southwest branch leading to Dore and the southern branch leading to Penguin Bay. Taking Blue home meant going off course. Lola needed to see her uncle as soon as possible. "Maybe we can find someone else to take him home," she said.

"It's possible we'll find someone in the Mouse Farmlands," Melvin said. Lola refolded the map, then looked to the sky. It was late afternoon. They needed to get going.

"I'll have to carry him." Lola opened her backpack. In order to make room for the penguin, she'd have to move a few items. "Would you carry these for me?" She handed the map to Melvin. Then she pulled out *The Tales of Tassie Island*. She didn't want the penguin to get it all fishy. "This is very important to me. Will you take good care of it?"

"Of course," Melvin said. He pointed to the piece of crumpled paper. "What's that?"

"It's a . . ." Lola paused. How wise would it be to tell someone she'd just met about her secret message? If it was meant to be shared then it wouldn't be called a secret. She tucked it into the side pouch on her pack. "It's nothing."

Melvin's eyes widened. "Ooh, do tell."

"It's something I'd rather not talk about right now." Melvin seemed to understand, for he asked no more questions. But his gaze remained glued to the side pouch.

"Sleepy!" Blue's outburst startled them both, especially as he slumped himself against Lola's leg.

"You can take a nap in here," Lola told him, tapping his shoulder to keep him awake. She arranged her cloak to make a soft nest. Then she picked Blue up and set him in the backpack. His head stuck out. Melvin helped get the pack onto Lola's back, then put Lola's belongings in his bucket and grabbed his shovel. Finally, they set out again. At first Lola wondered why the path smelled so fishy. Then she realized that the scent was traveling *with* her. Penguins were definitely fragrant. Fortunately, she didn't have to worry about Blue yelling in her ears because it only took a few minutes for her steps to rock him to sleep.

Despite the fact that Melvin seemed like a nice rat, and that he had been very kind and helpful, Lola was glad she hadn't shared her secret message. Her question about what it meant would have to wait until she was in her uncle's presence. And then she'd ask another big question—why had Bale Blackwater told her that a bloodthirsty brute had sent the message?

A strange sensation crept up her spine. She looked over her shoulder. The path behind was empty. And the only thing she could smell was penguin breath.

10

THE MISSING MESSAGE

Another night was falling over the Fairwater River. The trio stopped walking just as the moon began to rise and take precedence over the sun, its own light soon to illuminate the world. For supper, Lola found an abundance of grasses and ate the remaining apples and pears that Melvin had collected earlier. Melvin caught a giant crayfish, which he and Blue shared, along with a dozen small river fish. Blue dropped each fish into his beak before noisily gulping it down. Melvin, being fastidiously mannered, carefully shelled the crayfish onto a plate, then ate the tender flesh with a fork. He never went anywhere without his plate and proper utensils. Blue seemed unsure what to do with his half of the crayfish, tapping at the hard shell with his beak. Melvin took pity on him and passed him the already unshelled half, beginning the process anew.

"It's peaceful here," Melvin said as he looked out over the river.

Lola's fur wavered like the grasslands as a cool breeze passed by. A pair of stars twinkled.

Lola sighed. "My mum and dad would love this place. Wombats are keen on peace and quiet."

Blue burped, then grinned dopily in satisfaction, sending the scent of undigested seafood throughout the campsite.

"Blue," Lola said. "Remember what I taught you to do?" He nodded, then patted his round belly to show he was full. "Good job. Now it's time for bed." She expected some sort of tantrum about not wanting to go to sleep, but the little penguin yawned and his eyes drooped.

Having carried Blue in her backpack for most of the day, Lola was beyond exhausted. She desperately wanted to feel the warmth and closeness of a burrow. While Melvin went about his nightly grooming routine, which included a swamp-mud facial mask and a swamp-mud conditioning spritz, Lola began to dig. She made a shallow burrow and just as she finished removing the last few pawfuls of dirt, Blue squirmed his way inside. She couldn't blame him for not wanting to sleep alone.

She bid good night to Melvin, who'd set up his sleeping bag beneath the star-filled sky, and then she crawled into the burrow. Blue cuddled up against her. *Poor little fella*, she thought. When he started to sniffle for his parents, she said, "Want me to read you a bedtime story?" He squirmed eagerly. Despite his fishy scent, he was warm and fluffy, and it felt nice to cuddle with someone, for she was also deeply missing her family and home. She took out *The Tales of Tassie Island* and considered the choices. "The Tale of the Long Waddle" was her favorite story, but the wombats' exodus from their homeland to the Northern Forest contained scary scenes and she didn't want to get Blue all riled up. She also liked "The Ugly Hatchling," but it might make him sad to read about a mommy bird sitting on her eggs. And because the goal was to get Blue to fall asleep, she decided to read him the most boring part of the book—the table of contents.

"Chapter One, 'The Sleepy Volcano.' Chapter Two, 'The Golden City by the Bay.' Chapter Three . . .'"

It worked. Before she reached chapter seven, Blue's eyes had closed and so had hers.

Just as the sun began to rise, a loud exclamation, scented by fishy breath, woke her. "Hungry!" Lola opened her eyes to find Blue's beak about an inch from her nose. Then he waddled out of the burrow and stuck his face into the sleeping bag. "Hungry!"

"Oh, dreary days, what a surprise," Melvin replied with dry sarcasm.

Blue waddled back to Lola. "Brekkie!"

"Yes, we know," Lola said as she climbed into daylight. She picked a downy feather off her face, then rubbed her eyes and looked around.

The wide river gurgled and lapped gently against the rocky shore. Small ripples flittered across the surface, redirecting sparkling bursts of sunlight across the campsite and illuminating what shadows lingered from the night gone by. The trio had survived the night. And despite Lola's worrying, she'd gotten a decent sleep. They weren't being followed after all. It was just her imagination.

Blue started bouncing up and down, chanting, "Hungry, hungry, hungry!" He bumped into her backpack, which lay open on the ground. She must have forgotten to close it after removing her cloak last night. But why was the side pouch open? She reached into the pouch. The secret message was gone. She searched the entire pack. "Melvin?"

"I'll catch him something in a moment," he muttered, pulling the sleeping bag tighter around himself in an attempt to sleep a little longer.

She tugged on the corner of the bag. "Melvin, wake up." His head popped out, eyes blinking blearily in the sudden light. He looked different because his gray fur was all messy. "Did you take my secret message?"

He sat up. "You have a secret message?"

She frowned. "I mean that little piece of paper I wouldn't show you. Did you take it?"

"Lola, I wouldn't search through your private things." He rubbed sleep from his eyes, then stretched his arms.

She wanted to believe him. Maybe the message had fallen out along the way. Besides, why would Melvin care about her secret message? To him it would just be a crumpled piece of paper. He couldn't possibly know what it meant.

Or maybe Melvin wasn't what he seemed. Maybe he was as bad as those other swamp water rats who'd taken her family and neighbors. Maybe he was spying for the gold-toothed devil. This last thought made her stomach hurt. Everything was so confusing.

Melvin stopped stretching and stared at her with a look of concern. He seemed to know exactly what she was thinking because he said in a very serious tone, "Lola, I would never take anything from you. I promise."

For a long moment they looked at each other in awkward silence. Which was broken by a single word. "HUNGRY!"

"You're welcome to search through my belongings." Melvin grabbed the bucket by its handle and held it out to her. "I wish you would. I don't want you to think I'm like those other rats, who would do anything for food."

"I—I don't think that," she said, none too convincingly. The situation made her uncomfortable. She stood, shuffled in place, looked away. "I don't think you took it. Really, I don't. I know you're not like other rats."

"Good," he said. "Because it's very important to me that I be judged for *who* I am and not for what others *think* I am. For once, at least." He sighed and looked off to the horizon.

Though Lola and Melvin stood in close proximity, the space between them suddenly felt like a vast distance, as if they stood on opposite sides of the river. The truth was, Lola had never had a best friend before. During their trek, she'd begun to feel close to Melvin, as if she could tell him anything. As if he'd listen. As if they were friends. But now she wasn't so sure.

After breakfast, they resumed their walk. According to the map, they would soon reach the river's beginning and the start of the Royal Road. Lola and Melvin didn't speak much during their trek, and Lola was starting to wonder if they'd ever talk again when they came upon a glorious sight. Even though Lola was carrying Blue in her backpack, she broke into a run. A dock! With a paddle-wheel boat tied to it! She ran onto the dock, Melvin at her heels.

A sign was nailed to one of the posts:

**PADDLE-WHEEL BOAT FOR HIRE
SHOUT FOR SERVICE**

"This is the boat that took the wombats away," she told Melvin, gasping between breaths. But there was no cage on board. She sniffed, but no wombat scent could be found. "HELLOOO!" she called. "HELLOOO, IS ANYONE HERE?" Her gaze landed on a door that was built into the riverbank. A platypus dwelling, probably belonging to the boat's captain.

Lola took off her backpack and pulled Blue free. "Don't wander," she told him, setting him on the dock. Then she did a very unwombatish thing and knocked on the door. Knocking on a wombat's door was considered rude, for it would interrupt a wombat's peace and quiet and most assuredly result in some sort of conversation. But this was clearly too small to be a wombat's door.

But no one answered. Then Lola saw a little sign tucked behind the windowpane. ON VACATION. Melvin stepped up behind her. "Maybe that's why the Tassie devil was able to get her paws on the boat. Because the captain was away."

Lola nodded. It did seem to make sense. She sighed. "Let's get going. Where's Blue?"

Blue, who'd been told not to wander, was nowhere to be seen. A single downy feather lay in the place where he'd last been standing. They called his name over and over. Melvin climbed up on Lola's back to get a better view, his paw shading his eyes as he scanned the horizon. He rushed from one side of Lola to the other, stepping on her head at times as he searched. "Oh, hooly dooly," Lola said. "We shouldn't have left him alone."

Melvin suddenly jumped off her back and ran to the end of the dock. "There!" he said. Lola squinted into the distance. She gasped.

A little ball of fluff was floating downriver.

11

THE ROYAL ROAD

Blue didn't appear distressed. He floated on his back, smacking his webbed feet together in a happy way. The river's current flowed slowly, causing the penguin to bob gently, like a little blue ball. But Lola knew that the river would eventually narrow, the current becoming tumultuous, the rocks sharper, for she'd passed those sections on her journey.

"Blue!" Lola cried, her paws around her mouth. "Blue, swim to shore!" Then she remembered. "Hooly dooly! He can't swim."

Without another word, both she and Melvin raced to the end of the dock and dove. Well, Melvin dove. Headfirst, his arms outstretched, his body arced gracefully as he broke through the water's surface like a kingfisher. Lola, on the other hand, tumbled in, like a rock, landing with a splat on her stomach. But she quickly recovered and paddled her arms and legs with all she could muster. But Melvin proved the faster swimmer, especially with the current aiding the way.

"Got him!" he announced once he'd caught hold of Blue's foot.

"Wheeee hee hee!" Blue chortled, happily clapping his flippers. Using his tail as a rudder, Melvin pushed Blue toward the shore. Lola caught up and helped. When they reached the shallows, Blue scrambled to his feet as if nothing had happened. Lola and Melvin crawled out of the water, both gasping for breath.

"Fun!" Blue exclaimed as he shook his feathers. He was shivering a bit, his baby down apparently not good at keeping out the cold.

"Fun?" Lola said with alarm. "Blue, that river could have crushed you on some rocks, or carried you all the way to the ocean. If we hadn't seen you . . ." Lola stopped, realizing that she'd raised her voice. Blue's eyes got real wide and pooled with tears. She quickly pulled him into a hug. "Don't cry. It's okay. You're okay. Nothing bad happened."

"*Nothing* bad happened?" Melvin wasn't so forgiving. "Look at me." He motioned over his entire body. He did look a mess, his fur matted in clumps, his whiskers drooping.

Blue laughed and pointed his flipper at Melvin. "Funny!" Blue reached out, grabbed a tiny fish that was stuck to Melvin's leg, and popped it into his mouth.

"My young fellow," Melvin said as began to wring water from his fur. "It is customary to *thank* the critter who saved your life, not *insult* him." But Blue had already wandered off, distracted by a dragonfly.

"You don't look *that* bad," Lola said, fighting back a smile. "Just a bit . . . waterlogged." To her relief, Melvin returned the smile. Things were back to normal between them.

Once Melvin had combed himself dry and Blue was in the backpack nest, the trio continued their trek. Finally, after so many delays, they were on the Royal Road. With the river behind them, a vast sky stretched overhead in endless blue, like an ocean over the world—an ocean Lola felt she might drown under. After living beneath a protective tree canopy all her life, the openness felt dizzying. But she pressed on. Tucked into the backpack, his little face sticking out, Blue fell into a sudden nap, snoring loudly in Lola's ear. Babies were certainly annoying.

The Royal Road was the only road leading from the dock in the opposite direction of the swamp, which meant that the rat-drawn cart, with its wombat captives, had also traveled this way. A wagon rut was visible here and there, but no scent of wombat could Lola detect, and no tufts of wombat fur did she find. Until she spotted something—something that made her heart sing.

"What is it?" Melvin asked. He crouched next to Lola, who was staring at the ground.

"It's a wombat dropping," she told him.

"It's shaped like a cube."

"Yes." She beamed with happiness. "Do you know what that means?"

"That this particular wombat needs to see a doctor?"

Lola gave him a deadpan stare, and her whiskers twitched in response. "No, that's not what it means. It means that they were here. We haven't lost them after all. They might be a day or two ahead of us, but we haven't lost them." Her mum's droppings were perfect cubes; everyone knew that. Alice had left this on purpose, for Lola to find. So Lola wouldn't worry. So she wouldn't give up.

The road steepened, heading uphill. Lola's legs ached as she and Melvin hiked side by side. They took deep breaths as the road twisted and turned into switchbacks, still wide enough for a cart. Lola wanted to stop and rest, but she pushed forward, and when they reached the top a beautiful sight awaited them.

The world below appeared as a shallow, lumpy bowl encircled by mountains, most small, but a few tall and craggy with white, snowy tops. A patchwork of colors stretched across the center, reminding Lola of her mother's quilt. Rich forest greens, light mossy greens, and all the greens in between, along with yellows, oranges, and whites in perfect squares. The patches were formed as if they'd been drawn with a ruler.

"The Mouse Farmlands," Melvin said. He was winded, so he leaned on his shovel. "This is the breadbasket of Tassie Island and the homeland of the long-tailed mice."

"It's a story in my book," Lola realized. "'The Tale of the Wind-Swept Mice.' The story says that once the mice bickered and fought over the boundaries of their lands, destroying much of what they produced. But one mouse who'd had enough of the fighting took to the sky atop a firebird and burned a pattern into the valley, dividing it into equal portions. Then, with the help of the wind, the mice were swept up and flung across the land, each one landing safely in a patch to call their own, ending all conflict in the valley. That's how the patchwork was made."

Blue was deep asleep, his steady breaths warming the back of Lola's neck. She turned her head, about to tell him that he was missing the scenery, but Melvin put a finger to his mouth. "Don't wake him," Melvin whispered. "We don't want to disturb the lovely peace and quiet."

"You sound like a wombat," she teased. Then she turned serious. "Do you think the mice will be able to help me?"

"There's only one way to find out."

They began the descent into the valley, treading carefully so as not to skid on the rocky road. The air was warm and moist from a recent rain. When they reached the bottom, the road forked into three roads, with three brightly painted signs marking each.

THE EASTERN ROAD TO BLACK SWAN LAGOON
THE WESTERN ROAD TO THE CRUMBLING MOUNTAINS
THE ROYAL ROAD TO BOUNTY AND DORE

Lola hesitated, looking from one sign to the other. Due to the rain, any tracks that might have been left by a cart or pawprints that might have been left by marching swamp water rats had been washed away. "They could have taken any of these roads. How can we know which way to go?" she asked.

"We can't go in all three directions unless we split up and I don't think Blue's up to that." On cue, Blue snored even louder. "The only thing we know is that the gold-toothed devil said the queen had changed her laws. And she also said that someone was paying gold coin for the wombats. If the queen is involved . . ." He paused. "Then Dore must be the destination."

Lola hated the very thought that Queen Myra might be doing something so terrible. "But how can we be sure?"

"We can't."

Up until this point Lola had been comforted by the belief that she was following her mum and dad. That they were somewhere up ahead. But now they could have gone east or west, and if she continued south she could be walking away from them.

"Lola," Melvin said gently, for she stood frozen in indecision. "Lola?"

"I can't leave them. What if . . . ?" Her jaw trembled. Melvin stepped closer.

"There's only one road that leads to the queen and to your uncle. They'll know what to do," he said encouragingly.

"Yes." She nodded slowly. It was the right decision, the surest decision. But that didn't make it any easier.

As they walked south, they found signs poking out of the fields, indicating the type of crops growing. The first field was thick with tall grasses swaying in a gentle breeze. GOLDEN WHEAT. The next field was dotted with yellow fruit. MOUNTAIN PEPPERS. The third field was thick with green plants. SPRAWLING PIGFACE. There was signage aplenty, but no mice.

"Keep an eye out for anyone we can talk to," Lola said. Where was everyone?

Blue awoke with a snort and started wiggling and kicking. "I think he needs to stretch his legs." Melvin lifted him out of the backpack.

"Hungry!" Blue cried.

"I'm sorry, Blue, but there aren't any fish here," Lola told him. She pointed to a shiny beetle crawling along the road. "What about bugs? Will you eat bugs? Lots of birds like bugs."

Blue poked the beetle with his beak, then slurped it up. "Blah!" he said, spitting it back out. The beetle sat dazed for a moment, covered in penguin slobber, then continued on its way, seemingly none the worse for wear.

"What are we going to feed him?" Lola wondered.

"Let's hope they have something in town," Melvin said.

The day was hot, so they took a short rest beside a pond. "It's a real scorcher," Lola said. To Blue's disappointment, the pond was filled with lily pads and frogs, not fish. They all drank some water, and because there was no food for Blue, both Lola and

Melvin decided not to eat. They didn't want to upset the youngest member of their group. They took a few moments to cool their feet in the water. Then, at Lola's insistent urging, they left the cool water behind and continued down the road, the sun beating on their faces. Melvin tied his handkerchief over his head. "To prevent premature aging," he explained.

Small mouse-sized wheelbarrows and carts were parked in the fields, but still there were no mice to be seen. Lola grabbed Melvin's arm. "Are you thinking what I'm thinking?"

Melvin's tail twitched. "That the Tassie devil might have taken the mice, too?"

Lola nodded. Was someone paying coin for long-tailed mice *and* wombats? Could that someone be the queen? There was only one way to find out.

Just as late afternoon turned to evening and the colors of the Farmlands were beginning to fade to darker hues, the trio reached the outskirts of Bounty, the largest town in the Farmlands. Rows of little mouse houses, far too small for a wombat or a penguin, were lined up in perfect precision. Each house was made from pebbles and clay and topped with a thatched roof. Each window was filled with a small pane of glass. The tidy yards were surrounded by white picket fences. Each house had a welcome mat at the front door, colorful curtains in the windows, and a mailbox out front. The houses and yards were empty.

The Royal Road widened. Proper shop buildings now lined either side of the street, with small alleys cutting through to farther streets beyond. The first shop displayed tiny pairs of sandals in the window. The next had stacks of cookies and loaves of bread. There was a haberdashery with straw hats and a general store with bandanas and gardening gloves. But each shop had a CLOSED sign on its little door, and still there was no one in sight. "This is getting creepy," Melvin said.

Then music caught their ears—an upbeat tune accompanied by high-pitched singing. They followed the sound around a building and found themselves standing at the edge of a cobblestone square. Mice were everywhere! Some wore straw hats and bandanas, some wore bonnets. They were dancing and singing and enjoying mugs of frothy amber liquid that were being brought out on trays from an establishment called Stella's Star. Tables were set up along the perimeter of the square. A quartet of musicians played on a central stage. Strings of lanterns sent a warm glow over the revelers. Both Lola and Melvin smiled with relief. Not only were the mice fine, they were having a party.

Back in the burrows, the only music ever played was during the queen's birthday, when the wombats brought out their carved pipes and played the queen's birthday song. The farmland instruments were different, some with strings, some with bows, producing the loveliest music Lola had ever heard. Blue's head started bobbing and he marched in a circle, keeping time with the tune. Lola wanted to enjoy the moment but she was on a mission. She scanned the scene, trying to decide if someone was in charge. And that's when Blue began to wander off. "Blue." He paid her no mind so she hollered. "Blue!"

The music stopped. The dancing stopped. The mice turned to look, their gazes falling upon the three travelers.

12

STELLA'S STAR

With hundreds of mouse eyes upon him, Melvin shuffled back and forth, looking as uncomfortable as a worm dangling from a hook.

"Why are they staring at you?" Lola whispered to him.

"I'm not sure. They certainly don't look happy to see me." He curled his tail around himself. While most of the long-tailed mice stayed in a cluster, watching with narrowed eyes, one mouse set down a serving tray, then walked forward. She was twice the size of the average mouse and wore a lacey white apron. Like the others, she was brown in color with a long white tail. Though her size was nearly ratlike, her features were purely mouse, from the rounded ears to the delicate paws. She stopped in front of Melvin and gave him a long once-over.

"They're looking at you, they are, because rats often cause trouble around here," she told Melvin. "On account of us having so much food in Bounty."

Melvin cleared his throat. "I assure you, ma'am, I will not cause any trouble."

She frowned. "You're a swamp water rat, aren't you? If you've come looking for garbage, we don't have any, we don't. We compost everything in the Farmlands. So you might as well be on your way."

Melvin folded his arms, his discomfort turning to annoyance. "Oh, how terribly disappointing," he said. "Because as a swamp water rat I think of nothing else. It wouldn't be possible for me to possess a finer palate, or good taste, for that matter." His tone was sarcastic and a bit rude. His tail had dropped back to the ground, twitching agitatedly. Lola's mouth opened with surprise. She waited with apprehension. Would the mouse ask them to leave before Lola had asked any questions?

But to Lola's surprise, the mouse cocked her head. Was that a little twinkle in her eyes? She turned to the crowd. "Go on now," she called out. "Stop your gawking. I'll take care of these travelers, I will." With a wave of her paw, the music resumed and the mice returned to their festivities. The enormous mouse put her hands on her round hips. "I'm Stella, owner of Stella's Star and mayor of Bounty. What can I do for you?"

Lola stepped forward. "I'm Lola Budge and this is Melvin and Blue. We're looking for the other wombats. Did you see them?"

Stella frowned. "Wombats? You're the first wombat we've seen in ages, you are."

"My mum and dad and all my neighbors were taken from our burrows and put into a cage. The cage was put on a cart, and the cart was put onto a paddle-wheel boat, and the boat floated up the Fairwater River and then the cart was taken off the boat and pulled up the Royal Road. But we don't know if the cart took one of the other roads or if it came this way. Did you see it? Did it come through town? Did anyone see it?" Lola's words came faster and faster the longer she talked. "I really need to find them. Can you help me?"

A look of puzzlement spread across Stella's round face. "You're not a typical wombat, are you?"

"No, I'm not."

Stella looked at Melvin. "And you're not a typical swamp water rat."

"Thank you for noticing," Melvin said as he picked a downy penguin feather off his shoulder.

Blue waddled up to Stella, opened his beak wide, and cried, "HUNGRY!"

"But *that* is definitely a typical penguin." Stella chuckled and reached out to pat Blue's head. Her expression turned serious when she looked back at Lola. "Your story is a terrible one, it is. I'm sorry to hear about your family. But I haven't seen any wombats in town. And I'd know if they'd been here. Everyone comes to my establishment, they do, for food, drink, and merriment."

Had Lola's worry come true? Had the cart gone down one of the other roads? Her ears fell back and she glanced over her shoulder anxiously.

"But I'm confused, I am," Stella said, interrupting Lola's worries. "Who would put a bunch of wombats onto a cart?"

"A night monster," Melvin said.

"With a gold tooth," Lola added.

Stella took a sharp breath, then looked around, eyeing the dark alleys between the buildings. "Are you saying there's a Tassie devil on the loose?"

Lola nodded. "Yes. She's the one who took my family."

Stella's long tail stiffened. "We need to tell the queen. Right away."

A loud thud sounded as the door to Stella's Star flew open.

It wasn't loud enough to disturb the revelries, but it did draw Lola's attention.

"Oh, dread," Melvin grumbled, his face falling into his open paw as a pair of swamp water rats emerged. Bob and Stanley stumbled out, wiping their mouths with the backs of their paws. They wore their shovels on their backs and carried their buckets. A little mouse followed, shaking a fist at them. "You didn't pay for your brew, you didn't," he called. He also wore a lacey white apron.

"Pay?" Bob opened his mouth and belched. "Why should we pay? That sweet stuff was delicious."

"Delicious?" The waiter puffed out his tiny chest. "Of course it was delicious. We are known kingdom-wide for our berry brew, we are. It's the specialty of the house. Made from seven different berry juices."

Stanley snorted and, with the tip of his tail, poked the waiter in the chest. "Hey little mousy, delicious is a bad thing. We don't want delicious. We want disgusting."

"Oh really?" The mouse's snout twitched and he glared up at Stanley. "Are you a professional restaurant critic?"

"I should be," Stanley said with a chuckle. "Your brew was too fruity. And there were no dead flies floating in it. Thumbs down from me."

"Aye, that's a good one, Stanley, only you don't have any thumbs." Both rats broke into laughter, tottering on their feet as if about to fall over.

"All you rats are the same," the little waiter said. "Smelly—"

"What did you call us?" Bob whipped his shovel off his back and shook it at the waiter, who squealed with fear. Once again, the music stopped. The musicians, dancing couples, and frolicking youngsters turned and stared. A rare few began walking forward, seemingly unsure, but getting ready for a fight.

A long-suffering sigh came from Melvin as he and Lola watched the scene unfold.

Stella stomped over to the rats. "Your behavior won't be tolerated in this town, it won't. You owe coin for the drinks, you do. Delicious or disgusting, they aren't free."

Though Stella was large in mouse terms, Bob's muscular frame still towered over her. "I'm not paying for something I didn't like. Give us some rubbish and we'll happily pay."

Stella balled up her fists. Lola couldn't believe what she was seeing. Was Stella going to fight an enormous rat? "You have three seconds to pay before I consider you a thief," she warned. "One . . . two . . ."

After a few quick motions, Bob found himself facedown in the dirt, with Stella sitting cross-legged atop him. "Oi! You're crushing me!" Bob cried.

Stella pointed at Stanley. "You'll be next."

"Okay, okay," Stanley said, holding up his paws in a show of peace. His eyes roamed nervously over the slowly growing crowd of mice around them. "But we are a bit short on coin at the moment."

Melvin sighed again. Then he walked over to Stella. "Would you allow me to pay for their drinks by giving you some lovely products? I'm afraid I don't have any coin either."

And so Stella selected some paw cream, while the waiter chose some whisker cream, and they seemed satisfied. "You two can sleep in the field tonight, but don't come anywhere near my establishment again," Stella told Bob and Stanley.

Bob and Stanley collected their buckets and shovels.

"Whatcha still doing with the wombat?" Bob asked. "And where'd you pick up a baby penguin?"

"Not a baby!" Blue's pout seemed to grow fiercer each time he needed to repeat the phrase.

"It's a long story," Melvin said. "I suggest you two do as Miss Stella says and go sleep in the field. We can talk in the morning."

The musicians, who had been holding their instruments with bated breath, played again with renewed vigor. Dancers grabbed their partners and the little waiter began to fill empty mugs. "And that's why we rats have a bad reputation in this town," Melvin told Lola as they watched Bob and Stanley stumble toward the nearest field.

"Thank you for your help," Stella said to Melvin. "The least I can do is offer you some vittles." She hesitated. "I'm afraid I don't have anything *disgusting* on the menu, I don't."

"I assure you that my palate is quite sophisticated," Melvin said. "I will enjoy whatever you have to offer."

"So will I," Lola said, her stomach grumbling. "But penguins only eat one thing."

"Fish!" Blue hollered.

"I'll see what I can find, I will."

They sat at an outdoor table. It was tricky for Lola to balance on the little mouse-sized stool, so she pushed two together. Melvin tied a napkin around Blue's neck, and Blue clapped his flippers in anticipation of the meal to come. Stella returned with a plate of salad greens for Lola and a bowl of corn chowder for Melvin. He held it to his nose and sniffed. "Do I detect parsley and young onions?" He took a sip. "Yes. Delightful." The little waiter brought mugs of frothy berry brew. Stella opened a tin with a knife and a tangy fish scent filled the air.

"Fish!" Blue cheered.

"Anchovies," Stella told him, dumping the oily contents onto a plate. Blue slurped them up as fast as he could while Stella opened two more tins. "I keep them in the pantry, I do, for the messenger pelicans."

Lola, after first edging herself back from the especially smelly fish, pricked up her ears. Her eyes turned to Stella with a new-found sudden surge of hope. "I've been looking for a messenger pelican," Lola said. "Have you seen one around?"

"They were all called back to Dore last month, they were. The queen needed them."

"Why would Queen Myra need all the pelicans?" Melvin asked.

"I don't know, I don't."

A pair of mice waltzed past the table. "What are you celebrating?" Lola asked.

"We're celebrating the royal visit. The queen is coming to the Farmlands, she is. And she'll be stopping right here in Bounty."

Lola nearly choked on a crisp leaf of sprawling pigface. "The queen? Queen Myra? She's coming here?"

"It's true." Stella lifted her tail, then sat on a stool. She took a sip of brew. "She'll be here tomorrow. Her royal workers have finished laying the track that connects Dore to Bounty. Tomorrow morning Queen Myra will arrive on a train and visit our town."

"What's a train?" Lola and Melvin asked at the same time.

"I don't fully understand, I don't. But I've been told that it's a new way to travel. It's like a bunch of carts that are connected in a line, but instead of their wheels rolling over the ground, they roll on tracks. And the cart in front is powered by steam and it pulls the other carts."

Lola put a paw to her chin in confusion. She thought of the cart that had pulled her parents away, of dozens of them. All connected together and filled with wombats, rats, mice, and all the rest. At the front of the long, snakelike chain sat a large boiling pot where the Tassie devils clustered and prepared for their meal. Lola shuddered and shook herself free of the vision, knowing it couldn't really be anything like that. Not if the queen was coming with it, right?

"It's very exciting, it is. This train will carry our harvest to Dore much faster than we ever could by cart or wagon. Now the critters of Tassie Island will get the freshest food ever, they will."

If the queen was coming to the Farmlands, then perhaps Lola's travels were over. "I can talk to the queen tomorrow," she said, almost bouncing in happiness. "I can tell her about my family."

Stella patted Lola's paw. "Queen Myra will be very upset to hear what has happened. I'm sure she'll do everything she can. Our queen loves us. She's looking to the future, she is. She's building this train so all the peaceful critters who live on this island can be connected. Isn't that a lovely idea?"

Lola and Melvin exchanged a look of concern. Lola wanted, with all her heart, to believe that Queen Myra was a noble queen, as Lola had been taught. But she couldn't shake the nagging possibility that the queen already knew about the gold-toothed monster and the missing wombats. It was possible that the wombats had been taken under her orders. But they had no real proof yet, and it would be unfair to make such an accusation in public.

"Yes, I will tell her everything," Lola said. "And maybe she can help us get Blue back to Penguin Bay."

Stella set her mug aside. "As the mayor of Bounty, I will personally see to it that you get an audience with the queen, I will." Lola was so happy she jumped off her stools and threw her arms around Stella in a great big hug, engulfing the mouse almost entirely. Stella chuckled and smiled, but firmly pushed Lola away, wriggling free from the hug. "You are definitely *not* a typical wombat."

They finished the meal. Lola and Blue patted their bellies and smiled with satisfaction.

"Closing time!" Stella yelled. The music stopped and the musicians began to put their instruments away. The mice bid their farewells and scurried back to their homes, or inns and campsites for those visiting from the smaller villages.

While Melvin and Blue could have stayed in one of Stella's rooms, the only sleeping accommodation that would fit Lola was the storage warehouse. The double doors were massive, since a good deal of the fruits and vegetables were much larger than the mice themselves. Stacks of crates, cords of wheat, and baskets filled the space, all stuffed to bursting with fresh crops. Stella pointed to some piles of loose hay. "That should make a nice nest." She bid the travelers a good night. "I'll see you in the morning, I will. We're going to meet the queen!" After an excited squeal, she shut the doors behind her.

Lola was grateful to sleep inside. Grabbing pawfuls of hay, she made a comfy nest for her and Blue, covering both of them with her traveling cloak. Melvin lay next to them in his sleeping bag. But how would Lola be able to sleep with such anticipation running through her veins? Tomorrow she'd meet the queen. Tomorrow the queen would explain that everything had been a huge misunderstanding. Tomorrow everything would be better.

"Home?" Blue asked as he cuddled next to Lola.

"Not yet," Lola told him. "But soon." She didn't read from

The Tales of Tassie Island. Instead, as a full moon rose in the sky, covering the Mouse Farmlands in a soft glowing blanket, Lola told Blue a story about a queen named Myra, a good queen, who helped a little penguin find his way home.

But even now, doubt remained.

THE STEAMING DRAGON

Morning light shone through cracks in the warehouse's doorway. Lola blinked, slowly waking. Blue had moved in his sleep, rolling partially under Lola's head like an extra fluffy pillow—albeit a fishy one. She sat up, feeling a sense that something other than the sun had woken her. Something like . . .

Pawfalls?

She climbed out of the straw nest, hurried to the warehouse doorway, and opened the door. Dozens of mice were scurrying past, all heading in the same direction. And they appeared to be wearing their fanciest clothing, including bonnets and colorful overalls. "Where are you going?" she asked a mouse, whose long white tail was decorated with a pink ribbon.

"We're going to see the queen, we are," the little mouse squeaked, at first taken aback by the wombat's size. "The train's almost here."

Lola's heart thudded. She ran back inside. "Melvin! Blue! Get up! Get up! The train is coming! The queen!"

Blue rolled over and buried his face in Lola's cloak. Melvin, not one to hurry in the morning, began to grumble about how he didn't want to be seen by Her Royal Majesty in such a disheveled state and that he needed, at the very least, to comb his fur. Then he scratched his arm. Then his other arm. He bolted upright. "Oh, dreary days, I think I have a flea!"

Lola knew that her mother and father would tell her to polish her claws, scrub her nose, and pick straw from her fur, but that would take too long. "Please watch Blue," she called. "Don't let him wander." And off she went.

She followed the mice to the edge of a cornfield where a wooden platform had been built, with a roof to keep out the rain. A sign was tacked to one of the posts:

BOUNTY TRAIN STATION
ARRIVAL SCHEDULE: SOMETIME
DEPARTURE SCHEDULE: SOMETIME THEREAFTER

The mice pressed close together, some holding bouquets of flowers, others holding little welcome signs. Youngsters bounced up and down and everyone chatted excitedly. "The queen, the queen!" Lola wanted to bounce, too, but was afraid she might land on an innocent bystander. "Hellooo," she said, waving down at the little critters.

"Hellooo, hellooo," they hellooo-ed back.

Two long silvery strips of metal ran in front of the station and ran far into the distance, like an endless ladder lying on the ground. Lola was still having trouble imagining what the train looked like and how it moved. Steam-powered? What did that mean, exactly? She was about to ask the mice around her when a loud voice said, "Make way, make way. Your mayor is here, she is. Make way." The mice shuffled aside as Stella pushed through until she stood beside Lola. A sash was tied across her chest and read: MAYOR. "Are you excited to meet the queen?" she asked, looking up at Lola.

Lola could barely find the words to answer. She'd never dreamed that she'd actually meet Queen Myra. Why would she? She was supposed to live out her life in the Northern Forest with the other wombats, in peace and quiet. But now, on that very morning, she would speak to Her Royal Majesty. She would tell the horrible story about her family and the queen would make things right. Lola tried very hard to push away her doubts. Queen Myra would prove to be the gracious, loving queen that she'd always been. "I'm very excited," Lola replied with a quiver of her whiskers.

Stella smoothed her sash. "I'll give my welcoming speech, I will. Then I'll escort the queen on a tour of the town, making sure she stops at Stella's Star to sip my famous honey brew." Stella motioned Lola to lean closer. Then she stood on tiptoe and whispered in Lola's ear. "Once she's tasted it, I know she'll want to buy barrels for the palace. This visit will make me rich, it will. I'll open a chain of Stella's Stars throughout the kingdom."

Lola smiled, trying to show some enthusiasm for Stella's dream. But at that moment, all she could think about was her family. And the doubt that kept creeping back into her mind. She wrung her paws.

"Everything is going to work out, it is," Stella told her. "This is so exciting. I've never seen the queen up close."

"Me neither. But my uncle is her friend. He's the ambassador to the Northern Forest and the Realms Beyond."

Stella's mouth fell open. "Wait. Your uncle? Your uncle is Tobias Bottom?"

"Yes," Lola said proudly. But why was Stella looking so worried all of a sudden?

"Oh, Lola, I heard from the railroad workers that your uncle—"

A whistle sounded. Then the tracks began to vibrate. A ribbon of black smoke appeared in the distance, rising into the sky. Lola sniffed the air and furrowed her brow in worry. Both for the smoke and for what Stella had been about to say. "Don't you worry none," Stella said. "It's not fire. It's the train, it is."

"Stella, you were saying something about my uncle—?"

The whistle sounded again, closer this time. And that's when the train rounded the corn field and came into view. At first it reminded Lola of a dragon from a storybook, creeping along the ground, smoke and steam rising from its nostrils. But dragons were pretend, and this thing was very real.

It was the strangest contraption she'd ever seen. It looked like a bunch of wooden wagons had been strung together, with the first and biggest wagon pulling the others and spewing the plume of smoke. The second wagon carried a large pile of blackened rocks the same color as the smoke rising from the train's chimney. A thin metal roof served to protect the rocks, ensuring they remained unexposed to the rain. The other wagons were boxlike and empty, ready to be filled with goods. And at the end of the train, the cars were more like carriages and had doors and windows.

Chug, chug, chug, chug, chug.

A loud keening screech pierced the air. Lola fit her paws over her ears to blot out the metallic wail. As the train slowed, the sound quieted and Lola's paws relaxed. The train came to a full stop and the engine ceased, as did the plume of black smoke. Lola's gaze traveled down to the center carriage, which was painted gold and bore the initials "H.R.M." Her Royal Majesty.

The windows of this golden carriage were covered with velvet curtains. Lola could barely stand still, knowing Queen Myra was in there. Being the largest mammal in attendance, she would have the best view when the queen made her appearance.

A mouse squealed. Then another. The crowd began to shuffle in an agitated way, as if all the mice were being stirred in a giant pot. Something was frightening them. Lola and Stella stopped talking and looked down the length of the train. The windows in the passenger cars had opened and dozens of rats had stuck out their heads. Black rats, gray rats, brown rats, all the different kinds that lived in forests, in fields, and in swamps. A grizzled older rat held up his paws and began to lead the others in a song:

Who do we serve?

Queen Myra!

Who do we serve?

Our queen!

Who gives us piles of food to eat?

Food that's savory, food that's sweet

Food that makes our lives complete

Serving our queen is our favorite treat

Who do we serve?

Queen Myra!

Who do we serve?

Our queen!

Lola listened carefully to the song's lyrics. What she'd learned in the swamp seemed to be true. A promise of endless food was what every rat wanted—and they'd do anything to get it, whether that meant working for the queen or for a night monster.

"Coming through!" Bob and Stanley pushed their way through the crowd of mice, then called up to one of the train's open windows. "G'day mates. Are you all working for the queen?"

"We sure are," a balding rat told them over the noise of the singing. "We joined the Royal Guard. Soon as we're done in this town, we'll be heading back to Dore to eat our fill of whatever we want."

"Does that include garbage?" Bob asked.

"Sure does, if that's your liking."

"We want to join up immediately!" Stanley said.

"You'll have to talk to the overseer, but climb aboard."

Bob and Stanley grabbed the handrail, climbed the little stairs and joined the others in one of the carriages. It seemed as if their journey would have a happy ending, but what about Lola's? Her gaze settled on the golden carriage. "Why is the queen traveling with rats?" she asked Stella. "What do they do for her, exactly?"

"*That* is a good question, it is," Stella replied.

The singing continued for a few more moments until someone hollered, "Cease that infernal racket!"

The door to the golden carriage opened. Both Lola and Stella stiffened and held their breaths. Queen Myra was about to show herself. The mice began cheering again. "The queen! The queen!" They squealed, they bounced, they waved their little arms. Lola looked over her shoulder, hoping to find Melvin. Was he still doing his grooming? He was going to miss the queen.

But then, as if they'd all been dunked in cold river water, the entire crowd gasped. The world went silent.

Instead of Queen Myra disembarking as expected, a pair of nightmare creatures stepped out of the golden carriage.

14

A MONSTROUS PAIR

Though the farmland mice had never seen Tassie devils, they'd heard the stories and, like Lola, they carried an instinctual fear of predators. Squeals and shrieks filled the air as the crowd began to churn. Panic ensued as mice parents grabbed their youngsters and ran desperately into the nearest cornfield, disappearing into its dense forest of stalks and leaves.

"Hide, Lola, hide," Stella said, pushing Lola with all her might.

Stella was right. What if these monsters were collecting wombats, just like the gold-toothed one? Lola darted behind the train station's platform and crouched as low as she could, pressing her belly to the ground. Only a moment ago she'd been wishing that Melvin would hurry up and finish his morning grooming so he could meet the queen. Now she was grateful that he and Blue were safe in the warehouse.

Lola peered around a post to get a better look. Only one mouse was left standing on the platform, which was now littered with abandoned WELCOME signs and bouquets. Stella straightened herself to her full height, then stepped forward. "May I help you?"

"Yes, I will allow you to be of assistance." An authoritarian voice resonated from the shorter of the pair of Tassie devils who had disembarked from the train. Her white markings encircled her neck like a mane. She wore a shiny black robe embroidered with red thread that matched the color of her ears. "I am Overseer Rake, daughter of Rake, and this is Taskmaster Lash, son of Lash."

The taskmaster was different because his fur was pure white. The taskmaster held a ruffled black parasol. He stood under its shade, squinting against the sunlight through small darkened spectacles. He also wore a long black robe, but his was plain and wrapped tighter about himself.

Lola held as still as she could, hoping the pair wouldn't notice her. If Stella felt fear, she showed no signs of it as she faced the ferocious carnivores. "I'm Stella Star, I am, Mayor of Bounty. We had a welcoming committee for the queen, we did, but I'm afraid . . ." She looked around. "I'm afraid you scared them off. We haven't seen any Tassie devils in these parts in many generations."

Overseer Rake drew a deep breath through her teeth, then spoke in a tone dripping with self-assurance. "We are about to become a familiar presence."

What did that mean? Lola wondered. Did that mean more of them were leaving the mountain? The rats continued to hang out the windows, scratching themselves and watching the scene unfold.

"How is Her Majesty?" Stella asked, looking up and down the train. "Did she enjoy the trip?"

"The queen has sent us in her stead. She has more important matters to tend to." The overseer reached out and caught a fly in midair, examining it disdainfully before crushing it with her claws.

Queen Myra wasn't on the train? Lola clenched her jaw. What was she supposed to do now? How could she save her family?

Overseer Rake glared at Taskmaster Lash. "Must I remind you that time is of the essence? Deliver the proclamation."

"Yes, of course, Overseer." Taskmaster Lash bowed, without a hint of anger or distain for her snappy demand. He reached into a traveling case and pulled out a scroll, which he handed to Stella, daring to stick his paw into the sunlight for only a moment. "We are here to take possession of your fruits and vegetables."

Stella unrolled the scroll and quickly read it. "This is the queen's seal. She ordered this?"

Overseer Rake smiled, revealing her razor-sharp teeth. "You are not as simpleminded as you look. The entirety of your harvest will be taken, and an additional train convenience tax will be collected." She turned to face the train and clapped her paws three times. "Rouse yourselves, you slimy scoundrels! Report for duty!" The rats groaned and grumbled with displeasure as they disembarked. Bob and Stanley followed, but stood off to the side, scratching their heads and looking confused. Back in the swamp they'd told Lola that they didn't want to work for Tassie devils. But it was becoming apparent that working for the queen meant dealing with these bloodthirsty predators. Lola shook her head sadly. But why? Why was this happening?

Stella looked up from the scroll. "What are the mice supposed to eat if you take all the harvest? We'll starve, we will."

"It is not my concern if the mice do or do not starve." Overseer Rake ran a paw over her white collar. "Forthwith, all fruits and vegetables grown in the Mouse Farmlands are property of the crown."

Stella stood as tall as she could and pointed the scroll at the overseer. "See here. This makes no sense. I'm the mayor and I demand—"

In one swift motion, Overseer Rake uncoiled a whip from around her waist. She sent it outward with a loud *crack*, knocking the scroll from Stella's paw. The rats stopped squirming, their ears and snouts alert; Stanley and Bob in particular jumped at the sound. Lola's body stiffened. If the overseer flicked the whip again, Lola was prepared to run out, grab Stella, and carry her away to safety. Her heart pounded as fear pulsed through her.

The taskmaster crept forward, collected the scroll, and returned it to the case. "Collect the harvest, you vulturous varmints!" the overseer ordered. The rats scurried off, their bald tails twitching with anticipation. Bob and Stanley didn't follow. They looked around as if trying to figure out a new plan. The overseer glared at them. "Did you not hear me?"

"We came to work for the queen," Bob said.

"Is that so? Well, I speak for the queen. Anyone who disobeys my orders will be arrested." Overseer Rake raised her arm again and her whip smacked the air. "Fill the train, you swamp scum!" Bob and Stanley scurried to catch up with the others, confusion on their faces.

Despite the sparkling, cloudless sky, darkness descended over Lola—a thick blanket of anguish and despair. The air had never felt so heavy. How she longed to burrow into the ground, to welcome the cool, damp embrace of the earth. To sleep and forget. To wake and find that everything was different.

But the truth was evident. Tassie devils were on the loose, capturing wombats, forcing rats to steal—all under Queen Myra's orders. Peace and quiet would never come again if Lola simply dug a hole and retreated. She had to act. Now.

She scrambled to her feet and hurried out from behind the platform. The taskmaster's eyes widened. "Excuse me," Lola said.

Stella whipped around. "Lola, what are you doing? Go into the cornfield with the others. This is not the time to be unshy."

"I can't," Lola told her. "I need to do this." A musky scent wafted past. Is that what predators smelled like? She held back a shudder. "My name is Lola Budge and I need to get a message to the queen."

Overseer Rake slowly ran a paw along her whip. "You *need* to get a message to the queen?"

"Yes." Lola tried not to look at the whip. She tried not to tremble. She held herself as stiffly as she possibly could.

"Don't you dare hurt her," Stella said. "She's just a joey."

"Will you take me to the queen? Please." It felt wrong to use such a kind word. These monsters didn't deserve courtesy, but Lola needed their help, so she swallowed her pride and said it again. "Please."

"How intriguing," Overseer Rake said. "You are either a very brave wombat or a very stupid one. It would appear that you are not up-to-date on current matters." She held out her paw and snapped. Taskmaster Lash reached into his traveling case and handed a scroll to Rake, who unrolled it and turned it outward to face Lola and Stella.

WOMBATS WANTED (ALIVE)

BY ORDER OF HER MAJESTY, QUEEN MYRA.

ONE GOLD COIN REWARD PER WOMBAT

A sour taste filled Lola's mouth. The horrid truth had been confirmed—beloved Queen Myra had turned against her most loyal and peaceful citizens. Just as this realization hit her like a sharp slap to the face, Overseer Rake cried, "Grab her!" The taskmaster was quick. He reached out, his claws curling around Lola's arm. The overseer smiled. "You wombats are all the same. Easy prey, unadapted to modern times, you rely on the old methods to keep yourselves safe. Well, such times of hiding in burrows have long passed."

Lola struggled, but as she did, the taskmaster's claws pierced her skin. Stella, however, was quick. With a swift kick backward, she sent the parasol flying. As the rays of the sun fell upon him, he shrieked and released Lola. Stella pushed Lola with all her might. "Run!" And that's what Lola did. She bolted, as fast as her legs would carry her.

Overseer Rake growled at the taskmaster. "You're pathetic. You can't do anything right. I don't know why I keep you around!"

"My apologies, Overseer. My only wish is to serve you." He huffed, breathing heavily from the little scare. Overseer Rake had already moved on, turning her eyes to scan over the mob of rats.

"A crate of food for the rat who captures that joey!" Overseer Rake cried.

Three rats had returned carrying a basket of apples. Upon hearing the word "food," they dropped the basket and let out a hungry cheer. Lola didn't look behind. She didn't need to. She could hear galloping rat feet as they took up the chase. She needed to warn Melvin and Blue, but the produce warehouse would be filled with thieving rats by now. What if Melvin was forced to join the others? What would happen to Blue?

The rats leaped over the fallen fruit, scrambling on all fours to reach Lola first. She froze for a moment too long, and the first rat reached her, grabbing her fur and starting to climb up her body. Lola instinctively tried to shake him off, to no avail. Then

Stella was there, having grabbed the rat and thrown him to the ground.

"I told you to run!" Not waiting for a response, she pushed Lola hard in the side. It was enough to get her moving. As Lola rushed off, she heard Stella holler, "All right, lads, time for a beating, it is."

"Lola!" Melvin's and Blue's heads popped up from behind a stack of berry brew barrels. Lola skidded to a stop on the other side, hidden momentarily from rat view.

"Are you okay?" she asked breathlessly.

"Why yes, I'm fine. I got rid of that flea. But rats stormed into the warehouse while I was flossing my teeth and began carrying everything away. Blue and I came to find you but some mice told us to hide. Are there Tassie devils here? What's happening?"

"It's bad, Melvin. Very, very bad." She gasped for breath.

"Bad!" Blue hollered.

"I'm wanted. All wombats are wanted. Don't come with me or you'll be in danger."

"Don't come with you?" Melvin stepped out from the barrels. "We're in this together."

Blue seemed to embrace the same sentiment for he pecked at Lola's foot. "Lola!"

She didn't want to leave her friends. But even though penguins and rats weren't on WANTED posters, who knew what the overseer and the taskmaster might do? "Then let's go. Where's my backpack?"

"The rats took it all," Melvin said. "Your pack, my bucket and shovel. Everything."

Her storybook? Her letters?

Thudding sounds approached. Some rats were getting close. "Climb onto my back." Lola crouched as low as she could, pressing her belly into the dirt. With a grunt, Melvin managed to push Blue onto Lola's back. Then he climbed up, holding Blue tightly with one paw while the other gripped Lola's fur. "Hold tight," she said, and then she burst into a gallop.

Lola's claws left furrows in the ground as she galloped with even greater force. She barreled down a path that cut through a wheat field. The only thing she could hear was her heart thudding in her ears. Stalks whipped past on both sides. She veered left, then right, then left again. She'd lost her pursuers a scant two minutes ago. But for how long could she maintain the breakneck pace? Lola knew she couldn't go much farther, not with two critters clinging to her.

She pushed through the wheat, gasping for breath. A tall wooden building loomed ahead, painted white and topped with a vented roof. "I . . . I . . . I can't keep going."

"You're going to break a leg if you keep running like that," Melvin said. "We can hide here." He slid off Lola's back and helped Blue to the ground.

The building was a grain silo, waiting to be filled in late summer when the grains were ripe. The doorway was large enough for Lola to squeeze through. Streaks of light came through the roof's vents, forming bright rectangles on the floor. Lola sank onto the wooden floor. "I'll be okay. I just need to catch my breath." Blue sat next to her.

Voices rose in the distance. Lola's fur bristled. She suddenly felt the walls closing in around her, and not in the comforting way of a burrow. "We're trapped if they come here. We have to go somewhere else."

Melvin nodded. They turned toward the door but the voices closed in.

"Mates, these plants are broken. Looks like something big came this way."

"Big like a wombat?"

"Why are we chasing a joey? I can't remember."

"For food, of course. A crate for each of us."

"Oh, that's right."

The rats began arguing in earnest, slowing their approach. Melvin stealthily closed the door but there was no way to lock it.

"Look, there's a door," a rat said.

Lola's first thought was to barricade the door with her rump, but it wasn't the right fit. She scooped Blue into her arms and backed up, trying to hide in the deep shadowy recesses of the silo. "Be very quiet," she whispered. Blue looked at her with his watery eyes. Then he whimpered and began sucking on one of his flippers. Melvin grabbed a long wooden tool that was leaning with a few other tools. Holding it tightly in both hands, he brandished it threateningly even as his paws began to shake.

In a moment, the rats would stream in, their snouts sniffing, their eyes darting this way and that, searching for Lola. They might put her in a cage and take her to join her parents, but they might take her somewhere else. She had no way of knowing. She couldn't get caught. Not when her uncle was waiting. *T.B. is ready.*

If she walked out of the silo, the rats would take her. They'd never have to know about Blue and Melvin. "I see that look on your face," Melvin whispered. "You're not giving yourself up. Don't even think about it."

"Halt!"

Lola's ears pricked. The voice had come from just outside the door. She pulled Blue's flipper from his mouth and clasped the end of his beak shut so he couldn't have one of his outbursts. "Shhhh," she whispered. Melvin raised the threshing tool higher.

"What are you doing?" the voice asked.

"We're trying to catch a young wombat," a rat replied. "Overseer's orders."

"I have already searched this silo. The wombat is long gone. She outran you all. Return to the train, immediately."

Shuffling sounds and grumbles arose, followed by the pounding of paws. The rats were leaving. Lola and Melvin exchanged a surprised look. Someone had lied to the rats, someone who also had authority over the rats. But who?

The silo door creaked open wider. Melvin stepped protectively in front of Lola and Blue. The trio stared at the doorway. Lola felt as if she were living inside a scary story, waiting for the monster to appear. Blue pressed against Lola and whimpered.

A monster did appear. But it wasn't just a monster from a story. It was real. Very real.

15

SNARL, SON OF SNARL

The Tassie devil who stepped into the silo was smaller than the others Lola had seen. His ears were red, but the rest of him was pure black, with no white markings around his neck. He wore a black robe like the overseer's and the taskmaster's but had no whip around his waist.

Melvin raised the threshing tool. "Stay right there or I'll—"

He held up his paws. "I am unarmed. And I mean you no harm, I promise." He lowered his paws. "Though I understand you have no reason to trust me. Why should you? You only know my kind as predators, or worse, as monsters." He shook his head sadly, then sighed. "But I assure you, most of us have given up the old ways. We are decent critters who love peace and quiet almost as much as any wombat." He looked directly at Lola. To her surprise, she found kindness in his eyes.

Melvin slowly lowered his arms. "You're a youngster, like Lola."

He bowed. "I am Snarl, son of Snarl. And though I carry no weapons, I am a warrior for peace."

"A warrior for peace?" Lola asked.

"Precisely." Snarl straightened himself, his chin held high.

"I have been trained to disarm with words, using physical force only after such methods have failed. What sort of warrior are you?"

"I'm not a warrior," Lola said. "But I do like words."

"I'm not a warrior either," Melvin said. "I abhor confrontations of any sort." He raised the threshing tool again. "But I'll use this if I have to. Believe me, I will." His tail stiffened and rose above his head, like a snake ready to strike.

"I believe you. But as you can see . . ." Snarl held his arms aloft and turned in a slow circle. "I carry not a whip, nor a blade, nor even a rock. I promise you that I pose no physical threat. And my promise is as good as my life."

Blue, who'd been trembling in Lola's arms, suddenly hiccupped. Snarl lowered his paws and cocked his head. "Hello, little penguin. And hello, Lola, daughter of Alice." Lola held tight to Blue. "How . . . how do you know my name? How do you know my mum's name?"

"Though I have never met your mother, I know of her through shared acquaintances. I was sent to find her and escort her to Dore."

"You were supposed to *escort* my mum to Dore?" Lola shook her head. Was there straw in her ears? Had she heard him correctly? Her mother didn't travel beyond the trading post. And she certainly wouldn't go anywhere with a night monster. "I don't believe you."

"Nor do I," said Melvin, taking a step closer to Lola.

"I'm Blue!"

Snarl pressed the tips of his paws together. "I know this is confusing. And I can't tell you everything. But as you have noticed, there is a scattering of Tassie devils on the loose in the

125

land. I suppose you could call them . . . rebels, outcasts from our own society. Perhaps even more so than we have been from yours. My acquaintances needed your mother to get to Dore as soon as possible, but it was too risky to have her travel alone. And so they sent me. I chose a route off the beaten path and traveled mostly at night, for as you know, my kind tends to strike fear in most critters."

"Terrify," Melvin said. "I think that's a better word choice."

Snarl sighed. "Yes, you're right. *Terrify* most critters." He continued. "But when I arrived, the burrows were empty. I found fresh paw prints and followed them. That's when I spied you, Lola, crossing the river to the trading post in Fairwater. I listened, outside the window, to your conversation with the proprietors, and I learned about the horrid fate of your family. I'm sorry. We're sorry."

"We?" Melvin asked. "Who are you working for?"

Snarl didn't reply. "Lola, I—"

"Wait." She tightened her hold on Blue as that eerie sensation crept back up her spine. "After leaving the burrows, I kept hearing sounds. Were you following me?"

"Yes. I needed to know something. I found the message, and that's when I realized you had gotten it by mistake."

Found the message? So he was the one who'd taken her secret message. That explained why the pocket of her backpack had been opened. "*You* know about my secret message? Are you the one who sent it?" Lola frowned in disbelief. Suddenly, a piece of the puzzle clicked into place. "Wait a minute. *You're* the bloodthirsty brute who hired Bale Blackwater?"

"Bloodthirsty I am not," he bristled, flicking his head aside in a huff. "Nor do I consider myself a brute. As I have said, I carry no weapon of any sort. I am beholden to the Treaty of Mount Ossa, as is the vast majority of Tassie devils. To the pledge that we would no longer hunt. And that we would cast aside instinct and desire, choosing instead the calming structure provided by society and discipline" He placed his paws together once again and bowed.

His words were complex and confusing. Lola didn't know anything about their society, except that they were predators. And predators were bad. But though one of those predators stood only a few feet away, Lola's need to understand outweighed her fear.

She set Blue on the floor next to Melvin. Then she took a hesitant step forward. "Were you trying to trap my mum? Did you want her to think that her brother needed her? So you could catch her for gold coin?"

"No," he said, looking deeply into Lola's eyes. "I'm working *with* your mother."

"Working with her?" Lola clenched her paws. "That's impossible. My mum carves bowls, that's her work. She would never work with a . . . with a . . ."

"A monster?" He frowned.

"What do you want?" Melvin asked. "Why are you here?"

A whistle blew. Snarl turned, glanced outside, and turned back. "Listen to me, Lola. We don't have much time. You must go home, where it is safe. That's what I want. And that's what your mother would want, too. Go back to the burrows. You are too young."

"I'm the same age as you," she said defiantly. "I won't go home. And why should I? There's no one at home. Your kind took them away!"

Snarl nodded sadly. "Alas, there is a rebel band of Tassie

devils who cannot be trusted. Who wish to return to the old ways, no matter what the cost may be." His gaze turned to Melvin. "Take her somewhere safe, perhaps to Penguin Bay so you can return little Blue as well. Please. I will not be able to protect her if she makes her way to Dore."

Melvin leaned on the threshing tool. "I hate to break it to you, but Lola's no ordinary wombat. She speaks her mind and makes her own decisions."

"That's right," Lola said. "I'm going to find my family no matter how many devils try to stop me!"

A low growl thrummed in Snarl's throat. For a moment Lola saw the flash of temper she'd seen in others—a glimpse of razor-sharp teeth, a hint of fire in the eyes. But this reaction passed quickly and his composure returned. "Then go in peace, Lola," he said, his voice calm and steady. "But know that for now I cannot protect you. There are other things I must do." He bowed, and with a swift turn on his heels, he left the silo.

"Bye-bye," Blue called with a little wave.

Lola and Melvin rushed to the doorway, watching Snarl disappear among the stalks of wheat.

16

HOT AIR

In the distance, the train whistled multiple times as it departed, each issuance growing softer until the noise fell away entirely, leaving a heavy silence in its wake. A thin plume of black smoke faded into the horizon.

"Do you think the rats and devils left on the train?" Lola asked as she and Melvin stood in the silo's entryway.

"I hope so," he said as he set the threshing tool aside.

Blue squeezed between Lola and Melvin, then bounced down the steps, chasing a yellow butterfly that had caught his attention. "Don't wander," Lola called after him. She and Melvin looked at the field. The cornstalks swayed gracefully in the breeze as if nothing had changed. As if night monsters hadn't invaded the Farmlands. As if the queen hadn't turned against her most loyal subjects.

"Do you think there are good Tassie devils and bad Tassie devils?" Lola asked. "Like Snarl said."

Melvin folded his arms and looked out over the landscape. "It's possible. Just as there are swamp water rats who despise garbage and Northern Forest wombats who like to talk."

"Melvin?"

He turned his long snout toward her. "You don't have to say it."

"I do have to say it." Lola felt terribly guilty. She'd suspected Melvin of taking her secret message. But Melvin had led her out of the swamp, helped rescue Blue, and walked every step of this journey beside her. As the sun warmed her fur, she realized that not only did she trust him, but he'd become her friend, too. And maybe he could help her make sense of it all. "I'm sorry," she said. "I'm sorry I didn't trust you."

He waved a paw at her. "It's understandable that you'd suspect me. You thought we were alone out there. I was the only critter who could have taken it. Other than our loud companion."

Blue caught the butterfly and shoved it into his beak. "Blech!" he exclaimed as he spat it out. "Bad!" Then he started chasing a green butterfly, presumably thinking different colors had different flavors.

"I still don't understand all this fuss about a secret message," Melvin said. He sat on the top step and patted the space next to him. "Do tell."

"Okay, here goes." Lola also sat, then took a long breath. "Bale Blackwater is the platypus who carried the message upstream to the burrows. He said that it was a *secret* message and it needed a *secret* password. I said 'hooly dooly' because I always say that when I'm nervous, and 'hooly dooly' turned out to be the password, so Bale Blackwater gave me the message. Then, just before Bale swam away, he told me that a bloodthirsty brute had sent the message but he didn't say who or why."

"The bloodthirsty beast is Snarl, apparently. And the message was meant for your mum. What did it say?"

"'T.B. is ready.'"

"Who's T.B.?"

"I didn't figure that out until later. After Bale Blackwater left I heard these terrible sounds. That's when I saw all the wombats being carted away. My mum hollered at me to find my uncle. I didn't even know I had an uncle. So I ran back to the burrow and searched until I found some letters from my uncle, Tobias Bottom, and I learned that he's an ambassador in Dore. His initials are T.B., so I guessed that the message was about him. I figured that Mum wanted me to find Uncle Tobias because he could help free the wombats. But why would a Tassie devil send that message? That's the part that makes no sense."

"There are still too many missing pieces," Melvin said. "If what Snarl told us is true, and he sent the message, then he must have sent it on your uncle's behalf. That would mean he's working for your uncle."

Lola shook her head. "Maybe Snarl lied. Maybe he's working for the queen. She's the one who's letting those monsters leave Mount Ossa. She's the one who's paying gold coin for wombats. What if Queen Myra sent the message *pretending* it was from my uncle to trap my mum? What if she put my uncle in a cage, just like the others?" Lola couldn't believe what she was saying. She'd spent her entire life admiring the queen.

Melvin stopped grooming. "I agree with you that our queen is looking suspect. But why would she do these things?"

"I don't know. But at the very least I think we can trust my uncle to have been fighting against it. Still, there's only one way to find out and only one way I can help. I need to get to Dore, and fast." Lola scrambled to her paws.

"I?" Melvin asked, eyes widening. "Last time I counted there were three of us on this journey."

Even though she felt confused and scared, Lola tried to put on a brave face. "What the gold-toothed one said was true. There's a reward for wombats. I saw it with my own eyes. One gold coin for the capture of a wombat. And I met two Tassie devils who call themselves the overseer and the taskmaster. They will be looking for me. If you travel with me you'll be in danger. I should go alone."

Now it was Melvin's turn to scramble to his feet. "Alone?" He set his paws on his hips and looked at Lola the same way her father looked at her when she was caught talking to neighbors. "You listen to me, Lola Budge. I wouldn't be able to stand my own perfectly groomed reflection if I abandoned you. We're stronger together, or hadn't you noticed?"

A tear came to Lola's eye. She hadn't really wanted to be alone, but it had seemed like the right thing to do. She wrapped her arms around Melvin, enveloping him in a big furry hug. "Thank you." He hugged back, chuckling. When she released him, he looked a bit embarrassed and began anew the process of smoothing his gray fur.

"Do you see this?" he asked, pointing to a clump at his elbow. "I'm getting a mat. I can't believe those walking stomachs took all our stuff. How am I going to convince the critters of Dore that my swamp-mud products work if I look like every other swamp water rat?"

"Then we'd better get there before you completely fall apart," Lola teased. "Let's go." She looked toward the field. "Blue? Oh, hooly dooly. Blue!"

Melvin groaned. "Here we go again." He rushed down the stairs and into the field while Lola circled the outside of the silo, panic increasing with each step. That little penguin could disappear faster than a fish in a river. "Do you see him?"

"There's a little trampled path over here," Melvin called. He and Lola followed it through the field. A few fluffy gray feathers indicated that they were heading in the right direction. The stalks of wheat bent and wavered as they passed by. Lola felt bad that she was crushing more plants, but Blue had to be found. As far as she could tell, baby penguins had no defense mechanisms. They didn't have hard wombat rumps or sharp rat teeth.

"Blue!"

"I swear, I'm never going to be a parent," Melvin said, following in Lola's wake, his tail swishing agitatedly across the dirt. "Babies are more trouble than ticks. More annoying than bities."

A small wooden crate lay in the trampled path, exactly like the crates they'd seen earlier when they'd found Blue. This one contained sunflower seeds. They came to another crate with its lid fallen open. It was full of biscuits, most broken. Lola's mouth watered, but she kept walking. Several more crates were scattered among the stalks.

Then they came to a huge basket that was squarish in shape and as tall as Lola. Attached to the basket was a gaggle of ropes. Attached to these ropes was some fabric, which lay crumpled on the ground. The fabric was made from a hodgepodge of materials—shirts, vests, blankets, towels, even a few pairs of socks, all stitched together. Heavy stones hung off the side of the basket, and a pickaxe had been driven into the ground to serve as an anchor. Lola had no idea what she was looking at.

"Lola!" A familiar voice bellowed her name as a plump bundle of baby feathers waddled toward her. Lola scooped Blue into her arms. "You wandered off again, you bad little penguin."

"I fly! I fly!" He flapped his flippers, then pointed at the basket. Lola and Melvin looked at each other with a mixture of relief and confusion. "I fly!"

"Blue, I'm sorry, but you're the kind of bird who can't fly," Lola gently told him.

"Squwhaaaaat?"

The trio looked over at the giant basket, ears and noses twitching as they noticed the strange new scent. A black-feathered head with a wickedly curved, black-tipped beak poked up from within the basket. Both Lola and Melvin gasped, startled by the bird's sudden appearance. The bird's black feathers ruffled indignantly as he scowled at the three travelers. "Who said I can't fly?"

"Um, sorry for the confusion," Lola explained. "I wasn't saying that *you* can't fly. I was talking to Blue. He's a penguin and, well, penguins can't fly."

The head disappeared for a moment. Then a door opened in the side of the basket and a bird stepped out. Lola had to suppress a gasp of astonishment. The poor creature's left wing was gone, leaving him so unbalanced that he used his right wing as a sort of crutch.

"Are you saying there's something wrong with a bird who can't fly?" He puffed up his feathers again, eyes gleaming sharply in the light bouncing off his polished beak.

"Lola didn't mean to insult you," Melvin said, stepping between Lola and the sharp-beaked critter. "She was simply stating a fact. Penguins can't fly."

"That's right," Lola said, still holding tight to Blue.

The bird narrowed his black eyes and pointed his good wing at Melvin. "Well I think yer fulla beans! Everyone used to tell me that I couldn't fly 'cause I only got this one good wing. But I proved 'em wrong. I flew all the way across this island, I did. So I say, instead of crushing that little fella's dreams, why not give him a fair go? All he needs to do is get his pilot's license like the one I got here." He pointed to a tag that hung around his neck. Despite the bird's ominous beak, Lola and Melvin leaned forward to read the tag:

```
Ofissial Pilot Licens
4 Captain Bogart
to flie his hot air beloon
```

It didn't look official. It looked as if it had been written on a scrap piece of paper, and quite poorly at that. "What's a hot-air balloon?" Lola asked.

Captain Bogart pointed his wing at the large standing basket. "Yer looking at it. I invented it. Got tired of the other birds always picking on me 'cause I was grounded." His expression softened. "I don't expect you to understand. You don't know what it's like to be different from yer friends and family."

"Oh, believe me, we do," Melvin said.

Bogart cocked his head. "Now that you mention it, you don't look like a typical swamp water rat. And you, young lady, you're awful short for a wallaby."

"That's because I'm not a wallaby. I'm a wombat. I'm Lola, by the way. And this is Melvin and Blue."

"How does your balloon work?" Melvin asked.

Bogart began to strut around the contraption. "It's a genius idea, if I do say so myself. I fill the balloon with hot air and when the balloon is fully inflated, it rises into the sky."

"Seems a bit dangerous," Melvin whispered to Lola.

"How do you steer it?" Lola wondered. There didn't appear to be a wheel or oars.

"I catch the wind. It takes great skill." He pointed to his license. "But I don't expect you to understand. You don't have an official license like I do."

Melvin looked around at the strewn crates. "It looks like you crashed here."

"Squwhaaaaat?" The bird rustled his tail feathers. "I didn't crash. I landed here on purpose. In this place called . . ." He paused, mumbling to himself as he glanced at the tall stalks of wheat on all sides.

"The Mouse Farmlands," Lola said, partially interrupted as he repeated what she said a split second after.

"The Mouse Farmlands. Yes, of course. The Mouse Farmlands. Indeed, I knew that, of course. Right here, in the middle of this field, in this exact spot, is where I *planned* to land." He was certainly making a big deal about it.

Blue wiggled in Lola's arms, so she set him down. He immediately waddled over to one of the crates and poked his beak inside. "Captain Bogart," Lola asked. "Did you lose some baskets near the swamp?"

"Maybe. But I didn't crash up there, if that's what yer insinuating, missy."

"And did you happen to visit Penguin Bay before you landed, *on purpose*, near the swamp?"

"Yep. Bought myself some fish at the Penguin Fish Market."
He eyed them suspiciously.

Lola smiled at Melvin. "Blue must have climbed into the hot-air balloon to eat some of that fish. And then he probably fell asleep."

"Squwhaaaaat? That little bloke was a stowaway?"

Melvin shook his head in amazement. "Blue was telling us the truth after all. He did fly."

"I fly!" Blue pecked at the crate. "Hungry!"

Bogart seemed to have warmed up to the three travelers. He opened the crate and Blue hopped up and down with delight, for it was full of anchovies. "I gotta wait for the wind to change. Yer welcome to join me for lunch. I got some bikkies around here somewhere."

Lola remembered seeing the biscuits and she hurriedly collected that crate. Melvin was so hungry he didn't worry about the lack of napkins or utensils. The biscuits were dry, but neither complained, for the food was free and they were starving. Bogart and Blue shared the anchovies. Lola ate quickly, eager to get back to the Royal Road. No one said a word, too busy stuffing their faces, when Bogart suddenly stopped eating and put his good wing in the air. "You feel that?"

"It might be a flea," Melvin said. "I had one earlier." Bogart glanced worriedly at his wing for a second, before shaking his head and squinting at Melvin, annoyed.

"No, it's the wind. The wind's changing. Time to leave!" Bogart swallowed a herring and hobbled back inside the hot air balloon. Then his head popped up. He held a stick in his beak. The end of it was bright red and smoking.

"Watch out!" Lola cried. "That stick's on fire!"

"Squwhaaaaat?" Bogart held the stick with his wing. "I know it's on fire. It's supposed to be on fire." He disappeared into the depths of the basket.

"I just realized what kind of bird he is," Melvin told Lola. "He's a firehawk." When Lola looked at him with a puzzled expression, he continued. "Firehawks carry fire with them. It's how they hunt. Well, it's how they *used* to hunt. They used to carry burning sticks so they could set fields on fire. They'd wait at the edge of the fire for insects and lizards to flee the flames. Then they'd feast. But firehawks aren't allowed to spread fire anymore, not since the Great Burn."

"If he's not supposed to spread fire, then why does he have it?" Lola asked. Was this another law that Queen Myra had changed? She and Melvin crept up to the gondola and peered over its rim.

A potbelly furnace sat in the middle of the gondola. Bogart had set small pieces of kindling inside the furnace and was lighting them with his burning stick. A red flame flared for a moment, and then the kindling caught fire. The space above the furnace began to shimmer as hot air flowed out the top. At the sight of the flame, Lola's heart began to pound. "Why are you making fire?"

"Can't have a hot-air balloon without hot air," Bogart told her. He set his stick inside, then closed the furnace. The fire appeared to be trapped, held captive in the metal chamber. "Now I'll fill the balloon and be on my way."

"Where are you going?" Lola asked.

"To Dore."

"You're going to Dore?" Her eyes widened and her heart

pounded even faster. This was amazing news. "Can we go with you?"

"No." The reply was quick, clipped, as Bogart began to gather the large piece of piecemeal fabric.

"Please, Captain Bogart. Please can we—"

Melvin nudged Lola aside. "I don't think it's a good idea to fly with him. He obviously crashed this thing."

"I didn't crash," Bogart insisted. "I never crash. I just land *unexpectedly*." A metal ring had been sewn into the center of the fabric. Bogart held this ring over the furnace, and as he did so, the fabric began to billow.

"Why are you going to Dore?" Lola asked.

"To show my invention to the queen. If I can get her Royal Seal of Approval, then I can get a loan to make more hot-air balloons. I'll have a whole fleet of them flying around the island, giving tours and such. Think of all the critters who'd love to see Tassie from a bird's-eye view."

It sounded like a great idea, but Lola couldn't wait for the fleet—she needed a ride now. "Captain Bogart, my uncle is an ambassador. If you take us to Dore I'll introduce you. He knows the queen. He can help you get a Royal Seal of Approval, I'm sure of it."

"Yer uncle, eh?" Bogart let go of the fabric as it fully expanded into a giant balloon. It was an amazing sight as it rose into the air, inflating into an immense structure. As it filled, the seams began to stretch, revealing the stitching that held it together.

"Yes, my uncle Tobias, ambassador to the Northern Forest and the Realms Beyond."

Using his sharp beak and single wing, Bogart began to untangle the ropes until they hung in straight lines, attaching the balloon to the basket. "If you promise to get me a meeting, then you can come with me."

"Thank you!" Lola said.

"The wind doesn't wait. Hurry up and get into the gondola."

"What's a gondola?" Lola asked.

"This right here." He patted the large basket. Then he held open its door. Blue, who'd finished the last anchovy, waddled inside.

"Home!"

But Melvin stood frozen in place, wringing his paws nervously. "Rats aren't meant to fly."

Lola could tell he was scared. She was scared, too. There was fire on board, after all! "Melvin, this will get us to Dore much faster than walking. But if you're not going, then I'm not going. We're a team, remember?"

"Hurry, hurry, the wind, can't miss the wind!" Bogart hollered as he began to untie the hanging stones. One side of the gondola lifted a few inches. But Melvin didn't move. It appeared he had made up his mind.

With a disappointed sigh, Lola reached in to retrieve Blue, but Melvin suddenly pushed her inside. Then he stepped in and closed the door. She looked at him with surprise. "We're a team," he said. "But if we crash, I may never speak to you again."

"Deal," she said with a grateful smile.

She pressed against the gondola's side, keeping as much distance from the furnace as she could. Bogart hopped onto the gondola's rim, then pulled the pickaxe free. With a jolt, the balloon began to rise. A wave of panic rolled over Lola's body. Had she made the right decision? They were actually lifting into the air! Wombats, swamp water rats, and penguins didn't belong in the air. What had she done?

"Captain Bogart, you're forgetting all your crates," she told him.

"Can't add any more weight, not with a short, fat wallaby on board."

"Wombat," Lola reminded him again.

"Lola!" Blue climbed into her arms. Holding him tight, she held him up to get a better view. "I fly!"

"Yes, Blue, you fly," Lola said with amazement.

17

BIRD'S-EYE VIEW

Lola sat, wide-eyed and openmouthed, as the world below revealed itself. To her surprise, the height didn't bother her. Nor did the realization that fire was making this possible. She never would have guessed that she'd take so well to flying. After all, she was a burrow-dweller—a broad-shouldered, thick-bodied critter of the earth. But at that moment, gliding through the air, she felt as light as a feather. Her adventure was like one of the stories in her beloved book. And such was the excitement that she momentarily forgot that her book had been stolen by the overseer's rats.

The rolling patchwork of fields disappeared as the balloon floated southwest. Lola hoped that the long-tailed mice hadn't suffered much from the raid. Even if the rats had taken every piece of produce from the warehouses, fruits and vegetables were still growing in the fields, so surely the mice wouldn't starve. Would they? Lola would tell her uncle about the situation. She'd tell him how Stella had helped her and how unfair it was for the queen to take all the harvest. It was another part of the puzzle that didn't make sense.

"Melvin, look!" The balloon floated over a dense carpet of green. Lola had lived beneath a forest canopy her entire life, but to see it from a bird's-eye view was breathtaking. The treetops rustled as songbirds took off and landed. This world that existed between land and sky belonged to them.

I wish I had wings, Lola almost said, but then she remembered that the pilot only had one wing. She didn't want to offend him.

"Lola!" Blue tapped his flipper on her leg. He was eager to take in the view, so Lola picked him up so he could see. He spread his flippers wide, feeling the rush of the wind pass between his feathers. Lola laughed and moved him up and down, making him coo in happiness.

But Melvin did not look at the luscious scenery, for he was clearly not faring well. "I'm dizzy," he announced as he sat on the gondola floor, a grimace frozen on his face. "This thing feels so wobbly."

"You'll get used to it," Bogart said.

Melvin leaned back against the gondola's wall. "You sure this is safe? How long have you been flying, exactly?"

"A week, give or take a day." Bogart perched on the gondola's rim, his single wing sticking out into the air. He swept the wing from side to side, working simultaneously as rudder and sail.

"Only a week?" Melvin said with squeak. He grabbed the end of his tail and began nervously wringing it.

Captain Bogart cocked his little head and gave Melvin a long look of pity. "Scared of flying, are ya? Well, nothing to worry about, mate. The most natural thing a bird can do is fly, and that's what I'm doing. Just because I've only got one wing doesn't mean I don't have the instinct."

This made sense to Lola. Instinct was a powerful force. She'd never seen fire before this journey but she still had the instinct to avoid it. Her gaze darted to the furnace, which held the flame and its sparks within, like a monster trapped in a box. *As long as no one lets the monster out, everything will be okay*, Lola thought. And she had to admit that the warmth coming from the furnace felt nice against her back, especially as the air was growing colder the higher they flew.

"Hello!" Blue cried, waving his flipper at a passing pigeon. He pushed against Lola's arms, leaning over the gondola's rim so he could wave at more birds.

Pogart jumped onto the gondola's floor. "Since yer my first official passengers, this is a fine time to practice the safety announcement." He straightened himself to full height, cleared his throat, and hollered. "Attention passengers!" Lola, Blue, and Melvin all turned to look at him. "This is your captain speaking. Once we reach our cruising altitude, you will be free to move about the gondola, but until that time please remain seated with your arms, flippers, and legs inside at all times." He gave Lola a disapproving look. She pulled Blue away from the gondola's rim. "Also, please maintain an even weight distribution or we will tip over." He motioned for Lola to move a bit to the right. When she did, the gondola leveled. "During this journey we will be flying over water. Should the need arise, you may use one of the crates as a flotation device."

"Should the need arise?" Melvin asked with another squeak. "What does that mean? Do you expect us to crash? Is that what you're saying?" He wrung his tail faster.

"Don't get yer tail in a knot," Bogart said. "It's just a precaution."

"But there's only one crate," Lola pointed out, spooking Melvin into a new round of mumbles. "And there are four of us." Indeed, he'd left the other crates behind in the Farmlands.

"Aye, that does seem to be the case." Bogart scratched his

head. "Well then, I reckon you'll need to swim." He shrugged. "Anyhoo, our destination is Dore and our traveling time depends upon the fairness of the wind. Should we encounter any unexpected turbulence and you need to upchuck, please do so over the side. Thank you and enjoy your flight." He jumped back onto the rim and stuck out his wing again.

"Unexpected turbulence?" Melvin mumbled. "You know, I think I've changed my mind. I'd like to get off as soon as possible. I'll walk to Dore. Yes, that's what I'll do, I'll walk to Dore."

"Can't stop now. The wind's in our favor," Bogart said.

Lola wasn't sure how to help Melvin. He looked so frightened, his eyes wide, his nose trembling. He'd been so brave to join her and now he was miserable. She was about to sit next to him when Blue began to shiver.

"Cold!"

It was cold. *Very* cold, all of a sudden. Little Blue, with his downy baby feathers, wasn't prepared for the chill. And even though Lola had a thick coat of fur, the cold managed to pierce through to her skin. Melvin's teeth began to chatter. "It is cold," she said, her jaw trembling.

"Brrrrrr!" Blue hollered.

Lola wished she still had her cloak, which would be big enough to wrap around all three of them. Blue pressed against her, trying to burrow into her fur.

Then a lovely scent tickled her nose. It smelled like fresh rain. They'd reached the clouds. What would it be like to touch one? She reached up, on tiptoes, but the cloud was just a wisp of cold.

"Blimey, we're a bit high," Bogart said. His tone of alarm caught Melvin's attention. "No worries, I can fix this." Bogart opened the furnace so hot air was no longer flowing directly into the balloon. The gondola slowly leveled off, then began to descend. As it did, Lola's ears suddenly felt as if they were filled with something that was expanding and pressing deep within. She gulped, and when she did, there was a little popping sound in each ear and the feeling dissipated.

"Sleepy!" Blue's yawn smelled extra fishy thanks to the recent anchovy lunch. He wiggled out of Lola's arms.

"You need a nap," Lola told him, and he didn't protest. It had already been a long day for all of them. While standing on his blue webbed feet, he tucked his beak under his wing and closed his eyes. But the gondola rocked from side to side as they descended, causing Blue to topple over.

"Oh, make it stop," Melvin complained, his paw covering his mouth.

"Are you getting airsick, mate?" Bogart continued to deflate the balloon ever so slightly. "If yer gonna upchuck, do it over the side."

The rocking continued as the gondola swung from its ropes. "Sleepy," Blue repeated, rubbing his eyes. Lola looked around. She no longer had her cape or backpack, so she couldn't make a nest. But the wooden crate would make a snug bed. She walked toward it, and with the shifting of her weight, the gondola tipped.

"Ahhhh!" Melvin cried as he slid across the floor, Blue tumbling after him.

"Squwhaaaaat did I say about maintaining an even weight distribution?" Bogart shrieked as he fell off the rim and landed atop Melvin.

"Sorry," Lola said, darting back to her spot. The gondola

swung a few times on its ropes, then settled. Melvin put his paw to his mouth again and moaned.

"Again! Again!" Blue laughed and scampered to his webbed feet.

"*Don't* do it again," Melvin pleaded. His pink nose had turned a slightly greenish hue.

Despite Blue's enthusiasm, he couldn't hold back another yawn. He sat on Lola's lap, his head nodding sleepily.

Bogart seemed satisfied with the altitude and resumed his position as rudder. Lola wrapped her arms around Blue and stared at the passing sky. "Captain Bogart, is that a storm cloud over there?" she asked, pointing to a dark shadow that loomed on the horizon.

"Storm?" Melvin asked, wrapping his arms tightly around his knees. "Are we heading into a storm?"

"Now, now, don't jump to conclusions. I'm the captain of this balloon and I'll be the one to decide if it's a storm or not. This young wallaby doesn't know a storm cloud from a snow cloud."

"Wombat," Lola corrected.

"Bless you," he said, as if she'd sneezed. He grabbed a strange black object and held it to his eyes. "Ah, just as I thought. That's not a storm. That's a coal cloud. They've been burning coal day and night in Dore."

"What's coal?" Lola asked.

"It's a black rock, dug from the ground. It burns as good as wood but it stinks up the air."

"Why are they burning it?" Melvin asked through clenched teeth as he fought against his motion sickness.

"I don't know," Bogart said. "But the coal is delivered by

the wagonload. Actually, we're passing over the Royal Coal Mine right now if you'd like to take a look."

Lola lifted Blue carefully, for he'd fallen asleep. She set him into the empty crate. It made a nice makeshift bed. Then she stood and peered over the gondola's rim. The scenery had changed to a landscape of wooded hills, but ahead lay a large clearing. Several buildings were clustered at the edge of the clearing, near a dark hole that had been carved into a hillside. And outside this hole, two train cars sat on their train tracks. Lola squinted, then held her paw above her eyes, trying to get a better view.

"These binoculars will help," Bogart said, handing the strange black object to her. Lola looked at it quizzically. "Hold it up to your eyes," he explained. And so she did.

"Hooly dooly!" she exclaimed as the treetops rushed up to greet her. Everything was so close. She could see a stream of water running through a ravine. She could see the branches on the pine trees. She moved the binoculars. The hole in the hill wasn't a cave; it was a critter-made tunnel. A strangled sound caught in Lola's throat.

"Lola, what's the matter?" Melvin asked, pulling himself to his feet with great effort.

"Tassie devils," she said. Four sat on some rocks outside the tunnel's entrance. They appeared to be talking and sharing a jug.

"Night monsters?" Bogart said, his feathers rustling.

"Yes," Lola told him. "Some have left Mount Ossa." She gripped the binoculars so tightly, her paws began to ache. A pair of critters had emerged from the tunnel.

Lola gasped. "Wombats." She could barely find her voice. "There are . . . there are . . . wombats down there." She tried to hold the binoculars steady, but her arms began to tremble. The

148

wombats moved awkwardly, for a metal chain ran between them, attached to metal leg bands. Each wombat carried a bucket up to the first train car, then turned the bucket upside down. Round, black lumps fell into the car. Then one of the wombats stumbled and fell. A Tassie devil leaped off his rock and brandished his whip through the air. The wombat struggled, then got to his feet.

"Lola, what do you see?" Melvin asked.

"Aye, tell us."

"It's Mister Squat and Stout Junior. I'm sure it's them. They're my neighbors. Mister Squat!" Lola cried, leaning over the gondola's edge. "They are forcing them to dig coal. Hellooo! Mister Squat!" Then she looked back through the binoculars to see if they'd noticed her.

Mister Squat was looking up. But so were the devils. The one standing closest to Mister Squat pulled back her lips in a growl. Her gold tooth gleamed in the sunlight.

"Why would anyone force wombats to dig coal?" Lola asked.

Melvin pointed to Lola's paw. "Because you are designed for digging." He moved to Lola's side, the gondola tipping with the shifting weight. "Let me take a look." He took the binoculars with his shaky paws and surveyed the scene. "If I hadn't seen this with my own eyes I never would have believed it. Queen Myra has imprisoned her loyal subjects."

"Squwhaaaaat?" Bogart bristled his feathers. "How can you say such a thing about our queen?"

"We hope it's untrue," Melvin told him. "But we have reason to believe that Queen Myra is working with the Tassie devils."

"My mum and dad must be down there," Lola realized. "Captain Bogart, stop the balloon!"

Bogart shook his head. "I can't just stop a balloon. It doesn't work that way."

"Take us down. I have to get down there!" Lola was frantic. With every passing moment, the balloon was floating away from her family and neighbors. "Please!"

"Lola, if you go down there, they'll capture you, too," Melvin told her.

"I don't care, I don't care," Lola said, bursting into tears. She missed them with all her heart. Her quest forgotten, all that mattered at that moment was to see her mum and dad. "Please take me down."

"Don't do it," Melvin told their captain. He tried to be the voice of reason. "Lola, you know I'm on your team, but we don't know what those monsters would do to Blue. Or to Captain Bogart."

"I'm not keen on landing down there," Bogart said.

"So you're not going to help?" Lola glared angrily at Bogart and Melvin. "You won't take me down?"

Bogart shook his head. "It's not safe. A captain is responsible for the safety of his passengers. That's what I've always said, and so say I."

Feeling totally helpless, Lola watched as the mine disappeared from view. Tears stung her eyes. "Mum. Dad," she whimpered.

Melvin set his paw on her shoulder, but she brushed it off. She knew he was right. This was not a safe place to land, but her disappointment was like fire on her skin. "We know where they are," Melvin said gently. "That means we can rescue them." His words were reassuring, but then he leaned over the edge of the gondola and gagged. When he'd finished emptying his stomach, he looked at the captain. "Do you have a moistened towel? Or a glass of water?"

"No."

"No?" After a roll of his eyes, Melvin dabbed his mouth with the tip of his tail. "No napkin or kerchief. How humiliating." He settled back onto the floor, wrapped his arms around his knees, and groaned. "How much longer, Captain Bogart?"

"We'll be in Dore by morning," the bird said. "If the wind stays in our favor."

Melvin groaned again. "I never thought I'd say this, but if I had to choose between going on another hot-air balloon ride or being covered in swamp slime for the rest of my life, I'd choose the slime."

"What are you complaining about?" Captain Bogart asked crossly. "You're riding for free, aren't ya? And we haven't crashed, have we?"

"Is that the standard you set? That we haven't yet crashed?" Melvin asked, equally cross. "You might think about the comfort of your passengers and warn them, before liftoff, that they might get sick."

Bogart's feathers ruffled so much that he momentarily doubled in size. "Why, you—"

"Stop fighting!" Lola cried. She wiped another tear from her cheek. Both Bogart and Melvin settled down. But her outburst awoke Blue, who sat up and rubbed his eyes. "Story?"

Lola ignored him.

"Story!"

"No."

"Lola! Story!"

"No!" she hollered. "Go to sleep!"

Blue's eyes widened. With a little whimper, he curled into the crate and closed his eyes.

For the first time in her life, Lola didn't want to tell a story. She didn't want an audience holding on to her every word. She was done with stories. Stories were for books and this was real life. And in real life, unlike in a story, sometimes the ending wasn't happy.

"Lola," Melvin said gently.

"Leave me alone."

While Bogart tended to the furnace, Lola turned her face upward. "Please, wind," she whispered. "If you can hear me, please take us to Dore as quickly as possible."

As if listening, a sudden gust blew across her face, while another tucked itself beneath the gondola, lifting it and carrying it toward the golden city by the bay.

18

A PLATY'S CONFESSION

The night passed fretfully for everyone except Blue, who woke for another meal, pooped over the side of the gondola, and then went back to sleep. But Melvin tossed and turned. Lola didn't fare any better, for she couldn't stop imagining her parents being forced to dig for coal. And thinking about the queen who'd made this all happen. The queen she'd once loved.

These thoughts tormented Lola as the balloon floated through the night sky. Stars twinkled. Moonlight pooled on the gondola's floor. But on the horizon, where the golden city of Dore waited, the coal cloud hovered.

Since Melvin was still feeling the effects of air travel, he lay on the floor and curled into a ball. Lola and Captain Bogart had agreed to take turns keeping the furnace stoked. Bogart took his rest, settling onto the floor next to Melvin and tucking his sharp beak beneath his wing. For the first time in her life, Lola kept fire alive. She opened the furnace door and tossed in a piece of kindling. The hot air stung her face, but she swallowed her fear. Fire was a tool that would get her to Dore. Fire would deliver her to her uncle. Fire would help her rescue her parents.

Each passing hour moved slower than the last, like a grandfather clock winding down. The gondola's gentle rocking finally eased Lola into a state of relaxation. She stretched out her legs and the next thing she saw was Melvin standing over her, panic gripping his face. The sky behind him was tinged with the pinks and oranges of sunrise. "Lola, the fire's out!" Melvin cried. "We're falling!"

She could feel it in her stomach. Lola scrambled to her feet. The furnace was cold. She'd meant to close her eyes for only a moment, but she'd fallen asleep. Both she and Melvin looked up. The balloon was losing air. She peered over the gondola's rim. Water lay beneath them, the surface so smooth it caught the balloon's reflection. "We're going to crash," Melvin said. "I knew it. I knew we'd crash!"

"Squwhaaaaat?" Bogart wearily rubbed his eyes with his feathers. "I told you, I don't—" His eyes popped open. "What's happening? Why are we descending?"

"I fell asleep," Lola said. She grabbed three sticks and tossed them into the furnace. "Oh, hooly dooly, what have I done?"

Down, down, down they moved, the gondola plummeting through the air, the water rushing up to meet them. Lola's stomach felt strange, as if it had crawled into her throat.

"We have to slow down or we'll crash!" Bogart exclaimed. "Lighten the load! Lighten the load!" Melvin and Lola had to duck as Bogart leaped around the balloon and his wing swept overhead. He opened the gondola's door and began to push things overboard—the binoculars, a blanket, a crate.

"Blue!" Lola and Melvin cried, watching as the crate containing their little friend tumbled through the air, then splashed into the water.

"Oops, didn't mean to do that," Bogart said, not really paying attention as he relit the fire. His words came in clipped snippets. "But no worries. It's water. He's a penguin. We're not slowing down fast enough!"

"He can't swim," Lola said. "He still has his baby feathers." The lake was getting closer and closer, the water broken by patches of reeds. "I yelled at him," she said. "All he wanted was a story and I yelled at him." Where was the crate? Had it sunk to the bottom? There was only one way to know.

Before she could come to her senses, Lola flung herself over the edge and into the air. And at that moment, just before she began to plunge, she thought, *Maybe this wasn't such a good idea. I don't have wings.* Having swum most of her life, she wasn't afraid of the water. But she *was* afraid of falling. She fumbled around in the air, her body turning end over end as she tried to gain control. The blue water rushed toward her, and just before she hit the surface she managed to turn so that her armored wombat posterior entered the water first, absorbing most of the impact. A colossal tower of water rose up behind her.

Lola closed her eyes, swam a few strokes, and then popped her head out of the water. The sheer cold nearly took her breath away. The water tasted salty, and she spat out the mouthful quickly. She paddled in a circle, desperately looking for Blue. Something popped out of the water next to her. "Melvin?"

"Crikey, it's cold!" he said.

"You jumped out?"

"Of course I did. I'm not going to let Blue drown."

A voice called down from above. "Are you all right down there?" With most of the passenger weight now in the water, the balloon had stabilized. The sticks had finally caught fire and the balloon was starting to refill. Captain Bogart sat on the gondola's rim. "I'd lend some help but the wind seems to have changed course . . ." The balloon began to float up and away. "Good luck finding . . . the little . . . fella."

Lola pushed the hot-air balloon from her mind as she spun in circles. Where was the crate? A strand of seagrass wrapped around Lola's leg. She kicked it free. Then she dipped beneath the surface and opened her eyes, but the water was murky and the salt stung. She popped back to the surface.

"Blue!" she called. Melvin joined her. "Blue!"

"Oi! Ya lookin' for this baby penguin?"

"Not a baby!"

A platypus stood at the water's edge, a baby penguin bouncing beside him. With a groan of relief, Lola and Melvin swam to the shore, then collapsed as they tried to catch their breath. Blue waddled over and pecked Lola's face, his version of a kiss. Then he pecked Melvin's face. Melvin frowned. "You are a pest, do you know that?"

"Pest!" Blue clapped his flippers.

"But I do feel I should thank you for getting us out of that contraption," Melvin added. "I've never been happier to feel the ground beneath my feet."

Lola couldn't get angry at Blue for wandering, for this time it hadn't been his fault. And she'd been the one who'd set him in the crate. "I'm sorry I yelled at you," she said. Then she kissed him back.

Lola turned her attention to the platypus, who wore a pair

of swimming goggles, and gasped as she recognized him. "Bale Blackwater?" she asked.

His paw flew to the side of his head in a salute. "Bale Blackwater, Platypus Delivery Service, Northern Streams and Rivers Division."

"Hate to break it to you, but this isn't a stream or a river," Melvin said as he wrung salty water from his fur.

Bale pushed his goggles onto his forehead and scowled. "I know it's not a river. Ya sayin' I don't know it's not a river? I got electroreception." He snorted. "What're ya doin' here? One of ya need a delivery? Cause if ya don't need a delivery, then I got better things to do."

"I'm Lola. Lola Budge. Don't you remember me? You gave me a secret message in the Northern Forest."

Bale screwed up his face and stared at her. "A young wombat who talks too much? I remember you. What're ya doin' all the way down here?"

"Mister Blackwater, I'm here because of that message. You gave it to me but I think it was supposed to go to my mum."

"Wha'd ya say?" Bale stomped over to her, stood on tiptoes, then stuck his face in her face. She was well aware that his venomous spur was only inches away. "Ya sayin' I delivered to the wrong critter? That's a serious accusation, missy."

Melvin stopped grooming, his whiskers alert. "Sir, if you would kindly settle down."

"Settle down?" Bale stomped his foot. "She can't go around sayin' I delivered to the wrong critter. That would ruin me reputation. Ruin me chances of gettin' a Golden Platy."

"I didn't say it," Lola told him. "Someone else did. But I'm wondering . . . is it true?"

"Course it's not true, and I'll prove it!" Bale stomped over to his delivery bag, opened it, and began to rifle around in its contents. Then he pulled out a form. "Here it is, right here." He read it. "Deliver to Alice Budge, Northern Forest Burrows." His tail thwapped the ground and he gave Lola an I-told-you-so look. "And that's exactly what I did. Hmmmph."

"I'm sorry to tell you this, but I'm *Lola* Budge. Alice is my mum."

Bale Blackwater's expression fell until his eyes were wide and his beak hung open.

Lola also felt astonished. Snarl had told the truth. The message had been meant for Lola's mother. Did that mean everything else Snarl had said was true?

"Mister Blackwater, did a Tassie devil pay you to deliver that message?" Melvin asked.

It was quiet for a long moment, the only sounds made by Blue as he splashed in the shallows. Then, after a long sigh, Bale Blackwater sank onto a rock and buried his face in his paws. "Mister Blackwater?" Lola asked. "Are you okay?"

"No. I am not okay." His voice came even and low, no longer filled with the usual combative determination.

She stood next to him, her fur dripping. Up close, Bale's fur was sleek and glistening, as if it had been coated with oil. He smelled like salt water and mud. It was a nice scent. "Are you upset because you made a mistake?" she asked.

"Course I'm upset that I made a mistake," he grumbled as he raised his head. "Do you know why I'm here? Because I've been demoted to the Estuaries Division. The Platy Union brought me here on one of the steam ships, then dropped me off. No one wants to make deliveries in estuaries! There's no good clean water and too much muck. The only place worse would be the swamp."

He looked sheepishly at Melvin. "No offense intended, swamp water rat."

"No offense taken," said Melvin, who'd begun to comb through his fur with his paws. "But do tell, why did you get demoted?"

Bale sighed, resting his bill on one paw. "I got demoted because I'm terrible at me job."

His lack of defensiveness took Lola by surprise. This was a very different Bale Blackwater. Gone were his arrogance and blustery way of speaking. He looked small and sad, arms hanging limply at his sides. "I'm the worst delivery platypus in the history of the union. One more screwup and I'll get fired. I'll be the only member of me family who never got a Golden Platy."

"But you said you had three Golden Platys," Lola remembered.

His flat beak turned down in a pained expression. "I've never gotten a single one. There's somethin' wrong with me electroreception. It's wonky and makes it hard to catch me meals. That's why I've been late with me deliveries. I was supposed to be in the Northern Forest weeks earlier."

Melvin stopped grooming. "*Weeks* earlier? You're right, you are terrible at your job."

Lola took a step back, her thoughts spinning again. "If you'd come to the Northern Forest weeks earlier, then my mum might have gotten the message and everything might have been different. My uncle was trying to warn my mom, I'm sure of it. She would have had time to send a message back to him. And he would have told her about the escaped Tassie devils. My family, my neighbors would all be safe. I could be home, right now, curled up in my burrow." The last few words nearly caught in her throat.

"Did you say Tassie devils?" Bale Blackwater blinked at her.

"A gold-toothed one came and took my family." She pointed

at him. "And you heard her at the stream. You ran away, leaving me there by myself!"

"Now hold on, hold on." Bale spread his webbed paws in the air. "I don't know any gold-toothed Tassie devils. And I certainly didn't know one was gonna take yer family. The one that paid me to deliver the message was a youngster. I thought he'd come after me 'cause I was runnin' late. That's why I skedaddled."

"Wheeee!"

Lola looked over at Blue, who wiggled his bottom happily as he splashed in the shallows. He was a fluffy little reminder that time was of the essence. She needed to get him home to his family because there was nothing worse than not knowing if your loved one was safe. There was no time to blame Bale or be angry that he'd been late. "We gotta go," she said.

"Agreed," Melvin told her.

"Where ya goin?" Bale asked, looking dejectedly over his shoulder.

"To Dore."

"Well, yer in luck. The Royal Road is directly over that hill. And Dore itself isn't all that long after."

Finally, some good news!

Blue started kicking and hollering when Lola tried to coax him from the water. "Stop throwing a wobbly," she said as she picked him up. "We have to go."

"Why?"

"Because I said so," she said, an answer she'd heard countless times from her own parents. It seemed to work because Blue stopped kicking. Sometimes there is comfort in not knowing the exact reason why, comfort in trusting. With no backpack, it would be difficult to carry him the entire way, but she had no other choice. Melvin helped put Blue onto Lola's back, where he nestled against her fur. Then they began to walk away from the brackish bay, across hardened mud and up a sandy slope that was covered in clumps of tall grass.

"If ya ever need me, I'll make it up to ya," Bale called. "I'll give ya ten percent off delivery service if ya promise not to report me to the union." They kept walking. "Okay, how about thirty percent off?" Still kept walking.

"What good is a discount if you deliver your messages late and if you deliver them to the wrong critter?" Melvin called back.

"Okay, okay, I'll give ya a free delivery, just don't tell the Platy Union that I messed up."

Lola had no intention of ever talking to the Platy Union. She didn't even know where to find the organization. But this was an offer she couldn't refuse. She stopped in her tracks, then turned around. "You'll deliver a message for free?"

"Yes. Platy promise."

"And it won't be weeks late?"

"It'll be right on time."

"And it will be delivered to the correct critter?" Melvin added.

Bale's temper flared again. "Course it will!"

Lola nodded. "I'll hold you to that promise, Mister Blackwater."

19

OUTSIDE THE GATES

It was a long day's travel with little conversation. Lola's feet felt raw and her shoulders ached from carrying Blue. They made a few stops for water but otherwise plodded on, moving forward, pulled toward a destination like ants heading to their hill.

And all the while, the dark cloud hovered in the distance, marking the place where Dore stood.

Uncle Tobias is very near, Lola thought.

The Royal Road, which had been mostly dirt and gravel up to this point, now consisted of bricks laid between thin strips of well-trimmed green grass. Geometric patterns swiftly became the norm, the road itself turning into an art piece. This was the road's grand finale—a dazzling, dramatic welcome to the weary traveler.

A dark-green hedge grew on each side of the road. Dozens of white mice, wearing green gardening aprons and holding garden clippers, stood atop the hedge. Leaves flew here and there as they trimmed. Statues also lined the road, towering monuments to rulers past. "King TheoDore the Wise," Lola whispered to Blue as they stared up at the first king of Tassie Island. She'd read his story many times and recognized him from his long, braided chin hairs and the extra toe on his right foot. "Princess Amelia the Sure," she said as she moved to the next statue. This young royal held an arrow in her paw but stared into the distance with closed eyes. "She was born blind but she became a champion archer." Their stories began to dance in Lola's head. She'd read about them so many times and now here she was, in the place where they'd lived and breathed.

Since leaving Bale Blackwater, Lola had been trying to craft the words she'd say to her uncle. How do you tell someone you've never met that you are a blood relation *and* that you need immediate help? But surely, she consoled herself, as soon as she mentioned Alice and what had happened, he'd leap into action.

The busy mice paid the trio no mind. At the end of the hedges the road opened into a rectangular courtyard. A great tree stood in the center, cracked from lightning long ago. Various notices and proclamations hung from its lowest boughs.

BY ORDERS OF HER MAJESTY,

A TAX HAS BEEN LEVIED UPON ALL
BEYOND THE WALLS OF DORE

TO PAY FOR THE GLORIOUS NEW TRAIN.

BY ORDERS OF HER MAJESTY,

A TAX HAS BEEN LEVIED UPON ALL
BEYOND THE WALLS OF DORE

TO PAY FOR THE GRAND GOVERNOR'S BIRTHDAY
CELEBRATION.

BY ORDERS OF HER MAJESTY,

ALL MUSICIANS AND BAKERS ARE TO REPORT TO THE PALACE

IN PREPARATION FOR THE GRAND GOVERNOR'S BIRTHDAY CELEBRATION.

"I've never heard of the grand governor," Melvin said as they stood beneath the boughs. There were dozens of similar orders spread about, each looking brand new.

"Me neither," Lola told him. They continued farther into the courtyard, then stopped to take in their surroundings. A towering stone wall encircled Dore, built generations ago during the invasion. While the late afternoon sun warmed the sky behind the travelers, the sky before them had turned dark, as if a storm had parked itself above the city. But there was no howling wind, no thunder or lightning. This darkness carried a pungent odor, of smoke, ash, and other things that Lola couldn't identify. "What's that?" Melvin asked, pointing to the far edge of the courtyard.

"That's the train," Lola told him. It sat at the end of its tracks, empty of rats. But some of the wooden cars were filled with vegetables and fruits, confiscated from the Farmlands. Just as the queen had ordered.

"What an interesting contraption," Melvin said. "Imagine how it could carry my swamp skin products all over the kingdom." He began to walk toward it, but Lola grabbed his arm.

"Imagine how it could carry the Tassie devils all over the kingdom." There was a tense moment of silence, broken only by light snoring from her back. "We don't have time. We have to get inside the city."

They could only see one entry to Dore—two massive wooden

gates large enough to fit the mythological elephant. The gates were ornately carved and decorated with golden letters spelling D-O-R-E. But they were closed. A guardhouse flanked each gate and inside each guardhouse sat a white rat, fast asleep. Each rat wore a fancy navy-blue jacket and hat.

"Do you think we can sneak around those guards?" Lola whispered to Melvin.

"I bet we can. Rats are notoriously heavy sleepers."

"Home?" Blue hollered groggily as he clung to Lola's shoulder, awake from his nap at last.

"Shhhh," Lola told him. Fortunately, neither of the guard rats stirred. "We're almost there, Blue, but you've got to stay quiet. Really, really quiet. Do you understand?"

Blue opened his beak, a capitalized *YES* waiting to burst out, but Melvin was quicker and clamped the beak shut with his paw. Blue shook Melvin's paw free. Both Lola and Melvin glared at him. He glared back. Then his beak opened a tiny bit and he whispered, "Shhhh."

Melvin stifled a grin. "What a surprise. I had no idea he could say anything that wasn't followed by an exclamation point."

"Come on," Lola whispered back. Then they started toward the gates.

"Oi! The line's over here, mate!" a squeaky voice called, prompting Lola to spin around.

Sure enough, a line had formed to the right of the gates. About three dozen critters were standing in shade provided by the wall. At the front of the line were three mice holding flutes, an echidna holding a cake, and an elderly brushtail possum who was leaning on a cane. Melvin and Lola turned away from the snoozing guard rats and walked over to the critter who had called to them.

"What's this line for?" Melvin asked.

"We're waiting to be let in, we are," the mouse replied with a twitch of his round ears. "Been here all day, we have." His companions nodded in agreement.

"But we can't go in, we can't. Not without the grand governor's permission," another flute-carrying mouse said.

The echidna looked at them from beneath a pink bonnet. Her long gray snout trembled. "Oh dear, oh dear, I'm not sure if we'll ever get in. This is a terrible situation. Truly terrible." Her spikes drooped with worry.

The old brushtail possum spoke next. "These gates were never shut before. Used ta come and go as we pleased. What kind of city shuts its gates outside of a war?" A tiny fiddle was strapped to his back. "I'm a citizen. This is my royal city as much as the next critter's."

"I haven't seen my son in five weeks," a quoll said. He stood behind and loomed above the possum, grinding his teeth in worry. "He went into the city to work as a brickie and hasn't come home since. I want to see him, but they won't let me in."

"We need to complain to the queen, we do," said another mouse, her black tail twitching far above her head, tickling the echidna's snout.

"Wish that we could, but no one's seen Queen Myra in ages," the possum said. "She's abandoned us all."

Lola and Melvin shared a pained look. The possum had confirmed what they'd feared about the queen. She was up to something. "Why don't you just go inside?" Lola asked. "The guards are sleeping."

"Oh, there'd be terrible consequences if we broke the grand governor's rules," the echidna told her. The frosted cake she was carrying on a tray had the words "Happy Birthday" written on it. "Truly terrible."

Lola was about to ask about this mysterious grand governor and his terrible consequences when the possum took a pair of spectacles from his vest pocket, set them onto his long nose, and squinted at Lola. "Yer a wombat. Ya best not let one of those guards see ya. They'll take ya away. They'll stick ya out in Woop Woop and make ya do hard labor."

"Oh dear, oh dear," the echidna said, trembling so much that her cake wobbled on its platter. "Terrible times these are."

A noise drew everyone's attention. A cart pulled by a dozen rats entered the courtyard.

"You've got to hide," Melvin said. He turned in a quick circle. "But where?"

"Over here!" A wallaby waved from the end of the line and pointed at his cart, which contained loaves of bread.

"I'll stay and get information," Melvin told Lola, doing his best to push her away but not really accomplishing anything other than ruffling her fur. "Go!"

Lola hurried toward the wallaby, then ducked behind the cart with Blue still on her back. Melvin stayed at the front of the line to better observe. From her hiding place, Lola watched as the rats pulled the cart up to the gates. These rats were tan in color and smaller than the swamp water variety. The cart was filled to the brim with black rocks. "Coal delivery!" one of the rats hollered at a sleeping guard. Then he kicked the guardhouse wall.

Sluggishly, the white rat emerged. "There's no need to be rude about it," she said as she arranged her jacket. "I heard you." Then, with a loud grunt, she opened a smaller postern door that was set within one of the gates. If the guard hadn't opened it, Lola doubted she would have known it was there, so perfectly did it blend in with the rest of the wood. The rats pulled the cart through. Then the guard pushed the door closed.

"Hello!" the first mouse called to her. "We're here to play music for the grand governor's birthday, we are. Shouldn't you let us in?"

The rat guard put her paws on her hips and faced the line. "How many times must I tell you to stop bothering me? I don't make the rules around here. You have to wait for Overseer Rake."

Lola cringed as the sound of the overseer's voice filled her mind. *A crate of food for the rat who captures that joey.*

"Where is Overseer Rake?" the quoll called out.

"How am I supposed to know?" the guard called back. "They don't tell us anything. They just tell us to stay here and don't let anyone in." Then she entered the guardhouse and closed her eyes for another nap. All the while, the other rat guard snored.

Melvin hurried down the line until he reached the bread cart. Lola set Blue on the ground. He'd begun wiggling again and her shoulders ached from carrying him. "Did you hear?" Melvin asked.

"Yes," Lola replied. "Overseer Rake is one of the Tassie devils I saw at the train station in the Farmlands. She's the one who ordered the rats to chase me."

"Then we'd better hope we don't run into her," Melvin said.

The wallaby shook his head and muttered, "Never thought I'd see this day."

Lola kept hold of Blue's flipper so he wouldn't wander, though he started bouncing up and down instead. "We need to get past those guards. What can we do?"

Melvin made a *humph* sound. "I didn't endure all that dust and dirt and running and flying and falling just to be told that I can't come in." He ran his paws down his neck and chest, smoothing out his fur. "Wait for my signal."

Before Lola could ask any questions, Melvin made his way in the stealthy manner of all rats. He crept past the sleeping guards without a sound, then stood before the gates. Those in line watched with rapt attention, holding their breaths. Melvin grabbed the handle of the smaller door.

A trumpet blasted. The echidna shrieked, dropped her cake, and then rolled into a ball. The mice musicians squeaked and huddled together. The two rat guards opened their eyes, leaped to their feet, and ran to the gates. Melvin had already stepped out of the way, watching wide-eyed. A series of trumpet notes sounded, a tune that might announce the arrival of someone important. The waiting critters began to stir with anticipation as the guards pulled open the gigantic gates.

Lola gasped at what she saw. Then she ducked behind the cart, pulling Blue with her.

Overseer Rake strode forward, her long black robe swishing against her legs. Taskmaster Lash followed a few feet behind her, carrying his black parasol and a scroll, his dark spectacles covering his eyes. The trumpeter, a mouse, scurried ahead, raised his trumpet to his mouth, and blew another series of notes. The overseer nodded at the guards, then turned to face the line of critters. "I am Overseer Rake, appointed by the grand governor. Come forward one at a time and state your purpose."

The trio of flute-carrying mice scurried forward. "We're here to play for the grand governor's birthday, we are," one said.

"Give your names to Taskmaster Lash and you will be admitted." She snapped her paw. "Lash, why are you dawdling? Do your job!"

The taskmaster crept forward and bowed. "My apologies, Overseer."

The mice scurried to the taskmaster, who wrote their names onto his scroll with a feather pen. The overseer pointed at Melvin. "You there. Swamp water rat. Are you here to join the Royal Guard?"

"Uh . . . yes. Yes, I am," Melvin replied. If he could get inside, then he could find Lola's uncle. Lola's heart danced for a moment—a hopeful flutter, despite her own peril.

Taskmaster Lash held out his scroll. "Sign this contract of servitude and you may enter."

Contract of servitude? Lola stiffened.

Melvin glanced at the scroll and frowned. "This says that I agree to work for the grand governor until . . . *I die*?"

"Correct," the overseer said.

"That's an awfully long time," Melvin said.

"I doubt it. You swamp water rats have such a terrible diet, you don't tend to live long." She tapped her foot and looked down on him with a mixture of pity and disgust. "But do not concern yourself. There is a garbage pile with your name on it. And all that you see on the train will soon rot as well. Now sign, swamp scum."

Melvin puffed out his chest. "I am not scum."

Lola gulped. She was proud to see her friend defend himself, but at what cost?

Overseer Rake curled her upper lip into a sneer, bending down so her eyes were level with his. She spoke slow and deliberately, as a bully to her victim. "I suppose you believe that you are different from other rats. Did you come to Dore because you have dreams? Because you want to be something special?"

She stepped closer to Melvin and sniffed the air. "Well I'm here to tell you not to waste your time dreaming such things. Despite your soap and polish, I can still smell the swamp clinging to you." Melvin momentarily lost his proud composure. His ears drooped. He'd clearly been stung by the overseer's harsh words.

"Do you want to get into the city or not?" the taskmaster asked, bored and clearly uncaring about which path Melvin took.

Lola tensed and Blue whined quietly, pressing himself against Lola as she tightened her grip on his flipper. If Melvin signed, he'd be stuck in the Royal Guard for the rest of his life, doing who knew what and being rewarded with garbage. There had to be another way to get into the city. But time was ticking. Melvin stared at the scroll, then grabbed the pen. Lola's mouth fell open. He was going to do this for her?

"No!" she cried, darting from her hiding spot with Blue in tow. "Stop! Don't sign it!"

A grin spread over the overseer's face. Then she bared her carnivorous teeth and said, "My, my, my, what have we here?"

20

RAKE AND LASH

Overseer Rake pressed her paws together and stared at Lola with the satisfied look of a predator who had stumbled upon easy prey. Blue let out a little strangled sound, then buried his face in Lola's side. "Hello, young wombat. I do believe we have met before," Rake said in her sinister, confident voice.

"Yes," Lola replied. "I . . ." She held tight to Blue's flipper.

Melvin darted between them and tried to push Lola backward, away from Rake. "Lola? What are you doing? You need to get out of here," he warned, pushing with all his might. But, as before, Lola wouldn't budge.

"I can't let you sign that," she said. "I can't let you give up your dreams. Not for me, not for my family, not for anyone." She gently pushed Melvin aside, placing Blue in his care. Then she faced the enemy, squaring her shoulders. "My name is Lola Budge. I'm from the Northern Forest." The overseer's gaze was fierce, now even more than before, but Lola didn't have time to be intimidated. She was on a mission. "I want to see my uncle. I . . . I *demand* to see my uncle."

"You . . . *demand*?!" Overseer Rake's blazing eyes narrowed as she reached for her whip.

It took every bit of effort for Lola not to flinch. The overseer's whip reminded her of an angry bee, capable of stinging at any moment. *Stay calm. No sudden movements.* "My uncle's name is Tobias Bottom. He's an ambassador."

The taskmaster, who'd been listening, gasped. Tittering to himself, he anxiously twirled his parasol. "Did she say that her uncle is—?"

The overseer threw back her head and released a vicious screech. The trumpet-carrying mouse squealed and scurried away. The echidna, who'd poked her head out to see what was going on, tightened into a ball again. Everyone else went silent, including the pale taskmaster, who retreated a few steps. When the screech subsided, Overseer Rake closed her mouth and lowered her head to face Lola. No matter how many times she heard a Tassie devil growl, Lola had the same reaction— an overwhelming instinct to dig and hide. But she held her ground.

The overseer ran a paw along her whip's handle. "Grand Governor Tobias Bottom is not receiving visitors today."

"*Grand Governor* Bottom?" Melvin said in astonishment, his eyes narrowing with suspicion.

"Bottom!" Blue shouted.

Lola shook her head. "There must be some mistake. My uncle is an ambassador, not a governor."

"Well, *at the moment*, he is a governor." Then the overseer mumbled under her breath, "But not for long."

The taskmaster snickered and repeated, "But not for long."

Lola had no idea what the taskmaster was talking about. She was still confused by the new job title. "A governor?" Lola shifted her weight. "Are you sure?"

The taskmaster drew a sharp breath. "Did my red ears deceive me? Did that wombat just question our honorable overseer?" He looked to the trumpet-carrying mouse for assurance. The mouse nodded shakily, hiding behind his instrument.

The overseer leaned closer to Lola and asked, loudly and slowly, as if speaking to a critter who was hard of hearing, "Are *your* ears plugged with fur? Tobias Bottom, *grand governor* of Dore, is not receiving visitors."

"But he'll want to see me," she said. "I came here because . . . because he sent for me."

"An obvious deceit," the taskmaster said. He stepped closer to his boss. "You would know if the grand governor had sent for this joey. You have the governor's absolute trust."

"But no one knew he sent for me because it was a *secret* message," Lola insisted. Despite the fact that she didn't trust the taskmaster, she needed to do whatever it took to get through that gate. "I have proof." She reached for her backpack, but her ears sagged with disappointment as her paw closed around nothing. "I did have proof, but it was stolen."

"I can vouch for that," Melvin said as he struggled to keep Blue from wandering off.

"Just as I suspected," Taskmaster Lash said, tapping the parasol's handle with his razor-sharp claw—a claw that was even better cared for than Melvin's—polished to a shine and with a gleaming gilded tip. "This *wombat* is wasting your precious time, Overseer. Shall I send her to dig with the others of her kind?"

"No. Please, I must see my uncle," Lola pleaded.

"Lola is telling the truth," Melvin said. The overseer gazed upon him with an expression of pure annoyance. "Her uncle did send a message and that's why she's here. And I think you should let her see him because, well, you see, I've learned a lot about wombats and penguins over the last few days. Penguins love eating more than anything else in the world."

"Hungry!" Blue cried as he tried to pull his flipper free from Melvin's grip.

Melvin continued. "And while wombats love peace and quiet, they love their families more. A wombat will travel the length of an island to be reunited with a family member. I wouldn't want to be in your position when the grand governor finds out that you turned away his only niece. His *family*."

The overseer sneered, showing off her teeth. "How dare you speak to me in such a manner, you filthy creature."

If Melvin's feelings were hurt, he didn't show it. Instead, he spoke calmly. "Though my fur needs a good brushing and my whiskers need whisker oil, I am not filthy, having just recently plunged into an estuary." Then he bowed. "I am merely concerned for your welfare, Overseer. I wouldn't want you to *lose favor*."

The taskmaster sidled up to the overseer. "The rat makes a logical point. Maybe you should consider—"

Overseer Rake spun around. "I don't need you to tell me about logic. You follow me, remember? You were nothing without me."

"Yes, nothing," the taskmaster said, bowing low and again stepping away.

A low growl vibrated in the overseer's throat as she spun back and glared at Melvin. "We shall see what the grand governor has to say about this. He will be eating supper soon and will not be pleased with an interruption. If you have lied to me, you will all be dealt with in a very . . . *delicious* way."

Lola shuddered. The threat was clear. When their eyes met, the overseer licked her sharp teeth. With the whip hanging at her side, Overseer Rake tucked her paws into her long sleeves, then turned on her heels. "Follow me." Lola began to follow, with Blue and Melvin at her side. The overseer stopped. "*Only* the wombat."

"But they're my friends," Lola explained. "I'm going to ask my uncle to help them."

"Help them?" Overseer Rake's serious expression melted into bemusement. "Indeed, I am certain that the grand governor will *help* your friends." She laughed in an unsettlingly high-pitched way. "And you, Lash, you deal with these other creatures."

"Yes, Overseer."

The mouse blew his trumpet as the overseer walked back through the gates. The rat guards, who'd been leaning sleepily against the wall, bounded to attention. Taskmaster Lash pointed his scroll at the line of waiting critters. "You there. Have you come to play for the grand governor's birthday celebration? Step forward and sign the contract of servitude."

Before leaving, Lola caught the look on the taskmaster's face—one of adoration but also frustration for his boss. Not at all what she expected.

But there was no time to contemplate that strange relationship, for finally, Lola, Melvin, and Blue were entering the royal city of Dore—the golden city by the bay. The beautiful city that TheoDore the Wise built to symbolize the beauty of the island and the peace won for all the critters. Where furred, feathered, taloned, and clawed lived together in harmony. And where golden cobblestones led to the royal palace, where all critters were welcome to seek guidance. So much hope flooded Lola's body, she felt like she might burst.

But as soon as they passed through the gates, Lola's spirits plummeted anew.

21

WELCOME TO DORE

Dore was nothing like the beautiful and harmonious city in Lola's storybook.

First, it was dark. The smoky cloud that hovered overhead kept the sun from shining through. The darkness cast the streets in a somber, grayish color. Darkness had never bothered Lola, but this felt unnatural, like this entire world was nothing more than a lamplit cave.

Next, an acrid odor shot up Lola's nostrils. Its source was a large heap of festering food. A few swamp water rats, with bellies bloated, lay atop the heap, smiling with contentment as they digested. One waved at Melvin and motioned him over, but he politely declined. They passed another heap, then another. Lola tried covering her nose with her paws, but there was no way of avoiding the stink. How she longed for a forest breeze carrying the scent of soil and rain. Of moss and dew. Back home even sunlight had a lovely scent as it warmed the leaves, but here there was no fresh air to be found.

"Icky!" Blue whined. Melvin took pity on the little thing and pulled out a handkerchief to cover his beak with, keeping at least some of the smog out.

The road inside the city walls was covered with mud and stagnant pools of water where bities congregated. Lola scooped Blue into her arms to keep him from jumping in the puddles. "The drainage ditches are clogged," Melvin pointed out as they passed rotting piles of leaves. Barren, dead trees lined the road, their greenery choked by the smoke and lack of sunshine. If they couldn't survive these conditions, how could the critters?

They followed the overseer onto a makeshift sidewalk—a line of raised wooden planks set over the mud. But when a cart of coal barreled down the road, the cart's wheels churned up mud, splashing some onto Melvin's legs. "How rude," he said. Then he called out to the brown rats who were pulling the cart, "For your information, only swamp-water mud is good for the fur, and only when properly applied!" The rats didn't seem interested in this tidbit and they continued on their way.

The main street was lined with shops, but none appeared open for business. Their colorful awnings and painted signs had been torn down; some lay in the street. CANDLERY. PERFUMERY. HATTERY. Windows were broken; doors hung by a single hinge. Most of the stores appeared to have been looted. Melvin reached out and ran a paw along a windowsill. "Filthy," he told Lola. Soot coated everything. The air tasted smoky. Lola sniffed. The hair on her neck bristled. She could smell fire. It was near.

A pair of Tassie devils stood outside a café, supervising as rats carried out bags of flour and sugar. Like the others, they wore long black robes. "Get a move on," one of them ordered. "All the food goes to the palace kitchen. Straightaway." They bowed as the overseer walked past. But there were no signs of shopkeepers or customers. "Where is everyone?" Lola whispered.

"I don't know," Melvin whispered back, "but I'm getting a

bad feeling. Worse than the time I tried a bite of Stanley's rotten egg omelet—just to be polite, mind you."

Lola also had a bad feeling about the queen she'd been raised to admire. Queen Myra had let these monsters into Dore and the result was ugliness and destruction. How did Lola's uncle fit into all this? If he lived in the city, then surely he knew what was going on inside the walls. But he probably knew nothing about the fate of the wombats. He'd be shocked when Lola told him.

They took a sharp left, following Overseer Rake down another street.

"Look," Melvin said. They'd come to a tall brick building. A sign hung on the door.

FACTORY #1

Lola craned her neck and looked up toward the roof. Black smoke plumed out the building's chimney. Sounds of hammering and clanging could be heard. What was going on inside? The window was covered in soot, so Lola wiped a section clean using her forearm. Then she and Melvin pressed their faces to the glass. Blue climbed onto Lola's shoulder to get a better view.

It was crowded inside, with all sorts of critters hurrying about, all wearing dingy gray aprons. Not a single smile to be seen, only fretful, weary faces. "These working conditions should be against the law," Melvin said. "There's no fresh air in there. And they're all covered in soot. That's terrible for the complexion."

But Lola wasn't looking at the critters. Her gaze was frozen on the huge, gaping maw of a fireplace, which was being fed shovelfuls of coal. A large bubbling basin was suspended above the fire, filled with gleaming liquid. A wallaby tilted the basin and the liquid flowed into a stone mold. Strips of metal that had cooled enough were carefully lifted out of these molds with large tongs and placed at one end of a stone table. The first critter pounded the strip with a hammer before passing it along to the next critter, who did much the same.

"They're making train tracks," Lola realized. "That's what this is all about. My family was taken away because of the train. Everything is for the train. Why?"

"Another question for your uncle," Melvin said.

"Hurry up!" Overseer Rake commanded from the end of the street.

"Uh-oh," Lola said. "Hold tight, Blue." She and Melvin ran to catch up.

They left the factory behind, following the overseer around another corner, then another. Then they stopped in their tracks.

The royal palace stood before them. It appeared to be the only soot-free building in all of Dore, thanks to a contingency of mice who scurried here and there with rags and ladders, polishing every golden brick. Pairs of mice dangled from ropes in order to reach all the high nooks and crannies with mops. Dozens of street lanterns caressed the palace with a warm buttery glow. It was everything Lola had imagined, a golden welcome for the weary traveler.

Overseer Rake continued up a wide flight of stairs that led to the palace entrance. Mice scurried out of the way as she approached. Upon reaching the top, the overseer stopped momentarily at a short stone pillar. She looked at it, cringed, and then continued walking. When Lola reached the pillar, she smiled. Sitting atop the pillar for all to admire was a cubic dropping. Her uncle hadn't forgotten his wombat heritage. It was a proud display, though the overseer didn't seem to appreciate the significance.

"Ah," Melvin said when he spied the dropping. "Well-crafted right angles."

"It's a sign that my uncle is well and he's waiting for me," she said with certainty.

The double front doors opened into a vast foyer with walls and ceiling painted gold. A pair of mice mopped the golden floor. The overseer stepped right through their work, then kicked a bucket out of the way. The mice squeaked as soapy water splashed onto their faces. Lola reached down and righted the bucket and one of the little mice, who quietly thanked her.

The foyer narrowed into a hallway, which was lined with a bright-red carpet, soft beneath their paws. They padded along this carpet until the hallway opened into the throne room. The throne had been carved from the trunk of a single great gum tree, sanded and polished so each ring stood out from the others in a vibrant display ranging from golden to red. Here, the mice wore dainty black aprons and carried little feather dusters. Two wallabys were in the process of removing the queen's portrait from the wall, cradling it like a sick child. *Must need cleaning*, Lola thought.

"Hurry up!" the overseer called. When they caught up to her, she glared at them. "I will tell the grand governor of your arrival. But if you decide to leave before I return, I want you to know that I will personally *hunt you down*." She licked her lips menacingly. Lola shuddered. "Step aside," Overseer Rake ordered. A pair of white rats who'd been guarding a door slunk away at the overseer's command. She smoothed her embroidered robe, then entered the room, shutting the door behind her.

The rats gave Melvin a long, curious look. "You come for a job in the Royal Guard?" one of them asked.

"Is the Royal Guard looking for a stylist?"

"I don't know about that, but what I do know is if you work for the Royal Guard, the queen feeds you all the food you want. Fresh food, rotten food, whatever suits your palate."

"The queen feeds you?" Lola asked. "Have you met her?"

"Haven't seen her since we arrived," the other rat replied, scratching her head. "Come to think of it, no one has seen her. But we've been told that we're working for her, and the governor works for her, so there you go."

Melvin pulled Lola aside. "What's the plan?" he asked.

"To tell my uncle everything," Lola said. "He'll help us. I'm sure he doesn't know what the queen has done. He would never allow my parents to be taken from our burrow."

"Home," Blue whimpered as he slid off Lola's back.

"Soon, Blue, soon. My uncle will send you home."

One of the rat guards frowned at Lola. "No, he won't. He won't help you. He doesn't—"

"Shut it," the other rat told him. "Don't say anything bad about the grand governor or we won't get our supper."

The door swung open. Dazzling light, golden and warm, filtered into the hallway. Lola stood on tiptoe, trying to get a view inside. But the light was soon blocked by a lean silhouette. The overseer stepped out, looking more perturbed than ever. A growl hummed in her throat and one of her eyes twitched. "This doesn't look good," Melvin whispered.

Lola took Blue's flipper in case they needed to make a hasty retreat.

"The grand governor will see you," Overseer Rake said through clenched teeth. "*All of you.*"

22

THE GRAND GOVERNOR

Lola could barely contain her nerves. She felt tingly all over, but not in a good way like when anticipating a birthday present. Anxiety bubbled in her stomach. Worry. Dread. What if her uncle couldn't . . . ? What if her uncle *wouldn't* . . . ? She shook her head, trying to push the negative thoughts away. All she had at this moment was hope. And hope is what moved her feet forward, one at a time. An unshy wombat had traveled all the way to Dore and was about to meet another unshy wombat who'd made the same journey years ago. If only this meeting were under better circumstances.

This room was cozy and filled with luxurious possessions—a velvet sofa and a matching wingback chair, a table with a lace tablecloth, shelves filled with fancy vases and seashells. Crystal sconces held lit beeswax candles and a grandfather clock stood in the corner. There were marble statues, bejeweled boxes, and sparkling mirrors. Lola had never seen so many things crammed into one room. But what stood out most was the gold. Golden chains hung from the drapery; golden dishes, golden frames, and golden bowls gleamed. A desk drew Lola's gaze to the side of the room, for it had been carved in the way of wombats. Lola's heart jumped.

A wombat was seated behind the desk.

He was a fat wombat, in a midnight-blue dinner jacket. He wore gold rings on his fingers and a gold chain around his neck. His chin hairs were long and waxed into a pointed beard. Upon seeing Lola, he stood, stepped around the desk, and reached out his arms. "My dear niece. How delightful it is to meet you at last." His smile was kind, his voice inviting. "Come give your uncle a hug."

In an instant, all of Lola's anxiety and fear washed away. Lola rushed into her uncle's embrace without a word. At the feel of another wombat's arms around her, she burst into tears. He smelled familiar. He smelled *like home*. This was her uncle, her *unshy* uncle who was just like her. And he didn't seem to mind that the hug lasted a long time. Finally, he released his arms and stepped back. "Let me get a look at you," he said. "Well, well. You're the spitting image of your mum."

Lola sniffled and wiped her tears. "Thank you."

His gaze traveled beyond her face. "And who might these two critters be?"

"This is Melvin and Blue. They're my friends."

"A swamp water rat and a baby penguin are your friends?" He chuckled. "You don't hear that every day."

Blue took a deep breath, opened his beak wide and hollered, "Not a—"

"He's not a baby," Lola told her uncle. Blue looked up at her and smiled as best a penguin could.

"I stand corrected." Tobias chuckled, then waved his paw in a dismissive manner. "You may leave us, Rake."

In the joyous reunion, Lola had forgotten all about the overseer, who was still standing by the door, watching the scene. "Your Excellency," Overseer Rake said. "I don't think—"

"Leave us."

Overseer Rake growled with frustration, clenching her paws. Then she left the room, allowing the door to slam behind her.

"Devils," Tobias said with a shake of his head. "They think they know everything. They boast about their university and their intellectual pursuits, but in truth, they are extremely temperamental creatures, difficult to work with." He motioned to the velvet sofa. "Please sit down." When Lola and Melvin were settled, with Blue bouncing impatiently between them, Tobias sat in an overstuffed wing chair, folded his hands in his lap, and smiled. His broad face reminded Lola so much of her mother's. But his eyes were different. Not in their shape or color but in a way she couldn't sort out. "So, what brings you to Dore?"

"I got a message," Lola told him. "A *secret* message."

"A secret message?" His smile faded.

"Yes. It said 'T.B. is ready.' A platypus brought it up the stream to the burrows. It was supposed to be for my mum, but I got it instead."

"'T.B. is ready'?" he repeated slowly. "And you say this message was for Alice?"

"Yes. Mum was sleeping and I—I snuck out the burrow to explore. I do that sometimes." She paused, expecting a reprimand, but her uncle simply stared at her, waiting for her to continue. Lola scooted to the edge of the sofa. "I like to go out during the day because I'm unshy."

"I figured that out," he snorted. "You're here, after all. But what about this message?"

She continued. "But while I was at the stream, something terrible happened. A Tassie devil came to the burrows and took mum and dad and all the wombats. They're being forced to dig coal."

Tobias's eyes widened and his paw flew to his heart. "What are you saying? My dear sister and brother-in-law are digging coal?"

"Yes. And so is everyone else from the burrows. We saw them. We flew in a hot-air balloon and saw them."

"I flew!" Blue blurted. Then he bounced so high, Lola had to grab him so he wouldn't ricochet off the sofa.

"Grand Governor Bottom?" Melvin spoke for the first time since entering the room.

"Do you have something to say, young swamp water rat?"

"My name is *Melvin*," Melvin said with a twitch of his nose. "And according to information we've gathered, the queen is paying those monstrous creatures to collect wombats and take them to the coal mine."

Tobias gasped, a paw rushing to his mouth. "This can't be true."

Melvin's forehead furrowed and his tail swished slowly back and forth along the floor. "As the queen's grand governor, surely you knew of this. Why would you allow your own kind to be imprisoned and forced into hard labor?"

Lola was surprised by Melvin's directness. Her immediate reaction was to defend her family. "This is Queen Myra's doing, not my uncle's," she scolded Melvin. Then she turned to face Tobias. "But why would she do this? Wombats are her most loyal citizens. We love her." She wrapped her arms around Blue, stroking his fluffy head. "We thought she loved us, too."

A long moment of silence hung over the room. Then Tobias Bottom rose from his chair and began to pace, his paws clasped behind his back. He looked quite regal in his dinner jacket and shiny golden monocle chain. No one in the burrows dressed in such a fancy way. Everything about him, from his waxed chin hairs to his opulent surroundings, solidified Lola's beliefs. Her uncle was important. He'd help her, without a doubt. "This is heartbreaking news," he said. "I had no idea that wombats were being *forced* to dig coal. Of course, they are welcome to dig, if they choose to. After all, digging coal is an honorable job and provides an important resource to the kingdom. But never should any critter be forced to dig, or into any sort of profession that belies their interests." He rubbed the back of his neck. "I admit I haven't been paying attention to everything." He motioned toward his desk, which was covered in scrolls. "Being the grand governor comes with so much paperwork, it overwhelms me. I'd rather work on my collections. Did you see my rare seashells? They're worth a small fortune. I obtain them from the trade between the penguins and the dolphins who live out beyond the kelp forest."

"They are lovely," Melvin said, softening for a moment as he glanced over at the shells. "You have excellent taste."

"Thank you," Tobias said with a puff of his chest. "I wish I had more time for such artistic pursuits, but I've been very busy getting ready for my birthday party. Which is tomorrow." He clapped his paws. "But what good timing! You will be my special guests. The queen has declared it an official holiday."

"Really?" Lola beamed with pride. A member of her family had an official holiday. Now the wombats would sing songs to both the queen *and* to her uncle. "Will the queen be at your party? I have so many questions for her—"

"The queen?" Tobias interrupted. "She's away. We don't know when she'll be back. Or *if* she'll be back."

"If?" Melvin asked.

"Yes, I'm afraid the queen has been talking about retiring. She's worn out, the poor little thing. She wants to live in seclusion, free from the obligations of state."

While both Lola and Melvin were surprised by this information, Blue was completely uninterested. He kicked his feet, wiggling until he slid free of Lola's arms. Then he began to waddle around the room. Lola didn't have to worry about him wandering away because the door was closed, so she decided to let him stretch his little legs. She turned her focus back to her uncle.

"I didn't know that a queen could retire," Melvin said. "Who would take her place?"

"Well . . ." Tobias picked a downy feather from the air before it could land on his fancy jacket. "As Queen Myra is the last of her lineage, the duty of succession would fall to the grand governor."

"You?" Lola couldn't believe what she was hearing. Her uncle might become the next ruler of Tassie Island? "Wow, that's amazing! I'm so happy for you."

Tobias returned to the wingback chair. But as he sat, his expression turned serious once again. "Lola, my dearest niece, what happened after your parents were taken away? How did you come to be here?"

It was such a long story. Where should she begin? "The last thing mum said to me was to find my uncle. I found your letters to Mum and that's when I realized that the words 'T.B. is ready' meant that you, Tobias Bottom, were ready. That's why I set out for Dore." She spoke briefly of how she'd met Melvin and Blue. "But then a Tassie devil named Snarl, son of Snarl, told us that he'd actually been the one to send the message. That's very confusing. Why would he tell my mum that *you* are ready?" The words tumbled out of her mouth so quickly, as if caught by a rushing river's current. She took a deep breath and waited for her uncle to explain everything. To make everything right again.

"Your story is most troubling." Tobias fiddled with a shiny button on his jacket, gazing out the window, deep in thought. A long moment passed before he turned his face back to Lola. "I did not send that message. Nor do I know who this Snarl is. But I can tell you this—there are citizens who are working against Queen Myra because they disagree with her new progressive policies. This Snarl might be one of those rebels."

"He called himself a warrior for peace," Melvin said.

"Aha." Tobias pointed at Melvin. "Exactly. That's rebellious talk if ever I heard it. I will issue a warrant for his immediate arrest."

Lola's whiskers bristled. Snarl hadn't seemed dangerous. But clearly her uncle knew best in these matters. "Uncle Tobias, why would a Tassie devil send a message to my mum?"

"And when you say 'progressive policies,' what do you mean, exactly?" Melvin asked.

Tobias stroked his chin hairs. "My oh my. You two are quite the talkative pair. Those are excellent questions, but I think—"

"Baby!" Blue shouted. He'd somehow managed to open the front of the grandfather clock. His head was inside the clock, but his little rump stuck out, his tail feathers wiggling. "Baby!"

In the blink of an eye, Tobias leaped from his chair and lunged at the clock. It was a surprising feat of agility for a critter with such a wide body and short legs. He pulled Blue out of the clock, then shut the door and latched it. Then he held Blue aloft with both arms and said, in a parental way, "You should not wander. You might get into trouble." While his voice sounded calm, his eyes looked enraged. "That clock could have fallen over and flattened you, or your feathers could have gotten trapped between the moving gears."

"I'm sorry," Lola said, sliding off the sofa so she could collect Blue. "I'll try to keep him close."

"See that you do." Tobias placed Blue in Lola's arms, then hollered, "Attendants!"

Immediately, the door flew open and three mice popped in, each wearing a white apron. "Yes, Your Excellency?"

"Supper," he said. "For two wombats, a penguin, and a swamp water rat."

"Hungry!"

"While I am grateful for the meal, I think you should know that I don't eat garbage," Melvin said. "'May our feasts be ever rotten' is not a phrase I agree with."

"Did you hear that? Our guest does not eat garbage," Tobias told the attendants.

"Yes, we heard, Your Excellency." They scurried away.

Tobias ushered Lola, Melvin, and Blue to a dining table that was set into a nook beside a large picture window. The window was crystal clear except for a little mouse paw print that the window washer had left behind. The window overlooked the city. According to the grandfather clock it was past twilight, and indeed the city had grown darker. Outside, mice climbed the streetlamps, lighting them with torches. Lola felt strange about sitting down to enjoy a meal, what with her family still held captive at the coal mine. "Uncle Tobias—"

"Lola, sit. There is nothing we can do tonight. You've traveled far and you must eat, then rest. And there is still much I'd like to know."

Lola still had her own questions. So she sat with Blue on her lap. The meal service began with each tray of food carried by four mice, then lifted onto the table by an old wallaby dressed in a butler's vest. Warm peppermint tea, a salad of tender butter lettuce, a basket of winter wheat rolls, a platter of raw root vegetables, and a bowl of colorful little fish, some yellow, some blue.

"All the best that Tassie Island has to offer," Tobias boasted.

"Fish!" Blue cried, excitedly clapping his flippers.

Melvin tied a napkin around Blue's neck, then one around his own, and he took a delicate nibble of a roll. "Delightful," he said. "My compliments to the chef."

Lola picked up a bowl of grapes. "Uncle Tobias, did you carve this?"

"I was never interested in carving," he replied.

"I'm not interested in carving either," Lola said. She took a sip of tea but was too fidgety to eat. "Uncle Tobias?" He glanced up from his salad fork. "Can you please tell us why—?"

He gently patted her paw. "Lola, it would appear that you and I are like two peas in a pod. Uninterested in carving. Eager for conversation. Full of questions. We are rare wombats, we two. Perhaps you'd like to stay here in Dore, where your talents for talk can be put to use? Why would you return to the burrows, where good conversation is not appreciated?"

"But there's no one in the burrows, Uncle. That's why I'm here, remember?"

"Ah, yes." He selected a plump red radish from a bowl. "You have come here for answers, and answers I shall provide."

While Blue noisily slurped, both Lola and Melvin sat in tense anticipation. *Tell me*, Lola thought. *Tell me that you will help. That everything will go back to normal.*

Tobias Bottom, the grand governor of Dore, finished the radish, then spoke. "Queen Myra is trying to modernize Dore and all of Tassie Island. To move us from a pastoral, agricultural society into a new age. She believes that with the advent of the train and similar achievements, fewer critters will be needed out on the farms, and the city will prosper all the more. We will soon have the ability to travel to all parts of the island, from the deepest valley to the tallest mountain." He pointed out the window. "Factory number one is for the shaping and smelting of steel into railway tracks. Factory number two will soon follow so that more tracks can be made. The inhabitants of Dore are working together to create this brilliant future."

"Is that why all the shops are closed?" Melvin asked. "Because everyone is working in the factory?" Lola thought of the quoll who'd been waiting in line to find her bricklaying son.

"The shops are unimportant at the moment. The critters of Dore are united in our common cause, but they will open again soon, I'm sure. We are entering a new industrial age. With our factories supplying track, it won't be long before our train can crisscross Tassie Island. No place and no critter will be unreachable. We will be able to trade goods quicker. To deliver goods quicker."

"And collect taxes quicker," Melvin said.

Tobias narrowed his eyes. "Taxes pay for progress."

"Do they also pay for your collections?" Melvin asked. "For your luxurious attire?"

"Those in positions of importance have always lived in comfort. So progress affects us first, but the benefits will trickle down over time, as they always do."

"Is it progress to take all the food from the Farmlands and leave none for the mouse families?" Melvin asked.

"We need to feed the Royal Guard, and factory work is difficult, making them all the hungrier as well," Tobias replied. "Would you have them starve when they are doing important work for our society?"

"I would have no one starve," Melvin said. "The mice were left with nothing."

"You are young and therefore you know not of what you speak." Tobias speared a boiled turnip. "It is rebellious to question the queen. She is wise beyond her years."

This didn't seem like a good answer to Lola. She looked at her plate, filled with lovely lettuce leaves and radishes grown in the Farmlands. There'd been so many mice at the train station, young and old. What would they eat now that the warehouses were bare?

"What about the wombats?" Lola asked.

Tobias chewed for a moment, then reached out and patted Lola's paw again. "Queen Myra would never hurt the wombats. I'm sure this has all been a misunderstanding. A misheard order repeated dozens of times can often cease to resemble the original at all. I shall send out a proclamation at dawn. Any wombats who wish to return to the burrows will be let go. But those who wish to stay and dig for the queen and for the future of Tassie Island will be paid well."

This was amazing news. Her parents would be freed! "Thank you, Uncle Tobias." Her mother had spoken the truth. *Find your uncle. He'll know what to do.* Lola beamed with happiness.

But Melvin gave her a worried look. She knew what he was thinking. There was a darker question yet to be asked.

She furrowed her brow. "Uncle Tobias, why is the queen letting Tassie devils leave Mount Ossa? They . . . they're *hunters*."

Tobias calmly took a sip of tea. "Now, now, Lola. That was in the past. We are thinking about the glorious future. Those hunters have changed their ways. And they have many skills we can use. Overseer Rake offered the train and train-track design to us in exchange for leaving the mountain. Of course, we made her sign an oath of loyalty."

"Are you sure they won't hunt?" Lola asked.

"Do you think I would allow them to roam the palace if I thought they might hunt? Besides, we live peacefully among the quolls and firehawks without issue; I don't see how this is any different." He returned his teacup to its saucer. "Do not fret, my dear niece. They have given a solemn promise. And although they are temperamental critters, the overseer and her companions have proven to be skilled managers of our growing labor force."

"When you say labor force, do you mean rats?" Melvin asked.

"Indeed. The overseer knows how to control rats. I most certainly wouldn't be able to control them; they are such unruly creatures."

Melvin pushed away his plate. "That is a common misunderstanding. Rats are not aggressive or mean-spirited by nature. But they do think with their stomachs. Decent rats are being bribed into doing terrible things, like pillaging warehouses and stealing from shopkeepers. How can you—?"

In a sudden display of temper, Tobias smacked his paw on the table. "Enough!" This surprised everyone in the room, Blue most especially. He spat out a yellow fish. It skidded across the table until it came to rest beside Tobias's plate. With a scoff of disdain,

Tobias crumpled his napkin, tossed it onto the table, and then rang a silver bell, which emitted a crystal-clear note. "Rake!"

The overseer entered the room so quickly that Lola suspected she'd been listening at the door this entire time. Tobias pushed back his chair and stood. "Rake, my niece will be reunited with her parents as soon as possible. When does the next train depart for the coal mine?"

"In the morning, Your Excellency."

"Then she shall stay the night in one of our guest rooms."

The overseer curled her upper lip, revealing her razor-sharp teeth. "What about the swamp water rat and the penguin?"

Tobias raised his eyebrows at Melvin. "I assume you will want to join the other rats."

Melvin dabbed the corners of his mouth with the napkin. "No. I came here to open my own business. A grooming salon."

The overseer snorted. "A rat-owned business? I've never heard of such a thing."

"Well, now you have," Melvin said. "It only takes one critter to pave the way for others."

"You wish to pave the way for *swamp water rats*?" Tobias asked.

"Why not?" Melvin replied. "Rats should be allowed to follow their dreams as much the next critter."

"I see." Tobias tapped his foot on the carpet. "I see, I see. Rake? Can you think of a location for this new rat salon?"

Overseer Rake stepped forward. "As a matter of fact, I do know the perfect location." She smiled ever so slightly.

"Then escort our new entrepreneur to his future business site."

"Immediately, Your Excellency."

It seemed that everything was working out. Lola was to be reunited with her family, the wombats were to be set free, and Melvin was going to open his business. "Uncle Tobias, can you have someone take Blue back to Penguin Bay?"

"Yes, of course, Lola. I am happy to help your friends because any friends of yours are friends of mine. Overseer Rake will escort the penguin to one of our royal ships." He patted Lola's head in a fatherly way. "Now I'll give you a moment to say your good-byes." He and the overseer stepped into the hallway and began conversing in hushed voices.

"Goodbye?" Blue looked at Lola with his little black eyes, his beak turned down in a frown.

How Lola hated that word. "Yes," she told him, kneeling so she could kiss his fluffy cheek. "But this is a happy goodbye because you get to go home. And we'll see each other again. When the new train is finished, I can come visit you. And once Bogart makes more hot-air balloons, you can fly again, too." As she hugged him, a downy feather went up her nose and made her sneeze. That's when she realized that she'd gotten used to Blue's fishy scent and didn't mind it one bit.

She was trying to be upbeat, for she didn't want to start crying. She'd come to love Blue like a baby brother.

Melvin crouched beside her. "Lola, I'm not sure we can trust your uncle," he whispered.

"What do you mean?"

He looked over his shoulder. Tobias and Overseer Rake were still conversing in the hallway, their backs turned. "Why is the city such a mess? Why are all the shops closed? And why were they taking down the queen's portrait? I've had a feeling something was wrong ever since we showed up." Melvin didn't wait for Lola's response. He motioned for her to follow. They tiptoed over to the carved desk. "Look at all these papers. Queen Myra's name is not on any of them. But your uncle's name is here, and here, and here." He picked up a scroll. "This proclamation makes Tobias's birthday a royal holiday. And this one—" He gasped as he read it. "This one changes Tobias's title from grand governor to king. Why would the queen agree to this?"

"Because . . . because she likes my uncle and she misses her family?" But even as she said those words, she knew how naïve they sounded. But she wanted so desperately to believe her uncle. He was family. They shared blood. They shared personality traits. "He's going to help us. I know it. Please stop saying bad things about him." She didn't want to fight with Melvin, not as they were about to say their goodbyes. Her stomach had finally stopped hurting. Her worries were finally over. She was going to see her mum and dad. This was not the time to get caught up in suspicions.

"Time to go," Overseer Rake called as she and Tobias stepped back into the room. She reached for Blue, but the little penguin opened his beak and snapped at the overseer's paw.

"I'll take him," Melvin said. "Goodbye, Lola. I wish you the very best and hope we meet again one day." He sounded so formal, but when he hugged her, he whispered in her ear, "I'm going to get more information. In the meantime, be careful." He squeezed her tight. She squeezed back.

Then Melvin took Blue's flipper and they began to follow the overseer down the hallway.

"Goodbye," Lola said, waving sadly.

"Bye-bye, Lola!"

"Now, now, no need for tears," her uncle told her. "Your

friends will be taken care of. Let's get you to bed. You've had a very long journey and you have a train ride in the morning. Your parents will be so delighted to see you."

Lola watched her two friends walk away. Melvin turned to glance over his shoulder, a worried look on his face. Blue waved his little flipper halfheartedly. Then they were gone.

And even though Lola was with her uncle, in a palace filled with servants and guards, she suddenly felt very alone.

23

THROUGH THE WINDOW

"Your Excellency." A wallaby wearing a paint-splattered smock approached. He wearily wiped his forehead with his paw, leaving a streak of green in his fur. "Your portrait is finished."

"That is excellent news," Tobias said. "Hang it in the throne room and we will have the official unveiling tomorrow morning during the celebration."

"As you say." The painter bowed, then hopped away.

A portrait to be hung in the throne room? Lola remembered the document on her uncle's desk. And the queen's portrait, which had been taken off the wall. So it was true. Her uncle was going to rule Tassie Island!

"Come along, Lola, let's get you settled in for the night." The guard rats snapped to attention, barely even breathing until Tobias had gone past.

Lola followed her uncle up two flights of stairs. He climbed slowly, breathing heavily with his steps. He clearly spent more time sitting at his desk than climbing hills. Lola wondered if all the gold he was wearing was heavy. "This is the guest wing," he explained when they reached the landing. The hallway was lined

201

with doors that would fit the larger critters, but set within each door was a smaller door, perfect for smaller critters.

"Do you live here, in the palace?" Lola asked.

Tobias took a handkerchief from his jacket pocket and dabbed his nose. "When I was made ambassador to the Northern Forest and the Realms Beyond, I was given a mansion in which to live. But when Queen Myra made me grand governor, I moved into the palace." He stopped at a door halfway down the hall. "This should do." He opened it, revealing a lovely guest room. The bed, covered in white linens, sat in the center. The nightstand was golden, as was the chair. Tobias clapped his hands. A little mouse wearing a butler's vest scurried out of nowhere and hurried into the room. "We have a guest."

"Yes, Your Excellency." The butler mouse climbed onto the bed and began to turn down the sheets and fluff the pillows.

"I suppose you'd prefer a burrow," Tobias said with a disapproving but amused snort.

"Do you have one?" Lola asked hopefully.

Tobias Bottom held out his paw and adjusted some of his gold rings, chuckling idly. "My dear niece, take my advice, leave the burrow behind. Burrow-dwelling is *uncivilized* and best left to those who inhabit the Northern Forest and wish to be left alone. In Dore, one must elevate oneself to sleeping in an *aboveground* bedroom. And adjust to a daylight schedule." He checked his gold pocket watch. "The hour is late and I still have much to do to prepare for my birthday. I bid you good night." He reached for the doorknob.

"Uncle?"

"You are full of questions, aren't you?"

"How long will it take for your message to get to the mines?"

"My message?" He looked confused.

"Yes, your message. About setting the wombats free. So they don't have to work in the coal mine."

"Oh, yes, of course. The message that I intend to send by messenger pelican first thing in the morning." He looked away. "Shouldn't take too long, mere hours at most. Pelicans are swift flyers."

Finally, a messenger pelican. Everything was going to be fixed in the morning. Despite the sadness she felt at having said her goodbyes to Melvin and Blue, she was overjoyed at the prospect of seeing her mum and dad. Even grumpy Mister Squat. "Thank you for helping me and my friends," she said.

"You were very wise to come to me," he told her. "Now, enjoy your sleep."

Tobias waddled out of the room, closing the door firmly behind him. The sound of iron skidding across iron came from the doorway as a lock slid into place, followed by heavy departing pawfalls. Lola scowled with puzzlement. She tried to open the door. It wouldn't budge. Why had her uncle locked her inside? Was he trying to protect her from something? That made no sense because anyone could simply unlock the door from the outside and enter the bedroom.

Or had he locked her inside to keep her from wandering? Maybe that was a wise decision. Blue's wandering had always gotten him into trouble, and Lola's had as well. Wandering had led her to a stream and a mistakenly delivered secret message.

But even so, it didn't seem right to lock a guest in a bedroom.

She wandered over to the window and leaned on the sill. A small courtyard and a fountain lay below, the city roofs beyond. The window washers and brick polishers were done for the day, but another cart of coal was being wheeled down the street. Even at this late hour, factory number one was going at full steam, the windows alight with a reddish glow. Did those poor workers ever sleep? Queen Myra was treating her subjects most unfairly. If the queen was retiring, as Tobias said, surely he would be a kinder ruler. *Tomorrow.*

Lola's mouth stretched into a long yawn. Her eyelids grew heavy. The sooner she slept, the sooner she'd be reunited with her mum and dad. It still felt odd to sleep at night, but it had been another long day and she needed rest. She hefted herself onto the bed, then sank into the pillows. Queen Myra may have been doing many terrible things, but she certainly knew how to provide a lovely guest room. Lola rolled onto her side and closed her eyes. *Tomorrow.*

Yet sleep wouldn't come. Lola wondered how Melvin and Blue were doing. Wondered if her parents had given up hope of ever seeing her again. But most curiously, why had her uncle seemed so calm about everything she had told him? And why did he think that burrow-dwelling was so uncivilized? He had displayed his cubic dropping for all to see, so surely he was still proud of wombat traditions. *Tomorrow*, she thought one last time as her eyes closed.

She tossed and turned so much that she didn't hear the sounds outside the bedroom window, the small creaks of someone climbing a ladder. But the sudden *crack* of the window was another matter altogether.

Lola tossed the blankets aside and bolted upright. A dark shape was climbing in through the window. When it touched down on the carpet she could just make out the unmistakable red ears and long robe of a Tassie devil.

Lola opened her mouth to scream for help, but the critter lunged at her and put a paw over her mouth. "Shhhh. It's just me."

"Snmmmph?" Lola pulled the paw away, careful of the deadly claws. "Snarl? What are you doing here?"

"We need to leave, quickly. You are in danger. Your life is in danger. Rake is coming to get you."

"Get me?" Lola blinked in confusion. She slid off the bed. "But my uncle's going to help me. He's going to let my parents and neighbors leave the coal mine. He agrees that the wombats shouldn't be forced to dig so he's sending a message in the morning."

"He's lying to you." Snarl darted around the bed and pressed his paws against a large dresser. Then, showing surprising strength, he began to push the dresser across the room. "Your uncle signed the proclamation that sent the wombats to the mine in the first place."

"No, he didn't. He wouldn't have done that." Lola's words rang hollow, even to herself.

"He did. I saw the proclamation with my own eyes."

"Then it's the queen's fault," Lola insisted, grasping for the most logical explanation desperately. "She's retiring and she left him with too much paperwork. He didn't realize what he'd signed. It was an accident."

"The queen isn't retiring. She's missing." Snarl began pushing the dresser until it rested in front of the door.

"Missing?"

"Yes, and your uncle has taken over."

More pieces of the puzzle began to click into place. The critters outside the city wall had said the queen hadn't been seen in a long time. The posters hanging from the tree were about the grand governor, not about the queen. The stationery had Tobias's insignia, not the queen's.

And the queen's portrait was being replaced by Tobias's portrait.

If Tobias had taken over, then that would mean—

The heavy thuds of running paws echoed from the hallway, accompanied by fierce growling and screeching. The thuds came to a stop outside the bedroom door. The lock slid out of place, but as the door opened, it banged against the dresser. "Open up. Orders of the grand governor!" It was the overseer's voice.

Did her uncle want to see her again? But why would he have sent the overseer?

Snarl stood between Lola and the dresser, his arms outstretched. "Don't let them in," he said.

"But my uncle—!"

The pounding on her door grew louder and more forceful, the dresser shaking with each strike, shifting inch by inch. "The grand governor has sent me. Open this door, you grass-eater!"

Truth swept over Lola. Ugly, undeniable truth.

Snarl began to push the bed, but it was too heavy for him alone. Lola threw her weight into it, and together, they pushed it in front of the dresser. "That should hold them for a few. Follow me." Snarl leaped onto the windowsill. Then he swung nimbly onto the top rung of a ladder.

Lola didn't ask where they were going. She didn't need more questions and answers. Her Uncle Tobias had turned against his own kind and she knew this in her shattered heart. But there was no time to ponder why. She did not want to end up in Overseer Rake's paws. She heaved herself onto the sill, then poked her head out the window. Snarl was already waiting at the bottom of the ladder. He motioned for her to hurry. The pounding continued.

The dresser wobbled and the bed moved back a few inches. Soon, the overseer would be inside. Lola wasn't sure how to negotiate a ladder. But because her life was in danger, she had no choice but to learn the skill on the spot. She pushed her back legs out first, flailing around until they found the top rung. Slowly but steadily she began her descent. Each step was a careful maneuver, but once she began to dig her claws into the wood, she stopped slipping.

"Hurry!" Snarl called. The ladder tilted to one side, then the other. When she was halfway down she heard a cry of triumph from above and the scrabbling of paws on carpet. A head leaned out the window, growling down at her.

"You shall not escape me!" Overseer Rake cried. "Ow!" A stone bounced off the overseer's snout, followed by a second striking her forehead. Snarl had excellent aim, but the overseer was still standing.

Ignoring the last rungs, Lola jumped and landed next to Snarl, who pushed the ladder until it toppled. The overseer screeched, then pointed down at Snarl. Such was her anger that she could barely move her jaw to form words. "You will regret your actions, traitor!" Then she ducked back into the room. "To the courtyard!"

"Where do we go now?" Lola asked, her eyes wide with fear.

"Trust me," he said.

Only a few hours had passed since the street sweepers had gone to bed, but already a thin speckling of soot coated the cobblestones. The moon streamed through the smog in scattered beams, streaking the night like pillars of captured starlight. Lola and Snarl galloped from the courtyard. The side streets twisted around on themselves, letting the pair escape view in moments.

Turning down a narrow alley, they reached a stone hut with a sign: WAGON REPAIR. The night suddenly grew brighter in their wake with the arrival of torches and the sound of marching paws. "Hide," Snarl whispered, pulling Lola behind a wagon. The lights passed by. Lola peeked out just in time to see several long bald tails turn the corner and vanish.

"Royal Guard patrol," Snarl explained. "They are supposed to keep factory workers from leaving the city." Snarl reached out and pressed his paw against one of the hut's stones. A door opened inward. He stepped inside. Lola followed. The stone door closed.

Never in her wildest dreams or dreariest nightmares had Lola ever imagined that she'd trust her safety to a night monster. Yet here she was, standing with a feared predator, in utter darkness.

"What is this place?" she asked.

"It will take us under the palace."

A light sputtered into existence as Snarl struck a match. The flame was so close, Lola jumped back, hitting the wall. Snarl stuck the match into a lantern. Turning a small knob on the side of the square lantern, three of the sides closed up entirely and the last condensed into a small pinhole emitting only a narrow beam of light. This done, he knelt on the floor and pulled open a hidden trapdoor. "Stay close to me. It is quite the labyrinth down there."

Lola looked into the darkness below. An ancient stone staircase descended steeply, curving like a corkscrew and preventing her from getting a good view of what lay ahead. A few insects shuttled along the walls and ceiling. Once they were both on the stairs, Snarl reached back and closed the trapdoor. Lola took a deep breath, then began to follow Snarl.

"It stinks down here, worse than a swamp rat's meal," Snarl warned her. The damp air of the passageway was permeated by a lingering earthly decay, a scent that didn't bother Lola. In the small beam of Snarl's pinhole lantern, Lola caught glimpses of white fungus coating the walls. When they reached the bottom of the stairway, the passage opened up before them. Lola's feet squelched through stagnant water. A shiver darted up her spine when she felt something scuttle past. But with a few more steps the water disappeared and light greeted them.

"We are beneath the palace," Snarl said. It took a moment for Lola's eyes to adjust, and even longer for her to understand what she saw before her.

They stood in a vast, multidomed chamber with evenly spaced stone pillars that reached from floor to ceiling. Sconces held candles, their glow filling the space with flickering light. In the center of the chamber, a large group of critters had gathered—mostly mice, quolls, and echidnas. Many of those assembled wore grimy aprons and carried mops and brooms. Others were dressed as butlers and maids. They were milling about, chatting with one another. No one seemed shocked to see Snarl. A few tipped their caps to him. He bowed in return.

"Who are these critters?" Lola asked.

"They are members of the Resistance," he told her.

"The what?"

"The *Resistance*. I am also a member, as is your mother, Alice. We are dedicated to the preservation of peaceful cohabitation on Tassie Island and will resist anyone who tries to defy the Treaty of Mount Ossa."

Lola's jaw dropped. "My mum belonged to a resistance movement? But that can't be. My mum is a shy wombat. She likes to nap and forage and carve. And the only time she ever left the burrows was to go to the trading post to trade our bowls and spoons."

"Your mother may not have traveled to Dore, but she was in communication with her brother."

"She was?" When and how did this happen? Lola wondered. Did her mother sneak out of the burrow to send messages while Lola and her father were sleeping?

"Lola!"

Lola turned toward the voice and blinked in surprise. A gray rat pushed through the gathered critters and hurried toward her, accompanied by a ball of fluff. "Lola!" Blue cried, waddling as fast as he could until he was hugging her leg.

"I'm glad you're safe." Melvin also hugged her, his arms barely reaching around her shoulders.

"What are you doing here?" she asked in surprise. "You're supposed to be at your new salon, and Blue is supposed to be on a royal ship, sailing back to Penguin Bay." Melvin looked disheveled, as if he'd been tossed around, again, in a hot-air balloon. Then she noticed a thin line around Melvin's wrist where the fur had been worn off. She cupped his paw in both of hers so she could get a better look. "What happened?"

"Bad!" Blue squawked.

"Yes, bad," Melvin agreed, glancing sadly at Blue. "As soon as we left the palace we were handcuffed and taken to the tower and put into a jail cell. Fortunately, Snarl was able to sneak past the guards. He's surprisingly good at picking locks."

"I distracted the tower rats with putrid cheese rinds," Snarl explained.

Lola wanted to believe that Overseer Rake had put her friends in jail. But she knew who was in charge of the palace. "My uncle

Tobias did this." That statement nearly weighed her down with sadness. The last of her excuses washed away, Lola finally fully accepted how far her uncle had fallen.

"I'm afraid so," Snarl told her. "He never intended to help your friends. And the only help he might have given you was a stay in the dungeon, until you saw his way."

The entire chamber suddenly grew quiet and all the critters turned toward the center. A mouse had climbed onto a stool and stood on her hind legs so that everyone could see her. A tiny dust broom stuck out of her apron's pocket. "Welcome, everyone. I wanted to let you know that the recruitment is going well, it is. We've gained over three score more brothers and sisters this past month, and we'll need every one of them if this is to have a chance of working. Long live the queen!" She paused as the audience whooped and cheered, the sounds echoing off the walls.

The mouse continued. "Unfortunately, we are still missing the most important piece. The queen herself." The critters nodded solemnly. "She's been missing for over two months, she has, and we fear that time is running out. If factory production continues, the train tracks will soon reach all the way to Mount Ossa."

Frightened voices joined together, murmuring and fretting. A few of the echidnas rolled into quivering balls. Lola turned to Snarl. "A train to Mount Ossa?" she whispered.

"That is the deal Tobias made with the overseer and her followers. If they support him as grand governor, then he will make sure they have a train to the mountain."

"Why does the overseer want a train to go to Mount Ossa?"

"What the overseer wants is to control the island so she can control its laws. What she wants more than anything else is to bring back hunting."

Both Lola and Melvin shuddered. It was a terrible thing to imagine.

"But why is Tobias working with her? What does he get in return?" Melvin asked.

"Gold. The mountain is full of it," Snarl replied.

All of this chaos and fear and tragedy for gold? This made no sense to Lola.

A quoll stood and raised his paws, quieting the crowd. "As many of you know, we have stationed resistance fighters along the Mount Ossa line to cut the tracks behind the railway workers and destroy the supporting wooden struts. But we need more help. We need more critters to join the cause, and I fear that will not happen without Queen Myra. We must find her."

"Long live the queen!" everyone shouted.

Lola flinched, fearing the echoes might collapse the cavern with their voracity. Fortunately, the structure remained intact, with only a few motes of dust descending loftily from the ceiling.

The mouse, who was still standing atop the stool, clapped her paws for attention. "Everyone, everyone, I hear our leader's footsteps. Please quiet down."

Voices hushed again. Lola pricked her ears. Sure enough, steps approached—not the scurrying of a mouse, but the soft padding of much larger paws.

A door opened from one of the chamber walls and a wombat emerged. At first Lola gasped, worried that Tobias had found her. But then she realized this was not Tobias. The wombat's gaze fell immediately upon her.

"Hello, Lola," he said. "I am your uncle Teddy."

24

T.B. IS READY

Teddy Bottom was definitely Tobias's twin in size and shape, coloring, and even the long chin hairs. But unlike his twin, Teddy wasn't dressed in a fancy way, but with a simple cap on his head. He hadn't adorned himself with gold. And he didn't strut the way Tobias had. He walked humbly, his head lowered.

Snarl placed his paws together and bowed. "I retrieved Lola from the clutches of your brother, as you requested."

"Thank you," Teddy said. "You have, once again, proven to be a loyal friend." He returned his gaze to Lola. "I understand you got a message." His voice remained soft and gentle. "A message about me."

Lola found herself at a sudden loss for words. Her uncle. Her *other* uncle. "T.B. is ready" stood for *Teddy* Bottom, not Tobias Bottom. She'd forgotten all about Teddy. He was the shy brother who'd sought peace and quiet by working beneath the palace. At least that's what Tobias had written in his letter. Lola realized that her assumptions had been totally wrong.

"Wait a minute." Melvin furrowed his brow and gave her a deadpan stare. "You have a *second* uncle, with the same initials as the other? And that didn't seem important to mention?" Lola sheepishly turned her head away.

"And who might you be?" Teddy politely asked.

"I'm Melvin, Lola's friend. And this is Blue, a penguin we've been babysitting." Blue stuck his tongue out the side of his beak and blew a raspberry at Melvin. "I mean . . . *penguin*-sitting."

"I see. It is nice to meet each of you." Then Teddy rubbed his face wearily. "Please forgive me. You've come at a critical point in our operation and there's not much time to get acquainted." He sighed, as if he could feel the weight of the stone walls pressing down upon him.

"Am I to understand that you are the leader of the Resistance?" Melvin asked.

"Guilty as charged." He paused. "Though if things go well, I hope to never be charged, nor found guilty for that matter."

Lola wanted to shrink with shame. She'd judged her uncle without knowing him. She'd been influenced by the way Tobias had described him in the letters. *Lesser aspirations. A lowly mop-pusher.*

Lola had been wrong about trusting one uncle. Could she trust the other? "Uncle Teddy?" she said finally, her voice so quiet he had to lean forward. "Do you still sleep in a burrow?"

"Of course I do. And I still display my droppings. We must keep our traditions, especially in times such as these." He winked at her. And there it was, the thing that had been lacking in Tobias's eyes. A twinkle. But it faded. "I'm sorry you've come to Dore at such a dire time. I'm sure it's different than you imagined it would be."

"It's nothing like the stories in my book."

"*The Tales of Tassie Island*?"

"Yes," Lola said. "That's my favorite book."

"Mine too," Teddy said.

Lola's heart nearly burst with happiness. Here was the uncle she was meant to find. Here was the uncle she could trust. The uncle whose eyes twinkled just like her mother's eyes. "I'm sorry," she said. "I didn't know you sent the message. I thought—"

"You thought you could trust your powerful uncle because he is your blood relative. But blood, unlike a river, does not always flow in the same direction." The twinkle faded, replaced by a sad smile. "You have many questions, I know. Snarl is better at explaining." He lowered his eyes and stepped back, and Snarl stepped forward. The other critters had gathered around, their little faces turned up as Snarl spoke. He wasn't a monster in their eyes. He was one of them. Blue, however, apparently bored by politics and rebellions, sat on the floor, leaned against Lola, and closed his eyes.

"The foul plans of the rebel devils have been in the works for years now," Snarl said. "Most of my kind live in peace and contentment. But long have we hoped to rejoin the island, to live again with other critters. And when our engineers designed the train, we saw it as a possible way to begin trading goods, and thus gain trust.

"But the Overseer had other plans. She is one of the few who preach that the old bloodthirsty ways are better. And she found a partner inside the Tassie government—a wombat who is driven by greed and tempted by golden trinkets."

Lola swallowed hard. Everything seemed to come back to Tobias.

Snarl continued. "We thought Queen Myra could control the uprising, but it took most of us far too long to notice Tobias

Bottom's involvement. After the queen disappeared, Tobias issued a proclamation that the queen had promoted him to grand governor. This was a lie. He promoted himself. Then he declared that all critters in Dore would have to work in the factory, except for those who kept the palace clean, inside and out. Thus, all the shops closed and the shopkeepers were sent to the factory. Tobias declared that no one was allowed to enter or depart the city gates without permission. Then, to increase production, he offered a reward for the capture of the best diggers on the island—the wombats. More coal means faster production of the train tracks."

"Why would Uncle Tobias do this?" Lola asked, her eyes stinging with tears. "Why would he hurt his family? Doesn't he love us? Doesn't he love his sister?" Everyone looked at Teddy.

Teddy took a moment, folding his paws behind his back, then spoke. "When the three of us were joeys, Tobias and your mum were very close. They did everything together. Alice wanted to come to Dore with us, for she also wanted to seek her fortune, but your grandmother was ill at the time and Alice stayed at the burrow to care for her. I left because our mother begged me to keep an eye on Tobias. He'd always been unpredictable and prone to getting into trouble. Soon after we arrived in Dore, Tobias introduced himself to the queen. She was smitten by his charm and gave him a prominent position in the government as ambassador. And he quickly discovered the things that power could buy—delicious foods, a stately manor, golden rings." He paused again. Lola could tell that it took great effort for Teddy to tell this story. Maybe it was his shyness. Or maybe it was the heartbreak he must have felt, knowing his brother was a traitor. "Power corrupts, dear niece, and greed is all that remains of the Tobias I once knew."

"And so you formed this resistance?" Lola asked.

"We needed to find the queen. We still do." The mass of critters nodded in agreement.

Melvin folded his arms and looked apprehensive. "I don't mean to sound rude, but when you find the queen, how will you stand against Overseer Rake and her followers? And what about the Royal Guard? Rats are fiercely loyal to those who feed them. You have no weapons, no armor." Lola had been wondering the same thing. The little apron-wearing mice with their buckets and mops, and the trembling echidnas with their feather dusters, looked about as fierce as an army of baby penguins.

"That was why I sent for your mother," Teddy said. "We were hoping she might gain Tobias's trust and help find out where he has hidden the queen."

The question was finally answered! Lola nodded with understanding. If Bale Blackwater had gotten the message to Alice weeks ago, as Teddy had intended, then Alice could have saved the queen. And the queen would have stopped Tobias and Overseer Rake.

"Do you have any idea where she might be?" Lola asked.

"The queen's size has proved problematic," Snarl said. "Being a pygmy possum, the smallest mammal in our kingdom, she can easily be slipped under a hat or swept into a dustbin. She could be in countless places where other critters can't fit. It makes the search very difficult, especially because Tobias can move her so easily from location to location."

"Baby!" Blue cried, his eyes popping open.

Melvin sighed. "Blue, please be quiet."

Teddy raised his paws to get everyone's attention. "Is there any new information to report? Places we might have overlooked?"

"Baby!" Blue scampered to his feet.

"No one is calling you a baby," Melvin told him. "We're trying to solve a very important mystery and you're making a scene." He tried to grab Blue's flipper, but Blue slipped away.

"Baby, baby, baby!" The penguin began jumping up and down, evading Melvin's snatching paws as he tried to quiet the little upstart.

"Oh dear, oh dear, we've looked everywhere," one of the echidnas said.

A small platypus burst into tears. "The queen is gone."

"BABY! BABY! BABY!" Each of Blue's exclamations was louder than the last. He pecked at Lola's feet, trying to get her attention. Was he just being annoying? Or was he trying to tell her something?

Baby? The last time Blue had said that, he'd had his head stuck inside Tobias's grandfather clock.

A shiver ran down Lola's back. Her fur prickled, from the tips of her ears all the way down her legs.

Where would a wombat hide something small that he wanted to keep secret?

"Blue," she said, crouching in front of the little fella. "Blue. What did you see inside the grandfather clock? Did you see a very small critter?"

Blue nodded.

Could it be that Blue's wandering had come to good? Perhaps the greatest good in an entire generation? Lola looked up at her uncle's confused face. "Uncle Teddy, I think Blue found the queen!"

25

BLUE TO THE RESCUE

The room went dead silent in the wake of Lola's exclamation. Then everyone encircled Blue, looking at him with expectant and hopeful eyes.

"Was this baby the size of a plum?" Head nod. "Did this baby have a furry tail?" Head nod again. "Did this baby have big blue eyes?" Big head nod over and over.

"You found her?" Teddy said. "You . . . *found* her?" In a very unwombat-like way, he picked Blue up and held him above his head for all the critters to see. "He found her!"

"YAY!" everyone cheered. Blue clapped his flippers and kicked his webbed feet, sending feathers adrift like snowflakes. Lola and Melvin clapped along with him.

"Tonight we save the queen," Teddy said, setting Blue back on the stone floor. "Long may she live!"

"Long live the queen!" everyone cried.

The gathered maids, butlers, window washers, and floor sweepers began hugging one another. Happy tears were shed and the underground room suddenly felt warmer and brighter. Blue rushed into Lola's arms and she whispered to him, "Good boy. I'm so proud of you."

"Sir." Snarl stepped forward, his voice loud enough to interrupt the celebration. "We must act immediately, before Tobias moves Her Majesty to a new location."

"Agreed." Teddy waved his paws and the critters sat, their heads tilted up as he began to pace before them. "Resistance fighters, our goal is the same: to return Tassie Island to its peaceful existence by capturing the rebel devils. There are three dozen total, including the overseer and the taskmaster. I suggest we—"

Suddenly, the ground began to tremble. A pounding arose as if thunder were rolling in. Teddy grabbed Lola's arm and, with a burst of speed, yanked her toward the door he'd used to enter the chamber. "Get inside!" he said. Before she could ask what was going on, she was inside. Melvin next, then Blue. Then Snarl.

"Keep them safe," Teddy ordered Snarl. He thrust a candle into Snarl's paw.

The thunder increased in volume. Tassie devils began to stream into the chamber. Lola squealed at the terrifying sight. Melvin, too. Snarl threw himself against the door and pushed it closed. Then he slid three deadbolts into place. He, Lola, Blue, and Melvin stood in the darkness, listening to the sounds of scurrying on the other side. Voices filled the chamber, cries of fear. Then a voice rose above the others that made Lola shudder.

"My, my, my. What have we here?"

A small peephole had been drilled into the door, allowing whoever stood behind it to see into the underground chamber. Lola pressed her eye to the hole, watching as the events unfolded inside. "Wha—" Melvin clamped a paw around Blue's beak to keep him quiet. He and Snarl pressed their ears to the door to listen.

Over a dozen Tassie devils had surrounded Teddy and the others, pushing them toward the center so that they were huddled in a group. "Is this reception for me? Such a nice gathering of *tasty* critters." Overseer Rake presented everyone with an openmouthed grin, her tongue running slowly over her deadly fangs. But where was her shadow, the taskmaster?

Teddy, who towered above everyone, spoke in a calm manner. "Rake, there is no need to make threats," he said. "You know very well that if you ate any of us you would be breaking the law of the island."

"Breaking the law?" The overseer smoothed her long robe, then spoke in a sickly sweet manner. "You dare tell me about laws? You, who lead an organization that is attempting to overthrow the government, the very source of said laws?"

"You have misjudged us." Teddy clasped his paws behind his back. "We are but humble servants of the palace and have gathered for a birthday celebration."

"Liar!" the overseer cried in a burst of rage. "The grand governor's birthday isn't being held down here, in the bowels of the palace."

Teddy remained calm. "We are celebrating *my* birthday. Have you forgotten that the grand governor and I are twins? I was born first, so it seems fitting that I should celebrate first."

Overseer Rake narrowed her black eyes. "I do not see a cake. Nor presents."

"We *lowly* palace servants do not have the funds for such things," Teddy said humbly. The others nodded solemnly. "Now, call off your servants and leave us in peace. Please."

"I shall do no such thing." She pointed to a fat mouse who wore a window washer's cap. "You are a plump one. Perfect for a stew." She reached out and grabbed the mouse by the tail. The mouse squealed and kicked his legs.

Lola gasped, her paws flying to her mouth. "The overseer's going to eat a mouse. We've got to do something."

Snarl and Melvin could only hear what was happening. "Let me see," Snarl said. Lola was about to step aside but movement caught her eye. A looming shape had entered the chamber. Rays like sunlight announced his presence, the reflection of candlelight on gold.

"Uncle Tobias," Lola whispered.

Melvin and Snarl held their breaths, their ears still pressed to the door, trying to catch every word. Blue squeezed between them and pressed his little earhole to the wall.

Tobias Bottom, the grand governor of Dore, was dressed in his finery for his birthday celebration. Gold encircled his wrists, his fingers, his neck. His vest was embroidered with golden thread, his golden slippers were curled at the tips. He stood beside the overseer and looked quizzically at the scene. "Overseer Rake? What's going on down here?"

The overseer let go of the mouse's tail. The mouse darted behind Teddy. "This is the uprising I've been telling you about, Your Excellency," she said.

"Uprising, you say?" Tobias looked sadly at his twin. "Hello, my dear Teddy."

Teddy maintained a calm exterior. "Hello, Tobias. This is a surprise. You rarely leave your luxurious quarters. I see you've been using taxes to purchase more gold."

"How your government uses its hard-earned taxes is no concern of yours," Tobias said. "But is it true? Have you been leading some sort of ragtag conspiracy against me?"

Teddy did not reply.

"They are all traitors," the overseer hissed. "They are guilty of treason against you."

"We're not traitors, we're not!" The mouse who had delivered the earlier speech stepped forward and stood firmly in front of Tobias. "We're loyal to her majesty, Queen Myra, we are." Though she stood on her hind legs, her ears only reached to Tobias's knees.

"How dare you speak." Overseer Rake pulled out her whip and sent it lashing toward the mouse. But a large paw blocked the strike. Silence rolled over the chamber. Small beads of blood pooled on Teddy's outstretched paw, then dripped onto the cold stonework. The move infuriated the overseer, who let loose a shriek so loud even Tobias cringed. "Take them to the tower!" she ordered. "Toss them in with the pelicans!"

Pelicans? Lola scrunched her face. The messenger pelicans were imprisoned in a tower? Is that where they'd been all this time?

The critters began to shuffle. A few made a run for it, only to be grabbed. The others went peacefully, allowing themselves to be marched from the chamber, leaving Teddy and Tobias standing nearly nose to nose. Twins, on opposite sides of a deepening chasm.

Tobias shook his head. "Mine own brother conspiring against me? Oh, what a terrible world we live in where familial blood means nothing. And you poor little misbegotten mouse, how can you be loyal to the queen when she's long gone? I am your ruler; your loyalties should lie with me and me alone."

Lola wanted to holler at her uncle Tobias. *He* was the one who didn't care about family! And Teddy spoke her exact thoughts.

"Who are you to speak of familial blood? You, who tore our sister from her burrow and sent her to a coal mine."

Tobias frowned. "I had nothing to do with that. Yes, I agreed that wombats would make excellent coal diggers, but not against their will. It was a miscommunication."

"It's not too late," Teddy said. "You don't have to work for the rebels."

"Work for them?" Tobias snorted. "They work for me. I am the grand governor now. And with the queen's retirement, I will become king in her stead. I can show you the proclamation."

"A proclamation you forged," Teddy said. Tobias narrowed his eyes. "Brother, rethink this. The overseer is using you. She will turn on you."

"What do you know of politics? You chose to push a mop. I chose to move up in the world and in society. Soon, I will rule and make Dore the most beautiful golden city the world has ever seen."

Lola couldn't believe what she was seeing and hearing. Identical twins and yet so opposite.

"Overseer Rake will not turn on me, for I have given her what she wants."

Teddy's shoulders stiffened. "You'll allow her to hunt?"

"Hunt? Of course not." Tobias grimaced at the notion. He tucked his thumbs into his vest's lapel. "How little you must think of me, brother. I've promised freedom, transportation, and gold coin to buy whatever the devils desire."

"What they desire is meat."

"You're wrong." Tobias swallowed dryly. "The overseer has said nothing about hunting." A tremor of doubt ran beneath his words. "She's satisfied with the deal we've struck. You see, this is why

I am the grand governor. I know how to control Tassie devils. I would never allow hunting."

"Never allow hunting? Oh dear, oh dear." The overseer had reentered the chamber, followed by a tangle of her followers, who slinked in and surrounded the twins.

"They're back," Lola whispered to Snarl and Melvin. "Six of them."

"Teddy can't defend himself against six devils. I need to go back in there." Snarl reached for a deadbolt. Melvin grabbed his arm.

"You can't fight that many." He kept his voice hushed. "Teddy told us to save the queen. We can't save her if we get captured."

Snarl nodded. "You are correct."

"Baby," Blue whispered.

"Shhhh," Lola said. "Teddy is talking."

Melvin, Snarl, and Blue pressed their ears to the wall again.

"What's the meaning of this?" Tobias asked, his eyes widening.

"If you will not allow hunting, then I regret to inform you that this is the end of our relationship," Overseer Rake said with a truly joyous smile. "You and your brother will be taken to the tower, to join the other unfortunates."

Four Tassie devils lunged forward and grabbed Tobias. "How dare you!" he cried. "I'm the grand—"

"You are a grand fool. Even a rat would think twice before taking the deals you did," Overseer Rake said.

"Fool? Why, you—" Before Tobias could get out another word, the devils heaved him upon their shoulders and began carrying him from the chamber. Tobias kicked and fought, but they held tight. "Rake! I order you to call off your thugs! Rake!"

Overseer Rake did not respond. Rather, she calmly folded her arms behind her back and watched the proceedings.

"Rake! This will not stand! I own you, Raaaaaaaaa—" And his voice faded into the tunnel's depths. The remaining devils turned to Teddy. More agile than his brother, Teddy managed to get a couple of kicks in, sending one devil sprawling onto his back and another flying against the wall. But the rest soon mobbed him and tied his arms to his sides with a whip.

"The citizens of Dore will rise up and outnumber you," Teddy said, gasping as he tried to catch his breath.

"Outnumbered by mice? How terrifying." Overseer Rake laughed. "Besides, I have an army of rats at my disposal. Did you forget the Royal Guard?"

"Rats aren't evil. They've always been loyal to the queen."

"Ah, this is true. But I have learned that rats will work for whoever feeds them. The royal kitchen is currently overflowing with food for your brother's birthday party. Such an elaborate feast means scraps and waste the likes of which most rats have never seen." She began to strut slowly around Teddy. "Once I am satisfied that you and your fellow traitors are securely locked in the tower, I will open the royal kitchen to all rats, allowing them to gorge themselves. In exchange for their loyalty to me, of course. And by the time any of those rats wake up to what's happening around them, it'll be far too late for them to stop me."

"It's a good plan," Melvin whispered.

"Brilliant," Snarl agreed.

"And then the grand governor will get the biggest surprise of all. For his birthday celebration is about to become my coronation ceremony." Before Teddy could say another word, Overseer Rake clapped her paws. "Take him away!"

With his arms and legs firmly tied, Teddy couldn't defend himself. As the six Tassie devils carried him from the chamber, Teddy looked over his shoulder, straight at the spot in the wall where Lola and the others were hiding, and said one word.

"Baby!"

The overseer paused, taken aback. "What a strange thing to say."

But it wasn't strange, for Lola, Snarl, and Melvin knew exactly what he meant.

26

LONG LIVE THE RESISTANCE

With his final word, Teddy had made it very clear that he wanted Lola and her companions to save the queen. There was no time to lose.

Snarl held the candle aloft. Wax dripped down its side. The light flickered off the tunnel's walls and ceiling. "Follow me," he said. "This passage leads up to the servant's quarters. Use your paws along the wall to feel your way."

They moved as quickly as possible in the low light. "Cobwebs," Melvin said with disgust. "Right in my mouth. Blech."

"Blech!" Blue hollered, his voice echoing up the tunnel while he clung to Lola's back. The passage began to angle upward and formed a steep stairway. At the top they had to crouch beneath a low ceiling. Snarl grunted as he pushed something heavy. A section of the ceiling opened, and light filtered in.

It was a trapdoor, and once Snarl had climbed out, he reached back in and grabbed Blue. Lola climbed out, followed by Melvin. They emerged in flickering lamplight to the servants' quarters. The walls were lined with barrack-like rows of bunk beds, each tidily made. Snarl blew out his candle and set it aside. Everyone breathed a sigh of relief—one fishier than the others. For the moment, they were safe. "What do we do now?" Melvin asked as he picked strands of cobweb off his ears.

"The city will fall to Overseer Rake if we do not act quickly," Snarl said. "We need to get the queen, and find those with the strength to stand with us. Tobias's office is not far from here, just a few hallways and stairways. If we run into guard rats, I will tell them that you are my prisoners."

Lola didn't ask the question that frightened her the most—*What if the queen is no longer inside the grandfather clock?* If that were true, all might be lost.

"What do we do after we get the queen?" Lola asked. She set Blue on one of the beds, where he proceeded to bounce.

Snarl paused, deep in thought. "I am . . . unsure."

"We need the rats," Melvin said. Lola and Snarl looked at him expectantly, waiting for his explanation. "We could use the overseer's plans against her. We could spread the word, to all rats, that the queen is opening the royal kitchen to reward them with a feast. And to announce that she is not retiring and will rule the Royal Guard once again. But they must swear their loyalty to her and not to the overseer. That should work."

"Wheeee!" Blue hollered, still bouncing.

"But we'll need to spread the word to all rats, right away, before the overseer leaves the tower," Lola said. "How can we—?"

A deeper shadow fell over them. Snarl rushed to the window and opened it. Dawn had not yet come, but the amber glow of the factory and the glow of the streetlights revealed a large shape hovering above the palace courtyard. "That's Bogart's balloon," Lola said. "Hey, I have an idea." She stuck her head out the window. Melvin squeezed next to her. "Bogart! Captain Bogart!"

The gondola floated above them. Lola called once more and was answered with a "Squwhaaaaat?" A sharp-beaked bird hopped onto the gondola's rim and looked down at her. "Oh, it's you. Mighty good to see you. Did you find the baby penguin?"

"Not a baby!"

"Yes, we did," Lola said, thinking, *No thanks to you*. "He's fine."

Bogart smiled. "That's good news. I was worried about the little fella. Did you get me a meeting with the queen? So I can show her my astounding invention?"

"The queen's life is in danger," Lola told him. "Will you help us save her?"

"Save Queen Myra?" Bogart ruffled his black feathers and saluted with his good wing. "Captain Bogart at your service!" He jumped back into the gondola and began to release air, lowering the balloon until it hovered parallel to the window. "How can I help?"

Lola leaned on the sill. "We need you to fly all over the city and tell every rat you see to come to the palace kitchen, right away. Tell the rats that Queen Myra has returned and if they swear their loyalty to her, they can eat all the royal garbage they want. Can you do that?"

"Of course I can do that," Bogart said. "I have my pilot's license, don't I?" He indicated the cardboard tag hanging around his neck.

"Clever idea," Melvin told Lola with a pat to her shoulder.

Snarl squeezed between Lola and the window frame. Upon seeing him, Bogart's feathers ruffled again. "Squwhaaaaat is this?" He aimed his pointy beak.

"You can trust him," Melvin explained. "He's on our side."

"Hello, Captain Bogart. I am Snarl, son of Snarl, and I am a warrior of peace intent on saving our good queen. But I must insist that you allow Lola onto your vessel and take her away from the city, immediately."

"But—!" Lola began to protest.

"Snarl is right," Melvin said. "I can't believe I'm about to say this, but you'll be safer onboard that contraption. If you get captured, they might send you to the coal mine. Or they might do something worse. You're Teddy and Tobias's niece. The overseer might not show you any mercy."

"He speaks the truth," Snarl said.

Blue tugged on Lola's leg. "I fly?" he asked. She picked him up and he reached his flippers toward Bogart. "I fly!" He didn't seem to remember that he'd been pushed out of that same balloon less than a day ago.

Lola knew that Snarl and Melvin were thinking of her safety. But there was no way she was going to flee. She'd come all this way to save her family, and Queen Myra was the key to their future. To everyone's future. But Blue's safety was also her responsibility, and she didn't know what the overseer would do to him. So she gave him a little kiss on his feathery head. "Yes, you fly," she whispered. Then she gently tossed him into the gondola.

"Wheeee," he said as he landed with a soft thunk.

"I'll see you soon!" Lola called to him.

"Lola, aren't you going with him?" Snarl asked.

"No, I'm staying here. We have an entire city to save."

Snarl opened his mouth, but Melvin stopped him. "You can argue with Lola all day, but I know she won't change her mind. This is her family we're talking about. You've dealt with wombats. Are you telling me *you* can beat their stubbornness?"

Snarl sighed. "Understood."

"Remember, tell every rat you see that the royal kitchen is open to them, compliments of Queen Myra," Lola said. The balloon was beginning to rise again, but slowly, hovering only barely above the wall. "Captain Bogart, if you don't see us again, will you take Blue back to Penguin Bay?"

"Yes," Bogart said.

"And please don't push him overboard again!" she called, suddenly far more worried than she'd been moments before.

"And try not to crash!" Melvin yelled.

"Squwhaaaaat?" Bogart glared at him. "I never crash! I just land unexpectedly. Those are two very different things!" The balloon began to float over the rooftops, Bogart's lone wing pumping back and forth as he steered them through the near-windless air.

Lola felt odd not to have a baby penguin clinging to her back or holding on to her paw, and for a moment her heart ached. Had she made the right decision? Melvin patted her shoulder again. "He's definitely safer up there." She nodded, holding back a tear.

"We must make haste," Snarl said.

Melvin shook his head in amazement. "Who would have imagined that a Tassie devil, a swamp water rat, and a wombat would be the last hope for our island?"

"It's like a story," Lola realized.

"Let us hope this story has a happy ending." Snarl held out a paw. "Long live the resistance."

"Long live the resistance," Lola and Melvin chimed, placing their paws atop his. "And long live the queen."

27

BUCKETS AND SHOVELS

The palace was eerily quiet since most of the servants were members of the Resistance and had been taken away to the tower. With cautious steps, Lola and Melvin began to follow Snarl down the hall. Despite the fact that Lola was skilled at sneaking, her nerves were jittery. She'd snuck out of the burrow many times, but the future of a kingdom hadn't depended on her success. She thought of Josie and Rupert back at the trading post and wished she, too, could curl into a ball of spikes.

While walking, Melvin combed his fur with his claws. "I'm going to meet the queen," he whispered when Lola gave him a quizzical look. "I don't want to look like I just rolled out of my sleeping bag."

"You look fine," she assured him.

"Thank you. I know you're lying but that just proves you're my friend." He winked at her.

They had reached the end of the hallway when Snarl turned quickly and motioned for them to stop. Two white rats, each holding a short sword, marched down the connecting hallway with six palace mice scurrying in front.

"I haven't done anything, I haven't," one of the mice squeaked. "I was scrubbing the pots and pans, I was."

"We have orders to take everyone to the tower for questioning," a rat guard said.

"But I'm the royal pastry chef, I am," another mouse pleaded. She wore a chef's hat. "I need to finish icing the cake for the grand governor's birthday."

"Don't blame us, we're just following the overseer's orders," the second rat said, prodding the mouse with his foot. "Keep moving."

"That's right, keep moving. We don't get to eat if we don't do what the overseer says." And they passed by, not seeming to care one bit about Snarl and his companions.

"We need to open the royal kitchen so we can get the rats on our side," Snarl said, continuing around the corner now that the rats had left. "And we need to rescue the queen. But the kitchen and Tobias's office are at opposite sides of the palace."

A red carpet drew Lola's attention. She knew exactly where it led. "Melvin and I have been inside my uncle's office, but we've never been to the royal kitchen. We've also seen the grandfather clock. We'll go get the queen."

Snarl's black tail flicked. "I would take the time to argue with you, but there is no time. We must split up. I shall open the kitchen doors and alert any remaining servants of our plans. I doubt any will side with the overseer. Most will leap at the chance to help. You two will find the queen."

"Then what?" Melvin asked.

"Meet me outside in the courtyard." He pointed down a hallway. "We will take Queen Myra to the factory. The workers think she abandoned them and they will not rise up unless they see her. We need them to join our fight and help us round up the rebels."

It was a plan made in haste, and probably filled with flaws, but as Lola turned to face the red carpet, she felt a sudden rush of confidence. Why? Because she knew that the best stories came with the least expected heroes. The plan would work. It had to work. There was no other option.

In a few minutes, she and Melvin were facing Tobias's office door. The two white rats had been replaced by two gray rats. One was large with wide shoulders and was missing an ear. The other was shorter but equally muscular. Instead of swords, they each held a shovel.

"I'll handle this," Melvin said, shaking his head and sighing. Lola nodded, and followed alongside. "Hello, Bob. Hello, Stanley."

The taller rat scratched his rump. "Oi! It's Melvin. Hello, Melvin, good to see you." He jabbed the other rat with his elbow. "Stanley, look, it's Melvin, and that joey."

Stanley, who'd been asleep on his feet, awoke with a start. "Hey, Melvin. Did you join the Royal Guard?" He didn't wait for a reply. "Look at you. Not a speck of slime on you. You're still a disgrace to all rats."

"Thank you." Melvin rolled his eyes.

"Oh, that reminds me . . ." Bob leaned his shovel against the wall, then pushed his bucket aside, revealing another bucket that had a custom-made red covering with pockets. "I found this on the train after we raided the Farmlands. Been carrying it around in case I ran into you. Don't think too poorly of the rats who took this. They were just following orders so they could fill their stomachs. They meant no ill will toward you."

Melvin accepted his bucket with a smile. "My sleeping bag and my products are still inside. You did this for me?"

"Of course, mate," Bob said. "You might be an oddy, but you're one of us and we stick together." Then he handed Melvin a shovel.

"Did you happen to see Lola's backpack?" Melvin asked. Lola took a hopeful step forward. Her cloak? Her letters? Her book?

"Sorry," Bob said with a shrug. "So, what are you two doing here?"

"Lola and I have been invited to the grand governor's office for a meeting," Melvin said. "So if you'll just let us in . . ." He took a step forward. Bob and Stanley stepped closer together, blocking the way.

"No can do," Bob said. "No one is allowed inside, orders of the overseer."

"But I'm Tobias Bottom's niece," Lola said. "I have his permission to enter his office."

Stanley picked something green off his front tooth. "We follow the overseer's orders, not the governor's," he told her.

Melvin narrowed his eyes and looked slyly at his fellow swamp rat. "Stanley, are you telling me that you're working for a Tassie devil? You said you'd never work for one. You came here to work for the queen, remember?"

"The overseer feeds us better," Bob said. "So much rot and ruin, I'm getting fat." He patted his belly, which did look rounder. "And that other one told us to guard this door while he's inside getting ready for something."

"Other one?" Lola asked.

"Lash, the taskmaster," Bob said.

Lola and Melvin shared a pained expression. Why was

the taskmaster inside Tobias's office? There could only be one reason—he was looking for the queen. They had to get in there!

"We have good news for you," Lola said. "News about garbage." Bob and Stanley's ears perked, their tails standing at attention.

"Uh, that's right," Melvin said, taking the cue. "The queen has invited the Royal Guard to her kitchen to feast on Royal Garbage. The doors are opening as we speak."

"But the overseer is the one who feeds us," Bob said. "Not the queen."

"We've never even met the queen," Stanley said. "The overseer said she was dead."

"She's not dead," Lola insisted, her voice rising. "She's here, in Dore, and she's wants the Royal Guard to be loyal to her."

"She's going to feed you better than you ever imagined. The royal kitchen is open to you, right now, but you've got to hurry if you want to get the first pickings." Melvin pointed down the hallway.

Bob licked his lips. "You hear that, Stanley? We don't have to work for those devils."

"I heard." Stanley wiped a bit of drool from his chin. "It's our lucky day." They grabbed their buckets and shovels.

"You coming with us?" Bob asked Melvin.

"He's not coming with us," Stanley said. "Melvin hates garbage. Hey, Melvin, if we see a fresh piece of fruit with no bruises or wormholes, we'll save it for you."

"Thanks," Melvin said.

The two swamp water rats scurried away, their tails twitching with excitement as they sang. Other rats could be heard to slowly take up the call.

So raise your shovels to the sky

Then plunge them in the ground,

There's garbage to be found, mates,

There's garbage to be found.

"Now what do we do?" Melvin asked.

Lola's thoughts had been swirling around and around as she tried to work out the best next step. And she'd come to one conclusion. "I'll give myself up to the taskmaster. He'll take me to the tower, and then the coast will be clear for you to go inside and get the queen."

"No, that's too risky," Melvin said. "For all we know, Overseer Rake might be getting ready to hunt as we speak!"

"We don't have another choice." The queen had to be saved. The citizens of Dore had to see that Queen Myra was alive and well. Only then could they join together to defeat the rebels. Only then would Lola's family have a chance.

Lola was about to knock on Tobias's door when a voice on the other side said, "Who is singing?"

The knob began to turn. Melvin grabbed Lola's arm. "I have an idea," he whispered. "A better idea that might keep you from the tower." With all his strength, he pulled her behind a velvet window covering. She thought they were both going to hide, but he stepped back out.

"Stay there." What was he going to do? Lola peeked between the two drapes, watching as Melvin hurried toward Tobias's office door.

The door opened and the taskmaster appeared. His robe

brushed across the floor as he stepped into the hallway. His parasol was closed and hanging from his forearm. His pure white fur was always a shock to see. His intense gaze rested on Melvin. "Where are the guards?"

Melvin shrugged. "You know rats. They smelled food and took off."

The taskmaster made a *tch tch* sound and shook his head. "That does not surprise me. They are bound to their natures, as are most of us." He was about to turn away but hesitated. Then he narrowed his eyes. "I have seen you before. I would not forget such a well-groomed rat. You were outside the city gates, accompanying the niece of Tobias Bottom. Where is she?"

"The overseer is looking after her, so I'm sure she's fine."

The taskmaster considered this for a moment. His eyes softened, but there was some pain hidden behind them, too. "She is your friend?"

"Yes. My very good friend." Even though Lola already knew that she and Melvin shared this sentiment, it warmed her to hear his words, especially in such a dire moment.

"Friendship is important, as is loyalty. Especially in times like these." The taskmaster leaned on his parasol, gilded claws tapping like bells. "Why are you standing outside this door?"

"I'm the new royal barber. Tobias Bottom hired me to prepare him for his birthday celebration."

Brilliant, Lola thought.

The taskmaster waved his paw dismissively. "That celebration has been canceled. Thus you have no reason to be here."

"That's a shame. I brought all my special products." Melvin held up his bucket. "Luxurious skin conditioners, silky fur detanglers, ear gloss, and whisker cream." He pointed to the

239

taskmaster's paw. "I do notice some slight flaking around your claws. That can happen if you forget to moisturize. You might want to consider my mud treatment." Taskmaster Lash glanced at his paw. "I also see a bit of matting behind your ear." Lash anxiously felt behind his ear. "I have the perfect products for you. But if you're too busy to look your best . . ." Melvin shrugged.

Taskmaster Lash smoothed his white mane. "How much time would this take? I have *other matters* to attend to."

"One must not rush beauty," Melvin said. "But I'll do my best to be efficient."

"See that you are." Taskmaster Lash turned gracefully on his heels and headed back into Tobias's office. Melvin gave Lola a wide-eyed look. Then, with his bucket and shovel in paw, he followed the taskmaster, making sure to leave the door open a crack behind him.

Lola tiptoed forward, the red carpet so thick she didn't have to worry about her claws clicking. Through the door's crack, she watched Melvin get to work. He beckoned the taskmaster to a chair, then reached into his bucket and pulled out some of his swamp-mud products. Noticing a teakettle on the hearth, Melvin picked it up and poured the water onto a small white towel.

"All right, Taskmaster Lash, I'll place this warm towel over your face to reduce the puffiness around your eyes."

"Puffiness?" the taskmaster said in alarm.

"Extreme puffiness. Have you been experiencing stress?"

"Unimaginable stress," the taskmaster admitted, his expression drooping. "I have not been sleeping well. As the overseer's right-hand critter, so many responsibilities lie on my shoulders. Overtaking a kingdom and establishing a new government is not an easy feat."

"You certainly deserve some *me time*," Melvin said. "Please sit back and relax while I place this towel on your face. The heat will help to soothe your strained facial muscles. I do hope we're not too late to prevent early onset wrinkling."

The taskmaster sat back in the chair and closed his red eyes. Once the towel was in place, Melvin grabbed a file from his bucket and began to work on the Tassie devil's sharp nails. He looked over at the door and nodded at Lola.

She took a long breath, then crept into the office. Melvin kept the conversation going. "Stress isn't good for the skin. Especially delicate, sun-sensitive skin such as yours."

Lola's heart beat in her throat. The grandfather clock loomed on the other side of the room and she'd have to pass behind the taskmaster to get there, within mere inches of him. She imagined that it was morning and her parents were asleep in their nests. She'd never woken them, not once. She could do this.

But three steps into her journey, her foot knocked against one of the bookshelves, sending a book tumbling to the ground. She froze.

"What was—?" The taskmaster began to pull the towel from his eyes, but Melvin stopped him.

"I do sincerely apologize for that noise, sir. I'm a bit nervous. This is my first time working on fur that is so very exquisite."

"Not everyone would agree with you." Taskmaster Lash settled back down. "I am considered an oddity among my own critters."

"Then we have something in common," Melvin said, "for I, too, am considered an oddity."

"Indeed." The towel remained over his face, so his voice was slightly muffled as Lola crept past. "I would guess that due to your grooming habits you faced ridicule. Humiliation. Isolation?"

"Er, yes, at times." Melvin, taken aback, continued to file the nails. "How about you, sir?"

"It was challenging to be the only one who could not play outside in the sun, and even had to be careful with the full moon. Those who embraced the old ways considered me to be weak and unworthy of survival. I was often the target of their frustrations. But Rake, daughter of Rake, befriended me and kept me safe."

"And so you followed her here?" Melvin asked.

"Yes. I do what she asks. And when she stole the design for the train—"

"Stole?" Melvin asked. Lola froze, trying to remember. Her uncle had said that the overseer designed the train. But stealing the design did seem more fitting.

"Did I say stole?" Taskmaster Lash shifted his weight in the chair. Then he cleared his throat. "I owe my life to Overseer Rake. If she had not befriended me in my youth, I would not be here today. All I want is to be useful to her, you know?"

Lola was struck by this sad story. On the two occasions when she'd seen the overseer and the taskmaster together, she'd noticed that the overseer didn't treat the taskmaster kindly. That she ordered him around and was short-tempered with him. But now Lola understood the relationship. The taskmaster was being loyal to someone who had helped him, no matter what the cost.

Lola began moving again, this time far more carefully, toward the grandfather clock. Her paws shook slightly and her nose twitched. When she finally reached it, she scooted as close as possible. Then she looked over her shoulder. Melvin had changed the subject and was talking about his products and keeping his eye on Lola's progress at the same time. Lola settled onto her rump, then reached for the clock's doors. Why had the doors not been bolted or chained shut? Either Tobias had been overly confident in his supreme power or . . .

The queen was no longer inside.

Ever so slowly Lola opened them, trying to keep the scraping of wood on wood as quiet as possible.

Finally, the doors were fully open.

She held back a gasp.

28

THE TINIEST QUEEN

Queen Myra, the queen of Tassie Island, sat inside the clock's belly, a piece of fabric tied over her minuscule mouth. Her tiny wrists and feet were tied together by a piece of twine. She was the smallest mammal Lola had ever seen, about the size of a plum. Her fur was brown and the tip of her nose was bright red. Her round ears looked a bit too big for her little pointed face, as did her round eyes that blinked as light filtered in.

Lola wanted to cry. With relief. With joy. With sadness at seeing such a tiny critter in such a state. Her fur was matted and dirty, probably from weeks of being carted around to various dusty and cramped places. Lola wanted to tell the queen that things were going to be okay. That she'd come to rescue her. But she couldn't risk words.

Reaching in, Lola carefully began to undo the bindings. Some comforts had been provided for the queen—a silk pillow, a wool blanket. Delicately using one of her digging claws, Lola cut through the gag around the queen's mouth. Queen Myra inhaled deeply and appeared on the verge of coughing, but Lola held a claw up to her lips in warning. The queen gave a nod of understanding, for the taskmaster's voice could be heard as he complained about all the work he had to do in order to help the overseer take over the kingdom.

Lola held out her paw. The queen took a moment to stretch her little limbs. She brushed some dust from her golden gown. Then, displaying surprising dexterity for someone who appeared so delicate, she scrambled up Lola's arm and sat on her shoulder, taking stock of the room. Melvin, who'd been clipping hair around the taskmaster's ears, stopped and gawked. Then, ever so slightly, he dipped his head in a bow. The queen bowed in return.

"How much longer must this towel remain on my face?" the taskmaster asked.

Melvin lifted an edge. "Your eyes are still puffy, I'm afraid. I suggest we leave it a bit longer. But only if you want to look *presentable.*"

"*Of course* I want to look presentable!"

With the queen balanced on her shoulder, Lola began to retrace her steps. Several times she had to shuffle to one side or the other to avoid objects. Melvin, for his part, dutifully took care of the taskmaster, clipping around his ears to help obscure Lola's soft, padding pawsteps and the creak of the door. Before she made it to the hallway, she turned to look at Melvin. He bowed to the queen once more, then waved at Lola to go on. He would keep the taskmaster occupied. "Good luck," he mouthed. Lola hurried down the red carpet. It wasn't until they had turned many corners and passed down many hallways that Lola whispered, "Your Majesty, are you okay?"

The queen spoke. "What is your name, my dear?" Her voice was high and chirpy. It tickled Lola's ear but still managed to sound regal. If this hadn't been such a serious moment, Lola might have giggled.

Lola stopped walking. "I'm Lola Budge. My uncles, Teddy and Tobias, work for you." Queen Myra crawled down Lola's arm and stood in her paw.

"You are Teddy and Tobias's niece?" she asked.

"Yes, Your Majesty."

Her expression hardened. "Which of your uncles do you take after?"

"I am unshy like Uncle Tobias," Lola said honestly. "But I'm loyal to the crown like Uncle Teddy." Lola held her gaze steady as the queen looked her over. Then she waited, breath held, for the queen's reaction.

"We believe you," Queen Myra said. Her gaze softened again. Her red nose reminded Lola of a tiny berry. "And We are grateful to you for Our rescue. Tobias has been moving Us from one pocket to the other, from drawers to shoeboxes. It has been quite the ordeal and often rather smelly."

"Melvin helped, too. With your rescue. He was very excited to meet you."

"Ah, yes, the swamp water rat. He seems very clever." Her long whiskers bristled. "But now that We are rescued, We hope you have a plan."

It was going to take a bit of time for Lola to get used to the odd way the queen spoke. "Yes, Your Majesty, we have a plan." Lola told the queen about Snarl, the rats, and the royal kitchen with all the food for Tobias's birthday celebration.

"We are acquainted with Snarl, son of Snarl. But where is Teddy?"

"He's being held in the tower with the other members of the Resistance," Lola told her. "As are Tobias and most of the palace workers."

"Tobias? In the tower?"

"The overseer turned against him."

"Of course she did. Tobias should have seen this coming, but greed muddled his brain." The queen unfurled her long swirling tail. "So, all that is left of Our loyalists is a wombat joey, a well-groomed swamp water rat, and a young warrior of peace?"

"Yes," Lola said. "And a one-winged firehawk and a baby penguin." She could practically hear Blue correcting her.

To her surprise, Queen Myra smiled. "Sounds like the makings of a most entertaining story indeed. Shall We be about it then?"

Lola set the queen back on her shoulder, then hurried down the hallway. She told the queen that Snarl was going to meet them outside. The plan was to take the queen to the factory so she could free her workers. Then the citizens of Dore would chase the rebels from the city and free the prisoners in the tower. It was starting to sound as if it might actually work. The courtyard was within reach.

The pounding of many paws on stonework sent a rumbling echo through the palace halls. Lola jumped out of the way as dozens of rats, white, brown, and gray, rushed passed them. "To the royal kitchen!" they cheered, drool dripping from their mouths. "The queen is giving us all the food we want!" Bogart and Blue had been successful in spreading the word. As they ran past, not a single rat noticed their tiny queen, for they had one thing on their minds.

"Your Majesty, the rats will soon be on your side," Lola said.

"Then your plan is working. Onward to the factory," Queen Myra ordered. "We must set Our critters free! We know they'll join us right away."

Lola galloped out a side door and onto the palace grounds. But just as her paws touched down, she skidded to a stop. Where was Snarl? She sniffed the air for him but found not a trace. Morning had come, with tinges of orange and red filtering through the smoggy air as factory number one continued to spew. The street beyond the courtyard was lined with little houses, but the doors were barred shut and no candlelight flickered through the shuttered windows.

"What has happened to Our beautiful city?" the queen asked, her round eyes filling with tears. "This is Our fault. The train was supposed to be a lovely way to connect the farthest corners of Tassie Island." She coughed, a delicate sound.

"The train could still connect us, Your Majesty." Lola couldn't believe that she was consoling the queen of Tassie Island. "As long as it's not controlled by the wrong critters."

"We should have been wary of Tobias when he began to collect things. When he began to demand more gold coin. We knew the truth, but We didn't recognize his greed for the draconian avarice it had become. While We were stowed away in Tobias's office, We overheard many of his conversations. He should not have trusted Overseer Rake."

"Uncle Tobias has made terrible mistakes," Lola said. As angry as she was with her uncle, she realized that she was about to defend him. "But he didn't know that the overseerer wanted to use the train for hunting."

"I know that, my dear. Your uncle might be greedy and shallow, but he is not a monster." She reached out her tiny arm and patted Lola's cheek. It was such a delicate sensation, like a kiss from a butterfly.

At that moment, it was hard for Lola to imagine that she could ever forgive her uncle for what he'd helped do to her family. But she was grateful for the queen's kind words. "The train will be a good thing," Lola said. "As long as it's not being used to take food from the Farmlands. Or for hunting."

"Quite right. We must get control of it again."

To Lola's despair, there was still no sign of Snarl. What was he doing? It wouldn't take long for word to reach the overseer that the Royal Guard had turned against her. Then she and her rebels would leave the tower.

"Hang tight, Your Majesty," Lola said. As the tiny queen gripped Lola's fur, Lola increased her speed, barreling down the empty streets toward the factory. She skidded to a stop before the factory doors. To her surprise, the doors were not barred shut, which meant that the workers could leave at any time. Why didn't they? And then she saw the proclamation, nailed to the door and taped to all the windows.

BY ORDERS OF HER MAJESTY, QUEEN MYRA,

ALL CITIZENS OF DORE ARE TO REPORT TO FACTORY #1

TO WORK WITHOUT UNNECESSARY CESSATION UNTIL THE ROYAL TRAIN TRACK IS COMPLETED.

They did not leave because they were loyal to their queen. The overseer used their loyalty to her advantage.

"This is forged," the queen said with anger and despair.

"I know."

"We must tell them the truth. Please take Us inside."

A blast of hot air shot out as Lola opened the door. She flinched, feeling as if she were standing too close to an open flame. The queen turned away, pressing her face against Lola's neck. With trepidation, Lola stepped inside.

The fire was the first thing she saw, with its bloodred flames that were large enough to engulf a tree. Large enough to engulf a forest. To burn greatly. Lola's ears tried to curl in on themselves as overwhelming heat washed over her. She blinked her eyes quickly, for the smoke stung. Workers, dressed in their grimy aprons, with faces and fur covered in soot, shuffled about, their shoulders hunched, backs stooped. Many looked as if they hadn't slept in days. Others looked as thin as if they'd gone without food. It was noisy in there, as workers banged hammers against metal. As more coal was dumped into the furnace. Queen Myra stood on Lola's shoulder. "Attention!" she hollered in her high-pitched voice. No heads turned. "Attention!"

Lola put her paws around her mouth and hollered, "Hallooo!" But the critters continued to move sluggishly as they went about their work.

"Your Majesty, I think I know how to get their attention." Lola set the queen on a table. "I'll be right back." Then she moved toward the massive central furnace.

Two quolls were taking turns jumping up and down on a large bellows that fed air through a pipe into the glowing furnace. A single lever stuck out of the pipe. Despite her rising fear, Lola knew what she had to do. Ignoring the heavy smoke and raging heat, she pushed her weight against the lever. With a shuddering clang, it gave way. The air duct was sealed tight.

The fire began to dim. The flames flickered, gasping for life, then died. The factory interior would have darkened completely, but the open factory door allowed morning light to filter in.

Hammers slowed. Everyone paused in their work and looked over at Lola with a mixture of confusion and apprehension.

"What happened to the fire?"

"Oh dear, oh dear, we are under orders to work."

"If we don't work, we'll be thrown in the tower, we will."

Now was the time. Lola scooped the queen into her paw, then clambered atop a crate, standing high enough for all to see. "Your Majesty, they can hear you now," she said, then she placed the queen back on her shoulder. Silence fell over the factory. The critters gaped at the sight of their tiny ruler. But no one bowed. Instead, expressions changed from bewilderment to anger, and even disgust.

"My loyal subjects," Queen Myra said. "We are here because you have suffered a terrible wrong."

"Aye we have!"

"A wrong done by you!"

"Down with the queen!" The critters became agitated as "Down with the queen" rolled across the factory floor, repeated over and over.

"Please listen," Lola said, raising her paws to get their attention. "Her Majesty needs your help."

"Why should we help her? She's kept us from our homes, she has."

"She forced us to work here, she did."

"Down with Queen Myra!"

Lola could feel the queen shrink. "We have lost them. They hate Us," she said, her eyes filling with tears. "We have failed to protect Our critters."

Lola couldn't bear to see the queen looking so defeated, especially not after all she'd been through. "Please listen," she pleaded to the crowd. She did her best to be heard, despite the continuous grumbling. "I was just like you. I thought the queen had turned against us."

"She did!"

"She doesn't love us!"

The queen broke into sobs and pressed her face against Lola's neck.

"She does love you. Please listen," Lola pleaded again. But they wouldn't. Some turned their backs, while others glared. "This wasn't the queen's fault. My uncle, Tobias Bottom, betrayed her. He allowed the Tassie devils to leave Mount Ossa because he thought they would work for him. He thought they'd bring him gold. So he captured our queen and hid her away these long months."

A few stopped grumbling. A few turned to listen. The queen wiped her tears and whispered in Lola's ear, "You've got their attention. Go on, tell them the truth."

Lola nodded. "The truth is, Queen Myra has been imprisoned by Tobias. That's why you haven't seen her. The proclamation nailed to the front door of this factory was forged. The overseer is the one who has forced you to work here. She is the leader of a group of rebels who want to live like they used to live, long ago. As hunters."

The crowd gasped in unison. From her perch on Lola's shoulder, the queen nodded, urging Lola to continue. Her own tears, even in the heat of the furnace, were still slow to dry.

A young mouse stood at the front of the crowd, twisting his tail in a fretful way. "Do not worry," Lola said. "Queen Myra would never allow hunting. And most of those who live on Mount Ossa don't want to hunt, either. They want to live peacefully with us. The train was supposed to connect the island, but the overseer stole the designs and used them to gain favor with my uncle."

A trembling echidna stepped forward. "Oh dear, oh dear, if Tobias is your uncle, then how can we trust what you say?"

"Because my family was also imprisoned. And forced to dig coal. I came to Dore to get help from Uncle Tobias, but now I know the truth. That my uncle wanted to use the train to grow wealthy and to become the next king. And he was willing to send Queen Myra into exile, or imprison her. The queen is innocent but she needs your help. We must work together to rid our city of the rebels. And we must reestablish the old Royal Guard, if we're to prevent this from ever happening again."

"But what can we do?" a white mouse asked. "We're too small, we are, too weak and tired. We can't defeat such monsters."

Silence fell again, the critters looking at Lola, not at the queen, their soot-covered faces waiting for an answer. Waiting for a direction. Lola reached toward her back, but stopped when she remembered her book was not there. She closed her eyes and breathed, ignoring the acrid taste of smoke. She breathed evenly and deeply before confidently looking out over the crowd. Lola spoke the words that came naturally to her, as carving came naturally to her parents. "Gather ye round and prick your ears, for a tale is about to be told."

This was not a story to lull them to sleep. Not a story to entertain. Lola needed to stir them, to ignite their feelings of injustice, to bring about action. She raised her voice and spoke the opening lines from a story they would all know.

"In the time before Dore, when critters lived for themselves and distrusted all others, invaders sailed across the sea and landed on our shores. Then they roamed the island, taking what they pleased. Only those who could take to the sky or dive beneath the waves were safe. It was a terrible time, dark and desperate. Until came TheoDore the Small."

At the name of the first king, the critters settled their rumps onto the factory floor. Pointed ears and round ears turned in Lola's direction. Black eyes and brown eyes gazed up at her. She'd never had an audience of this size. She paused, a lump in her throat.

"Lola, they are still listening to you," the queen whispered. "Help them understand that the story is real."

Lola swallowed hard, then found her voice. "Though he knew he was the smallest of the small, TheoDore bravely went to the invader's leader and asked him to stop the hunts. The leader laughed and said, *Why should I listen to you? You are insignificant.* Small and humble though he was, TheoDore believed that strength could be found in alliance, and so he began to gather a clan. *Alone we are weak*, he told them. *But together we are strong.* The clan grew and word spread throughout the island, and those who were frightened traveled to join TheoDore in his village by the bay. Together they built a glorious city, a shining beacon of peace where no critter would live in fear of being hunted. And those who loved him made him king, and set him upon the first throne, and named the city Dore. And TheoDore the Small became known as King TheoDore the Wise.

"His descendants have sworn to continue his legacy as long as they live. Ever since those days of chaos, the family of TheoDore has shouldered the burden of the throne. They take the same vow and carry the same blood as the one who saved us all. Their clan keeps watch lest the times of chaos reign once more."

That was the end of the tale, as written in her storybook. Now Lola had to add her own words. "Queen Myra, the greatest granddaughter of King TheoDore, would never betray you. But would you betray her by turning against her in this time of chaos? Or would you join together, as our ancestors did, to save our island?"

The critters sat in silence. Many had ears turned down with tears of shame in their eyes. But there was something else behind the shame, something that grew as disjointed chanting began. Slowly louder, more confident and sure. And hope glistened behind the tears as cheering arose, loud enough to shake the foundations of the factory itself.

"Alone we are weak! Together we are strong! Long live Queen Myra. Long live Dore!"

The queen once again whispered in Lola's ear. "Thank you." Then she held up her paws and silence fell again. This time the gathered critters gazed upon their queen with renewed faith and hope. "My loyal friends and beloved subjects," she said. "The invaders have returned, but they are not here to stay. We know that you are tired from the work they forced upon you, but from all this work surely you've gained strength as well, strength enough to fight back. Not for Us, nor for Our ancestors, but for your families. If we are going to chase the renegades from our city, then let's be about it!"

With a cheer, the critters tossed their aprons aside and followed Lola from the factory. One by one they emerged, taking deep breaths of cool morning air. Mice, quolls, and echidnas, a ragtag, soot-covered crew, determined nonetheless to face the enemy. They brought their great forge hammers, lengths of steel

29

CRASH LANDING

Overseer Rake stood at the end of the cobblestone street, flanked on each side by her rebels. With whips and daggers in paw, they walked toward Lola and the queen, snarling and baring their teeth. The hems of their black robes swept through the sooty street. The factory workers drew closer together, tightening into a frightened cluster behind Lola. The overseer and her rebels stopped a few feet away.

"You must all be confused," Overseer Rake said, her fingers tapping her whip's handle. "Workers are supposed to be *inside* the factory."

"You do not rule these critters," Queen Myra said, making her voice as loud as she could. Lola scooped the queen into her palm and held her out so she could face the overseer. "They are free by Our command. You are a rebel who has no place here. You are to return immediately to Mount Ossa, where your peers will decide on a suitable punishment."

The other devils growled, then waited to see what their leader would do. Overseer Rake remained calm, though the blaze in her eyes reminded Lola of the factory's furnace—yet somehow cold as ice. "You may have ruled us in the past but you can no longer hide behind your palace wall." A smirk spread across her face. "The descendants of TheoDore are no longer in control of the city that bears their name, much less the island itself. This is the second age of Tassie Island and you will bow to me."

"Never," Queen Myra said, her furry chin held high.

"Very well, I suppose you needn't bow. Cowering in fear would be much more satisfying." Overseer Rake threw back her head and shrieked—the same chill-inducing shriek that Lola had heard, what seemed like a lifetime ago, in the burrow. It was the sound that had the power to make her heart stop beating. To turn her legs to jelly. To obliterate any sense of hope.

It was the sound of a predator claiming its prey. And the overseer's glare had dropped to the queen.

"No!" Lola cried, pulling the queen close and cupping her with both paws. "I won't let you hurt her!"

"I am more than happy to take you down first." With a sweeping motion, the overseer raised her whip to the sky. Lola turned away to protect the queen, preparing to feel the whip against her back. She closed her eyes and held the queen tightly between her paws. She whispered how sorry she was to the little monarch. The whip snaked back and darted forward, but something rushed past her and stood in the way. That's when a clang filled the air. The shriek cut off in surprise.

Lola turned around. Melvin stood before her, holding a shovel aloft in both paws. He'd blocked the overseer's whip, which left only a small dent in the shovel head. At first the overseer didn't react. She stood in a state of shock, her mouth hanging open. The other rebels growled and shifted with agitation, waiting for her order to strike.

"How dare you protect my prey," the overseer said to Melvin, almost too shocked for anger. "Lower your shovel and get back to your station. You are a disgrace to all rats."

"So I've been told," Melvin said, but he did not flinch.

Overseer Rake yanked on her whip. It rushed across the ground from below Melvin's shovel and returned to her side. "All of you, return to the factory!"

The factory workers seemed to gather courage, for they began to step forward. "Never," a quoll said.

"We don't take orders from you, we don't," a mouse said.

"Oh dear, oh dear," an echidna said.

"Then you will all pay the price!" The overseer tossed back her head again, another shriek filling the air. Her devils joined her, their whips raised high. But then, with a sudden shift in her demeanor, the overseer stopped shrieking. She stood, her face still turned to the sky, her eyes widening as a shadow fell over her. "What the—"

A large basket landed on top of Overseer Rake. With a gargled sound, she disappeared beneath its weight. The rebels fell into silence. Lola couldn't believe her eyes.

"Squwhaaaaat's going on?" Captain Bogart stuck his head out of the gondola. Everyone stared back at him with expressions of utter disbelief. Completely unaware of what had happened, Bogart hopped onto the gondola's rim and waved his wing. "G'day mates. Is this my welcoming party?"

No one replied, all eyes fixed upon the place where the overseer had stood.

"Oi. What's everyone looking at?" the captain asked. Then he turned and spied the Tassie devils. With a strangled sound, he ducked back into the gondola. "Blue! We need that fire going again right away!"

Queen Myra jumped from Lola's paw, then scampered down Lola's leg. Holding the hem of her gown so she wouldn't trip, she scurried across the cobblestones. One of the overseer's paws stuck out from beneath the gondola. The queen placed her ear against the overseer's wrist. Breaths were held. Everyone waited for the news. "There is a pulse," Queen Myra reported. "The overseer is weakened, but alive."

"Still alive," the rebels murmured, gripping their whips. But without a leader they seemed unsure of what to do next. The critters of Dore, against all their instincts, shook their fists at the rebels, who were now faced with something wholly alien to them—the banding together of their prey. The Tassie devils paused momentarily in their advance. Emboldened by the devils' hesitation, the citizens of Dore took another step, then another, and yet another still. Lola watched as another miracle occurred before her eyes—the rebels took a step back. One of them turned and ran. And there, at last, they broke. More cheering followed as they ran to make their escape.

Their claws clattering loudly against the cobblestones, the critters surged forward to give chase. But soon the devils were putting on the brakes. Coming down the road in front of them was a contingent of bloated but determined rats, with a familiar devil at their head. A similar pounding came from surrounding alleyways as rats poured in from all sides, pincering the rebels between them, who threw down their arms in surrender.

A great cheer that shook the very ground arose from the critters on all sides. Many began celebrating, while still others stepped toward their foe. Taking up their discarded whips, and chains from the forge, they tied the rebels together.

Several quolls helped lift Bogart's balloon off the overseer's unconscious body. Following the queen's orders, four rats carried the overseer to the tower. Snarl stepped forward and bowed before the queen. "Your Majesty, it is good to see you again. Please forgive my tardiness. The rats would not leave until the royal kitchen was picked clean."

"Sounds about right," Melvin mumbled.

"You are, of course, forgiven, Snarl." The queen laughed. "Just this once, you understand?"

Snarl chuckled as he stood once more, looking around. "Where is the taskmaster?"

"Taskmaster Lash is in Tobias's office," Melvin explained. "I tied him up with some drapery cords. But his skin is glowing, thanks to the lovely facial I gave him."

"Excellent work, everyone," Queen Myra said. "Snarl, son of Snarl, please accompany these rebellious devils to the tower and free Teddy and the Resistance. And free the messenger pelicans, too. Then send Teddy and his crew directly to the mine to capture the remaining rebels and free the wombats."

"Immediately, Your Majesty." Snarl bowed and hurried away.

Queen Myra looked up at Lola. "Do not worry, my dear. You will soon be reunited with your loved ones." Tears sprang into Lola's eyes.

A feathered face peered over the gondola's rim. "Are they gone?"

"Yes," Melvin said.

The gondola's door sprang open and out popped a little bundle of blue. "Lola!"

Lola swept Blue off his webbed feet and pulled him into a happy embrace. "Home?" he asked.

"Yes, Blue, you will go home very, very soon. Everything is going to work out." She nuzzled her face against his feathers.

"Ahem." Captain Bogart hobbled toward them, then swept his wing into a graceful bow. "Your Majesty, it's an honor to meet you. Please allow me to introduce myself. I am Captain Bogart, captain and inventor of this hot-air balloon. I should like to discuss a business proposition with you."

Queen Myra smile graciously. "You may not have noticed, Captain Bogart, but We are in the middle of squashing a rebel uprising. Business propositions will have to wait. But We do thank you. Your crash landing was immensely helpful to Our city."

"Squwhaaaaat?" Bogart puffed out his feathers. "I'm a licensed pilot, Your Majesty. I never crash."

Lola and Melvin shared a knowing look.

Queen Myra stood on a cobblestone, her gown torn and stained. The factory no longer spewing black smoke, blue sky peeking through, a ray of sunshine falling upon her. It was as if she glowed. And that was how Lola felt, warm and standing in that pool of sunshine. It fell over her and Melvin, who smiled and lifted his face to the sun. Blue began to wiggle until Lola set him down. He took a cautious step, then another, and then leaned over and put his face very close to the queen.

"Baby," he whispered. Then he pecked her on the head.

30

A NEW TALE

Winter had come to Tassie Island in darkness and rain. A bright waxing moon peeked from behind the gray cloud cover, but it was only clouds that obscured it, not smog, nor smoke, nor billowing plume of blackening soot. Factory number one sat silent, its giant furnace cold and bolted shut. The first rains of autumn had been welcome, as they helped wash away the remaining soot. But even so, today was giving them all a spot of particularly bothersome weather.

But not everyone was feeling the gloom.

Lola couldn't stop smiling as she looked around. Inside the palace, the crystal chandeliers glistened with candlelight and the mantels and doorways were decked with boughs and red berries. It was the queen's birthday, and messenger pelicans had been sent all over the island, delivering special invitations. By boat and hot-air balloon, by train and cart, the honored guests had arrived and were now gathered within the grand hall. Despite the roaring winds and freezing rain that rattled the windows, inside the air was warm and filled with the lovely scent of freshly baked winter wheat bread.

While waiting for the grand meal to be served, guests mingled.

Melvin was speaking softly to several merchants, who had taken some interest in both the way he carried himself and his finely groomed coat. Lola had never doubted that her friend's grooming salon would take off. Business could not be better. And it didn't hurt that his most famous client was the queen herself.

Captain Bogart kept worriedly glancing out the window into the storm, checking on his balloon. Queen Myra had commissioned him to make three more for tours between Dore and Penguin Bay. The balloons were expected to be ready come spring, and quite a few penguins had applied for Bogart's pilot training program. In Bogart's opinion, flightless birds made the most enthusiastic pilots.

The regal notes of a trumpet drew everyone's attention and the guests moved to take their seats, finding the tables laden with food for every sort of critter. Moss salads and root-vegetable stews, worms and earwigs, anchovies and rotten leftovers. Members of the Royal Guard sat at the flanking tables. The contingent made of swamp water rats sat together with forks raised. "May our feasts be ever rotten!" they said with a raucous cheer. Prominent members of the citizenry sat at the other tables. But the center table was reserved for the guests of honor.

"You're to sit here," a butler mouse told Lola, ushering her to the head of the table.

"There must be some mistake," Lola said.

"No mistake. Queen Myra insisted. This is your seat."

Lola sat, then looked down the length of the table as the other guests took their assigned seats. Captain Jeb and Josie and Rupert from the Fairwater Trading Post gazed hungrily at the enormous platter of worms that had been set before them. Captain Bogart sat next to Stella from Stella's Star, who'd provided barrels of her berry brew for the celebration. Blue, along with his mother and father, sat across the table, next to Bale Blackwater. "Blasted! Why are there so many feathers in me worms?" Bale complained, as cranky as ever.

"We're molting!" Blue's parents exclaimed, bouncing on their chairs as excitedly as their son, whose baby feathers were almost all gone.

Snarl, son of Snarl, was the next at the table, alongside Teddy Bottom. Snarl had recently returned from a trip to Mount Ossa, where he'd attended a meeting of the Tassie Devil Council. Teddy was eager for news. "There is disagreement as to the handling of the rebels," Snarl reported. "Not all is harmonious. And while the taskmaster claims remorse, I do not fully believe him."

"What about Overseer Rake?" Teddy asked.

"We do not have prisons on the mountain, so she is free to live among us. But she has not shown any remorse for her actions and continues to preach a return to the old ways."

"That is troubling news," Teddy said.

"If they come back, we'll fight them, we will," Stella said, pounding a fist onto the table.

"Oh dear, oh dear," mumbled Josie, her quills aquiver.

A paw reached out and patted Teddy's paw. "Perhaps we should not speak of politics tonight." The gentle voice belonged to Lola's mother, who sat next to Lola's father.

"I agree," Arthur said as he grabbed a sprig of parsley. "Politics upset one's digestion." In the months that had passed since the wombats were freed from the coal mine, Lola had spent much time asking questions. Her mother had known that things were amiss in Dore because she'd kept in contact with Teddy. And she'd known that she might have to leave her family behind for a time in order to better protect them. But even after being captured, she had never given up hope or put a stopper to her plans.

When Teddy and his crew had arrived at the mines to free the wombats, they were surprised at what they saw. Alice had led the others in a scheme, pretending they had struck gold. Though skeptical at first, the gold-toothed devil and her comrades had rushed into the mine, heedless of their captives. Alice then led the wombats to seal the entrance. Teddy arrived to find them filing away at their bindings while the devils yelled from behind a barricade of stone and wood.

Melvin took his seat next to Alice and Arthur Budge. Looking well groomed, as usual.

When the meal was finished there were belly pats all around. Then the notes of the trumpet sounded again and all heads turned to the pygmy possum of the hour. Many could not see the queen immediately, but knew she had arrived because four members of her newly appointed Order of the Shovel were following her. These swamp water rats had been given a special place of importance as the queen's personal guard and their ordinary shovels had been replaced with golden ones, made after the melting of objects from the grand governor's office.

Bob and Stanley smiled proudly as they stood on either side of the tiny throne, which was elevated high enough for all to see. Bob gently lifted the queen and placed her on the velvet cushion. She wore a simple crown of woven greenery that matched her forest-green grown.

The Great Hall grew hushed as she rose from her throne to speak in her high-pitched, lilting voice.

"Our subjects, Our people, Our friends. This last year has been a hard one like none since the days of Our greatest grandfather, King TheoDore the Wise, who banished hunting from our land. We are ashamed that it was during Our rule, under Our watch, that an uprising occurred. Many of you suffered. Some of you were forced to work in factories and mines, others had livelihoods stolen." She paused for a moment, as if holding back tears. "But We can say that some good has come from this tragedy. We learned that not all Tassie devils were keen to return to the savage past. Some, in fact, actively worked to stop that from happening. Which is why here, on Our birthday, I have decided to begin a process of reintegration for those who are willing to live peacefully alongside all other critters of our land." Some mumbling arose. The queen raised her paws. "We understand your concern, but We have enlisted the help of a critter who has proven his loyalty. Tonight, We wish to honor Snarl, son of Snarl, with his new title, ambassador to Mount Ossa."

Applause arose as Snarl stood, placed his paws together, and bowed. Lola beamed. It was almost impossible to remember how frightened she'd been when she'd first seen him standing in the doorway of the grain silo. He was one of the most peaceful critters she'd ever met.

"Tonight We wish to present another ambassadorship, one that has become vacant—the position of ambassador to the Northern Burrows and the Realms Beyond." Again there was a bit of mumbling. Lola fidgeted. That was her uncle's old job. He'd abused his power and brought the island to the brink of chaos. Who would the queen choose to take his place? Lola had no idea.

"The ambassadorship is hereby granted to Alice Budge."

Applause filled the hall. Lola jumped to her feet and cheered. "There's goes my peace and quiet," Arthur said with an amused expression.

"Guess that means you'll be visiting Dore quite often," Melvin said to Lola.

"I guess so. Maybe I'll even live here someday," she said, which made her even happier.

When the applause had faded and critters had settled once again, the queen continued. "Before Our royal chef brings out Our royal birthday cake, there is one more honor We wish to present." Silence fell and all faces turned up, eagerly awaiting this unexpected news. "Lola, Melvin, and Blue, would you please join Us beside Our throne?"

Lola and Melvin shared a surprised expression. Lola's heart did a little pitter-patter dance. She had no idea what was about to happen. "Go on," her mother said, giving her a gentle nudge.

"Lola!" Blue exclaimed as he hopped off his chair and waddled up to her. She lifted him into her arms and carried him up the stairs. Melvin delicately dabbed bread crumbs from his whiskers, then joined them. Queen Myra nodded at Bob, who reached into his golden bucket and pulled out a book. It was a copy of *The Tales of Tassie Island*, but it wasn't the copy that she'd lost so many months ago. This one appeared to be brand-new. He held it out to her. She set Blue next to Melvin, then took the book.

"This is a new edition of Our most beloved book," the queen explained. "We understand that it is your favorite book as well."

"Yes, Your Majesty," Lola said. "I love this book. I read it every morning before I went to sleep in my burrow."

"Please turn to the marked page."

A satin bookmark peeked out from the book. With a trembling paw, Lola opened the pages. What she saw nearly took her breath away. "Oh, hooly dooly," she whispered.

31

LOLA THE UNSHY

And there, beneath the chapter title, was an illustration of a wombat, a swamp water rat, and a baby penguin.

"In honor of the journey that Lola Budge took to save her family and her home, and in honor of those who helped her along the way, We have commissioned a new story that will be told forevermore," Queen Myra said.

Lola turned the page toward the audience so they could see the lovely drawing. Applause filled the air again. It was the most perfect moment in Lola's life. "I'm a story," she told Melvin. "*We're* a story."

"We're not just a story," he said with a flourish of his paw. "We're the stuff of legend."

The Royal Chef wheeled in the royal birthday cake. Merriment and feasting commenced. A cast of characters united in camaraderie, friendship, and love.

"Lola! Cake?" Blue bounced at her feet. Then he waddled over to the cart and bounced even higher, trying to get a better view.

"Uh-oh, he's wandering again," Melvin said, rushing over to grab him before a disaster could occur. Lola saw much of her own inquisitive nature in Blue and remembered a time when she, too, had been scolded for being inquisitive. But that felt like a lifetime ago.

Lola hugged the book to her chest and chuckled to herself. She may not be like other wombats, but . . .

She wouldn't have it any other way.

EPILOGUE

Bale Blackwater had promised Lola that if she ever needed a message delivered, he'd give her a free delivery. And he was going to keep that promise. So he made his way down, down, down, into the bowels of the palace, his messenger bag strapped to his back, his webbed feet slapping the stone floor. He was in an extra cranky mood. He was supposed to deliver messages in the water, not on land.

"Oi! You there!"

There was no one down there but a single wombat, who turned around at the sound of Bale's voice. He was a stout critter, with chin hairs waxed into a pointed beard.

"Are you addressing me?" He set aside his mop and wiped his paws on his plain apron.

Bale came to a stop, then scratched his head. "Course I'm addressin' you. Do ya see any other critter standin' about?"

The wombat frowned. "Is there something you want?"

"Course there's somethin' I want. I'm here ta deliver a message." Bale reached into his messenger bag and pulled out an envelope. "But I gotta make sure yer the right wombat. Cause if I deliver to the wrong wombat again, I'll get fired from the union for sure." He smacked his flat tail against the floor.

The wombat sighed. "Well? I can't stand here all day. I have a floor to mop."

Bale looked at the envelope. "It's addressed to Uncle Tobias."

The wombat's eyes widened with surprise. "It is? I'm Uncle Tobias."

"Ya sure about that? Like I said, I can't make another mistake."

The wombat held out his paw. "I'm very sure."

"Well I reckon ya know who ya are." Bale handed over the letter. "All right, mate, have a g'day. But don't be expectin' me to come down here again. Being out of water for this long makes me feel as cross as a frog in a sock!" And with that, he spun on his feet and waddled away.

The wombat stared at the unexpected envelope for a long moment. Then he opened it. And this is what he found.

Dear Uncle Tobias,

Enclosed is a ticket for a hot-air balloon ride from

Dore to the burrows. We will be expecting you for a

family foraging as soon as you can join us.

Signed, your niece, Lola

Tobias Bottom read the message again and again and again.

And, despite the grimy apron and overwhelming stench of dirty mop water, he felt richer than he'd ever felt in his entire life.

A FEW WORDS FROM THE AUTHORS

While this story is loosely based on the beautiful part of the world called Tasmania, it is a fantasy, which means we took liberties. Many, many liberties. For that is the joy of writing fiction and the special joy of writing fantasy. We made stuff up. Of course we did. Wombats don't carve bowls and spoons.

And so, there are times when we created our own terrains for the purpose of world-building. We made the island swampier than it actually is. We made the island smaller than it actually is. And there are times when we brought in critters that don't normally live in Tasmania, and times when we modified existing species, like turning the Australian swamp rat into a garbage-eating, stinky critter, when in fact they are quite clean and cute. And, though Tasmanian devils are native to the island, we chose to make them invaders to up the tension of the story.

Most of our writing was done in coffeehouses, to which we thank the owners of Hot Shots Java in Poulsbo, WA, and Cups in Bainbridge Island, WA.

We are grateful to our Tasmanian reader, Jodi Haines.

And to our publishing team: Michael Bourret (Literary Agent), Erin Stein (Editor Extraordinaire), Carolyn Bull (Designer), Ilana Worrell (Production Editor), Raymond Ernesto Colón (Production Manager), Janine Barlow (Copyeditor), and Cory Godbey (Cover Artist).

And a big thank you to Brian Jacques, whose *Redwall* books inspired us to embark on this journey. We both got to meet him a few years before he died and it was an honor.

But we also want to thank each other, for it is not every mother and son who can sit down, day after day, to create a novel together, and still be on speaking terms when the process is finished. But we made it through. Thank you, Walker. Thank you, Mom.

Happy Reading!

ABOUT THE AUTHORS

SUZANNE SELFORS is a best-selling, award-winning author of over thirty books for young readers, including *Wish Upon a Sleepover* and *Fortune's Magic Farm*. She lives on an island in the Pacific Northwest where wombat sightings are extremely rare. This is her first book cowritten with her son. Visit her online at www.suzanneselfors.com.

WALKER RANSON studied engineering at Gonzaga University and worked as a pizza chef before finally admitting to his family and friends that what he really wanted to do was be a writer. This is his first published novel. Walker currently works as a bookseller at an independent bookstore and is writing his next novel. Visit him online at www.walkerranson.com.